the *Anatomy*

of *Jane*

AMELIA LeFAY

The Anatomy of Jane

Copyright © 2015 by Amelia LeFay

ISBN-13: 978-1544053462

ISBN-10: 1544053460

NYLA Publishing

350 7th Avenue, Suite 2003, NY 10001, New York.

http://www.nyliterary.com

Dedication

Dedicated to

Alessandra Torre,
Jodi, Christy, and
last, but not least, you
Suebee, for always having my back.

Thank you all for your support!
I would never have written this book without you all!

"Life gives us something that we could hardly imagine."

—Marcel Proust

Prologue

SATURDAY

I never met my parents, but I'd like to think they would have wanted more for me than just stale peanuts, glitter push-up bras, and body shots. However, since they left me in a crack house somewhere on Fremont Avenue, I'm pretty sure their bar wasn't very high to begin with…but a girl can dream right? After all, the only things I had left were my stupid dreams.

"Damn it's cold," I muttered to myself, zipping my leather jacket up to my neck, hugging my arms around myself as I waited on the corner.

"Hey! Sweetheart, please don't tell me you're leaving'?"

Ignore him.

"I'm talking to you sexy."

I'm not here. Please leave me alone!

"Hey, bitch!" He grabbed on to my arm and pulled me to him. "Why you bein' so unfriendly?"

I still didn't look at him. Instead I stared at the taxis as they passed. Men around here were like wild dogs, and if you made eye contact, you'd have to beat them back with a stick.

"I'm off the clock, but if you're looking for a friend, I suggest you head inside." I took a deep breath and ripped my arm away.

"Well, I'm not inside—"

"Aye, Gavin. What did I tell you about messing with my girls?" I knew that voice. I hated the rough sandpaper sound of it almost as much as I hated the gallon of Axe body spray he dipped himself in every night before coming out.

When he stepped behind me, it took all my effort not to gag.

"We were just having a chat—"

"Chat with someone else; either come in or get lost," Allen barked at him, and just like that, the asshole let go before wandering into the back door of the Bunny Rabbit. That wasn't a metaphor for something but the actual name for the strip club – I mean 'gentlemen's club' – where I worked. The Bunny

Rabbit was Allen's dream ticket to becoming the next Hugh Hefner...only he would want to be a perverted old man.

"You're being difficult *Janie.*" I hated that too, how he thought it was cute to add on to the end of everyone's name.

"How is asking for a raise being difficult?" I finally turned to him but had to look down, partially because of the heels I was wearing and also because he was so damn short. At five foot six, which was really five-four without the lifts in his damn shoes, he was almost always the shortest man in the club. Sometimes the girls said he looked like a kid waiting for his mother to get off work. The fact that he was only twenty-five and had a round, child-like face didn't really help either. The only positive thing was...give me a second and I'll think of something.

"Janie—"

"And for the record, I'm not one of your girls! I don't strip. I'm a bartender *and* your manager *and* accountant *and* the girls' tailor—"

"I get it. You do a lot."

"I do everything!" I screamed, lifting my hands up for him to see all the bandages I had been collecting on my fingertips. "See! This one I got from sewing Jasmine's bra back together. Do you know how hard it is to sew through sequins, Allen? Too fucking hard!"

"Jane—"

"And this one—" I pointed to the bandage on my thumb. "Is the price I paid for your stupid attempt to save money on a fucking stapler, Allen! Your fifty cent stapler bit me."

"I get it!" he yelled and I folded my arm back over my chest looking away from him and glaring at the John Hancock tower in the distance. "I get it, Jane. I know you do a lot, and you know I'm grateful—"

"No, I don't. People show gratefulness with money in our line of work. No money means ungratefulness." Well, it actually meant no service, but I was too upset right now to frame it better.

He sighed, "You're so damn stubborn."

"As a mule," I agreed.

"Do you know how much it costs to run a business in this—"

"I know, but if you cut out the Jell-O shots that no one drinks, stop serving the shrimp which only end up on the floor, and change all the lights to LED bulbs, we could save three hundred dollars a month. My earning an extra two hundred would mean my not having to choose between groceries and my damn electricity bill."

I had only started to do the books about a month ago, and I almost cried when I realized how much money I wasn't making by keeping my clothes on. On top of that, I knew exactly how much he made from the other girls while I was struggling day in and day fucking out.

We both came from the same group home, but he was a year younger than me. Part of me still saw him as my brother. I'm not really sure why. Maybe it was because I was a quiet child, and he always stood up for me, even when he would get beaten up for it.

Usually, parents who adopt loved their newborns, but I was a 'drug' baby and that was just like having the plague. No one would touch me. I was passed around from one group home to another until I left at eighteen, and Allen came to find me. He helped me find work as a waitress, a janitor, a barista and things like that until he opened his club three years ago.

"Look, how about we talk about this later? You know it gets crazy on the weekends here—"

"Jane!" Before he could finish, Lady poked her dark head outside the door and I could see that the purple glitter star she had on her left boob was smeared. "Jane, thank god! The snap on my bra broke, and my boobs look lopsided. Can you help me?"

"Don't you have another one?" Allen snapped at her. Lady placed her hand on her hip, rolled her eyes and popped the bubble gum she was chewing.

"Yea, but if Crystal gets pissed at me havin' a better Supergirl costume, I'ma tell her it was you who told me to change."

"Supergirl?" he questioned, and this time I rolled my eyes.

"It's Heroes Night," I reminded him. How could he forget his own stupid ideas?

"Right, Hold on—"

"My set is in five. Jane, please." She begged me.

"Jane...please," Allen added already walking to the back door. "I swear we will work this out tomorrow. We need you tonight. It's Saturday—"

"Jane," Crystal called again. "Please...please...please—"

"Fine!" They were like kids, so damned annoying! Turning back to Allen, I stuck my finger in his face. "If you do not give me a raise tomorrow, I'm quitting for good just so you know."

He raised his hands in surrender and like a weakling I caved before adjusting my purse strap and heading inside behind Lady. I didn't need to look at Allen to know that he was now back in his own oblivious world, most likely erasing the conversation we just had from his mind.

Entering the girls' dressing room, I reached into my bag and pulled out the saving graces of all strip clubs everywhere. "I have a glue gun, a sewing kit, push up pads and body glitter. Who's first?" I asked when their grinning faces turned to face me.

I was like a dirty Mary Poppins.

SUNDAY

"You're here," Allen said when I walked into the almost empty club. Angel worked on Sundays. She was one of the older girls but could work a pole better than anyone else. She always started her Sunday afternoon routine in white, but by six, she'd be in red with devil horns.

"I'm here. Yesterday you said we would talk about my raise," I started moving over to the bar putting my bag on the glass counter and sitting down. "So let's talk."

"Janie—"

"Don't Janie me, Allen. You promised—"

"Did you get it in writing?" He smiled and I glared at him. "Jane, we don't have the funds—"

"Bullshit Allen! Why are you doing this to me? We are basically family."

"There is no money Jane! It's gone. I lost it," he snapped, and the moment he said it, I knew he regretted it. He tried to avoid my gaze by moving to the other side of the bar where he pretended to clean the counter.

"Allen what do you mean? *You lost it?*"

No answer. Instead, he threw the towel down sighing deeply, as he ran his hands through his thick curls. "I invested in some…"

"Stop bullshitting me, Allen. How exactly did you lose everything?"

"Have you ever wondered how I was able to open a club at twenty-one?" he asked.

"No." Because I knew it wasn't legit and knowing stuff like that was how people ended up in 'car accidents'. I'd seen enough shady shit go down in the Bunny Rabbit to know better than poking around into things that weren't my business. But Allen unfortunately, was my business, so, "Now I *am* wondering. What happened?"

"Three years ago, I made a deal with Aaron—"

"Fucking hell, Allen." Just hearing the name made my stomach drop. I had no idea who Aaron was, nor had I ever met him, but I did hear his name here and there. He handled all the drugs out of Boston. He was like the monster under the bed or in the shadows; you fucked with him and he killed you. Period. The end. "What was the deal?"

"Jane...I—"

"Let me guess. You let him use the club as a place to clean his money, and he gave you a small loan to start your own club? What happened with the deal? Did you lose his money?"

"How did you—"

"I'm not a fucking idiot, but you might be!" My head was on fire. "How much?"

"A lot."

"Numbers Allen, speak in numbers."

"Two hundred."

"Two hundred?"

"Two hundred and ten thousand."

My mouth must have fallen to the ground because I couldn't feel my face. In fact, I think my soul was leaving my body. "Please repeat that."

"Two hundred and ten thousand—"

"How is that possible?"

"He also had products here."

I nodded casually now and reached for my bag. "Well Allen, thank you for the explanation. It's been interesting working for you, but I'm going to just quit before getting sucked into your shit storm—"

"You're kind of already in it," he said when I moved to walk away.

"What?"

"Your name, I put you as co-owner."

"Come again?"

He nodded his head. "When I first opened up, I put you as co-owner just in case anything ever happened to me. You're my only family—"

The moment he said that, I marched around the counter, pulled my arm back then punched him as hard as I could across the face sending his ass to the ground.

"Ah fucking hell, Jane!" he yelled gripping his nose. Pulling my leg back, I kicked him in the side. "Jane! Stop! Jane!"

I was about to kill him, but Tommy, the bouncer, pulled me back. However, this didn't stop me from struggling. "Let me go! Let me go! I'm going to kill that little bastard! Are you kidding me! Not only am I getting screwed as an employee, just barely making minimum wage, but I'm now a co-fucking owner with a massive debt! Are you kidding me?"

"Jane, calm down." Tommy pulled me back away from him. "Breathe! In through the nose and out through the mouth."

Doing what he said, I breathed…angrily, like a raging bull, but I breathed. I hated to admit it, but it did make me feel better…but only a little.

"Tommy, I'm good."

"Are you sure?"

"Yea, thanks." I nodded when he set me back on my feet, releasing his grip.

"Jane—"

"I don't want to hear from you." I pointed to Allen when he came over to me, blood now staining the ridiculous zebra striped shirt he was wearing. "Talk to whoever the fuck you need to talk to, and get me out of this shit, Allen, or I swear to god if they don't kill you, I will. Got me?"

"Okay."

Nodding, I grabbed my things and headed toward the door, but I paused and turned back to him. "Oh, and I quit!"

Mary Poppins was flying far, far away.

MONDAY

"I'll take anything. Mary, please!" I begged her, at this point I was ready to rub her shoulders and be her footstool. Okay, may be not to that extent, but I really needed a job.

"Jane, I love you, you know I do. And I will be forever grateful to you for helping me get away from Ryan—"

"But..." There is usually a 'but' after these types of statements.

"But you've never done well with authority."

"That's not true!"

She made a face at me before reaching for her phone. "Hello, Mary's Magnificent Maids, how can we help you? Yes...of course...yes. No, *thank you.*"

Two years ago, Mary was known as 'Spice', and was the only stripper I had ever met that could do a split in the air, while turning, in six-inch heels. You couldn't tell now with her buttoned up ruffled shirt and cardigan. She looked more like a principal with her red hair tied into a bun and her glasses resting on her nose. But I was proud of her.

"Sorry, what were you saying?" she asked when she hung up the phone.

"I was saying I don't have a problem with authority."

"Jane, you pulled a gun on my ex-husband."

"First of all, it was a fake gun. Second, he was abusing you and little Andy." How could she hold that against me?

"Okay then, what about the time you threw a drink at one of the guys at the bar?"

"I—"

"Or the time you threatened to drag one of the girls by her hair if she didn't stop stealing."

"You are making me sound like some violent, crazy person. Each I did—"

"Some things should be done to protect others. I know, Jane. You are a good person, heck you're probably one of the most decent people I know. But this is my business. I can't take the risk of you attacking someone or being rude to them if one of my clients, for example, asks you to re-clean her windows. I've worked really hard to get to this point in my life. This job is all about good references."

"Mary I swear you won't hear a peep out of me okay? I'll work twice as hard as anyone else. I really need this job."

She sighed and tucked her red hair behind her ear. "Fine"

"YES!" Thank you, Jesus.

"Ground rules. No cursing. No personal shit. And most importantly you do whatever the client wants, as far as it is legal." The way she added that last bit didn't go unnoticed.

"I got it. You won't regret it. I promise."

"God, I hope so," she muttered ripping a piece of paper before handing to me. "I just got this client from another service."

"I thought a maid's client list was as personal as an escort's. Why would someone else give you their client?"

"Apparently the maid is retiring, and the other service is closing. The other owner just so happened to be a former guest of mine at the club and is giving me his clients. This is a good starting point to see whether or not you can hack it. The maid is leaving tomorrow, so you can get the keys from her. You clean twice a week: Tuesday and Saturday."

"Thank you so much and any other clients, please send them my way," I said to her as I moved towards the doors.

"And Jane…"

"Yeah?"

"You should try smiling more. You're beautiful when you aren't scowling at the world."

"Smile, got it." I even flashed my teeth before leaving. When I stepped out of her office, I came face to face with my own reflection in the elevator doors.

I smiled at that moment, but I couldn't take myself seriously. The great thing about being pretty was that it made for great tips, but it also encouraged assholes to get handy. The bastards were even worse if they recognized me outside the club. So I always kept my light auburn hair in a ponytail, wore my Patriots baseball cap, and I used no other make-up than cat-eye liner. Some people love their boobs, skin or legs, but I've always loved my eyes. They weren't sexy or eye-catching, just plain old hazel brown, but supposedly brown-eyed people had, at least, one parent with brown eyes. I didn't know my parents, but one of them had brown eyes. At least, I knew something.

When the elevator came, I glanced back down at the address in my hands.

2829 W Rowling Street

Boston, Massachusetts

It was time to see how the other half actually lived.

TUESDAY

"You need to sign this," the older maid said in a thick German accent, before handing me a pen and clipboard. She made me feel like I had entered a clinic instead of a penthouse. She stood outside the doors like a guard dog, but I couldn't look away from the mole above her lip, which sprouted hair.

"Sign," She shoved it into my chest.

"Okay. Okay." Putting my bag down to read... "A non-disclosure agreement." Why?

"No sign. No work," she said again.

"I get that, but why? Should I get a lawyer or something?"

She just crossed her arms and narrowed her eyes at me. I read it quickly; it was simple and straightforward enough.

"Fine. Here," I said handing her back the clipboard. She nodded and tucked it under her arm before turning around to open the door.

"Code 03140902. No remember, the police come after three times."

"03140902," I repeated the numbers as the door opened to expose an awe-inspiring view. Wall to wall windows revealed a private pool and the whole of Boston. I couldn't look away.

"Pain in the ass," said the German lady while shaking her head at the wall of glass. I realized I still didn't know her name. "You clean the windows. Wiper is in the closet."

The moment she said it, the view I was admiring vanished. All I saw now was all the effort it would take to keep the windows clean.

"Come on." She waved me further across dark wood flooring giving me a quick tour. "Living room, you clean. Laundry, the clothes to be washed in the blue basket. Dry, in the red basket. Kitchen, you clean. Pots and knives you clean with this, nothing else." She showed me the unmarked cleaning products under the sink "Understand?"

"Understood," I nodded staring at the state of the art stainless steel kitchen. I noticed everything was colored in gray, blue and off-white, and perfectly placed like one of those model homes.

Great, I thought, *these people must be neat freaks.*

Don't complain, Jane. Remember you need the job.

"Upstairs." The unnamed German lady moved around me and up the spiral staircase.

"Three rooms," she said when he reached the upper level. "Master room, you clean. The spare room, you clean. Private room, you not clean."

"This one, not clean?" I asked to point to the cream door.

"No." She waved her finger at me.

Raising my hands up in defense I said, "Okay I got it, but believe me, there is nothing behind those doors that would actually shock me. It could be Christian Grey's room and I wouldn't even blink an eye."

"Who?"

I laughed. "Never mind."

"You understand?" she asked me.

"Yes."

"Yes. Okay. Goodbye." She replied by taking off her apron, handing it to me and marching down the stairs.

I followed her. "You're leaving?"

"Yes. You clean. I leave. Goodbye." She started to happily pack her bags and whistle. Yes, the woman was whistling and heading toward the door. When it closed, I stood in the middle of the penthouse and took a deep breath. I then did what any good maid would do. I got gloves. Cleaning toilets may be boring enough but it was still better than rubbing glitter on a woman's breast...to me anyway.

This was my new life.

Jane Chapman, the penthouse housemaid.

1

One month.

Twelve days.

And far too many hours to count.

That's how long I had been cleaning the penthouse at 2829 W Rowling Street without having any idea who lived there. If it weren't for the damn laundry left for me every week, I'd think I was working for ghosts. The penthouse was never that dirty. True, there may be a tie or sock left somewhere, or a cup left on the table or in the sink plus the normal dust, but other than that,

I had never actually met the owner. There weren't any pictures, yet I couldn't stop my imagination from running. There was something about the room hidden behind the forbidden cream-colored door that kept me guessing. So I had come to irrational conclusions: I was working for a serial killer, or one of those men who secretly collected blow-up dolls. Anything, I thought, creepy enough to keep me from going inside.

"Maybe he's a rich doctor who harvests human body parts?" I muttered to myself. I had only realized it was *he* because of the boxer briefs in his laundry. I bobbed my head to Bon Jovi blaring through my headphones before perfectly folding the newly ironed white shirts. I was so focused on my little world and wasn't expecting anything or anyone that when I did turn around and saw him...them... I nearly screamed.

"Take my hand and we'll make it..." The music rang in my ears as I stood frozen in the hall. I was unable to tear my eyes away from them as they ripped each other's clothes off.

It was two men. No, better, two models that I must have dreamt up. Well over six foot, one with dirty light brown hair, the other's jet black, shirts off, ivory arms locked around each other, their sculpted chests and abs rubbing together. They kissed like they needed to breathe through each other's mouths, while their tongues circled. The dark haired one reached into the pants of the other and grabbed the other man's cock, which was now standing proud and thick...I mean tall. He kissed the side of the other man's cheek and down his neck.

The more I watched the hotter my body became. This was so fucking hot, and I couldn't look away. I wasn't sure if it was even real. The lighter haired man didn't just stop at the nape of his lover's neck. He kisses fell in a quick line down the center of his lover's abs, all the while he never stopped stroking his partner's cock. Even from where I was standing, I could see it was throbbing.

Oh, my god. My mouth dropped open as he started to lick the cock's tip and sides like it was an ice cream cone melting in his hand, and he wasn't going to waste a drop.

"Ah..." Shit! Fuck! I moaned. I didn't mean to. I wanted to take it back, but I was caught. The dark haired man's blue eyes focused on me, as he got up from the floor. He was pissed but his lover only looked me over. Before either of them could say anything, I ran down the stairs screaming, "Sorry!"

I didn't even think. I just kept moving and quickly closed the door behind me.

"Jesus." I leaned back in the elevator trying to calm down, but erotic images kept flashing in my mind.

I'd never be able to get that scene out of my mind or listen to Bon Jovi again. *"Livin' on a Prayer..."* was still playing in my ears.

I made it all the way to the first floor before reaching for my bag to discover two things: I was still holding on to the client's shirts, and two, I had left my purse.

Why God, why? I couldn't leave without my bus pass or house keys, so I had to go back upstairs. I couldn't do it, and I didn't know why. I'd seen people getting off dozens of times. I'd even known that a few men had jacked off at the Bunny Rabbit. Shit like this didn't faze me, but right now, I was reacting abnormally, and I had no idea why.

"Why? It doesn't matter," I whispered to myself. I just needed to get my things.

Turning back around, I re-entered the security lobby and took a seat. I would wait an hour. I didn't want to interrupt.

"Ms. Chapman?" The security man called from behind the desk.

"Yes?"

"Mr. Emerson said you forgot your things and to tell you to come up."

"Thanks," I muttered to myself, moving back toward the elevators, hoping I still had a job when I went up.

Of course, I would still have a job. I didn't do anything. Who cares if they are having sex; it's their place, right? Wait. Was one of them not out yet? Was that the reason for the non-disclosure? Or were they having an affair? Were the two men married? Or maybe he was a politician? Someone high up the food chain? The dark haired one pulled off a tie...

Yes, Jane, in your little world all men in suits work for the government?

"Urgh..." I groaned and rubbed the side of my head. I was trying to fight back the headache I was giving myself when the elevator opened.

I stared at the double doors at the end of the hall with the padlock.

"03140902."

"Error, Password Denied." And just as I was about to panic, the door opened slightly. Staring down at me with brightest green eyes was the light haired man, and a sexy five o'clock shadow. He took the shirts from me at the same time his eyes wandered down my body for what seemed like forever. They finally settled on my face and he smirked.

"Hello Ms. Chapman," he said with a thick English accent that made me feel like he was trying to seduce me just by saying 'hello'. He opened the door wider, exposing his bare chest to me, forcing me to not only stare once again at his body but also the tattoos he had collected. I couldn't help but look. He had a five star constellation on his inner biceps, a dreamcatcher on his shoulder, Chinese lettering on the side of his abs, a cross on his chest and hovering over it were Roman numerals.

"You done staring, sweetheart?" he asked.

"You stared, too," I impulsively said, and the moment I did, I regretted it. This was what Mary was talking about: my secret annoying desire to always get the last word in.

"Touché," he said while one of his eyebrows rose. "Are you going to come in?"

"Yes, shit. Sorry." What is wrong with me?

My eyes immediately went to the man now standing at the window. He was dark-haired, clean-shaven, but the same blue eyes which had glared at me earlier were focused on his phone. He checked something before nodding. I noticed in the few minutes that I was gone that he had managed to put back on his shirt and tie.

"I got it, Nick. Yeah, I'll read it before coming in. Tell Carrie that I want to go over the program when I get—I don't fucking care if she's done it. I'm saying we are doing it again, so do it again." His voice was calm yet harsh, a slight Boston accent. Which meant he had grown up here but was most likely trained to speak 'properly.' He hung up then stared back at me. I noticed he looked me over just like the other one.

"You're the maid?" he asked like he couldn't believe it.

"Yes."

"How long does it take for you to clean this damn place all by yourself?"

"I'm sorry, but is there anything I can refer to you two as?" It would, at least make me feel like less of an outsider. "Or 'Boss' just works," I added in when neither of them answered.

"You don't know who I am?" Angry eyes glared at me causing his lover to snicker as he came over falling back on the couch.

"Should I?" I knew it. He was a goddamn politician.

"I'm Maxwell Emerson," he finally stated. I was sure I had heard that name before, but I wasn't sure. He reached down and took the remote control, turning on the large flat screen to the left of me. I wasn't sure what he was trying to show me until he appeared on screen in a fitted black suit and navy tie as part of some news report intro.

"Good afternoon ladies and gentlemen, I'm Michael Madison, and we are going to get right to it. Only a day after Maxwell Emerson broke the story on the Emerson Report *on Governor MacDowell's scandal, the district attorney has released a statement that they will be prosecuting—"*

"She got it, you damn show off." His lover groaned and turned off the television. When I turned back, he winked at me. "If you like, you can call me 'Boss'. I like the way you say it."

I was confused. It felt like he was flirting with me, but in my line of work, I hadn't come across many gay men. Maybe my radar wasn't as sharp as it should have been.

"The Brit here is Wesley Uhler, head chef of the Wes Hill—
"

"This is the asshole who charges almost three hundred dollars per fucking person?" I snapped remembering how many times I saw receipts from there. Allen had the habit of trying to live the high life at the expense of his club and most importantly me. I was so angry that it took me a second to notice the expressions on their faces. The words I had just said came back into my head, and I wished the ground would open up so I could just sink away from here.

"I'm so…"

"No, it's alright," Wesley laughed, shaking his head. "It's meant to be ridiculous. The higher the price, the greater the desire people have to eat there. It also helps that I'm a half decent cook."

"Don't be humble. It doesn't look good on you," Maxwell muttered reaching on the table for a printed piece of paper.

"Fine *love*, I'm a fucking badass in the kitchen, and if you ate at my restaurant, Ms. Chapman, you'd orgasm with every damn bite."

My breath was stuck in my throat, as I stared back at him. I could feel my ears getting hot. However, Max stepped into my line of sight, and his eyes were hard, sharp and unwavering. He flashed the document he had picked up.

"Now that we have been introduced, I hope you recall this," he said and I saw my signature on the non-disclosure I had signed a month ago. "I didn't call you back up here for us to make nice and get along. You saw something today and I never want it repeated to anyone. Because if I do, so help me God, it will be the end of you. Are we clear?"

His nostrils flared, and in one second, he went from being cool and collected to almost manic. He looked like he'd even consider killing me if I didn't agree.

"I know how to keep my mouth shut," I replied doing my best to stand up confidently against him.

"Good. That's it for the day. Take your things and get out. The new passcode will be emailed to you."

I nodded reaching for my purse and jacket. I didn't look back. My mind was spinning. I just needed air…and to get as far away as possible from Wesley and Maxwell.

They were opposites, like fire and ice, and I couldn't take the swift temperature changes.

The moment she shut the door, I turned to him. "What the fuck was that?"

"What?" he asked casually getting off on the couch.

"Don't play dumb. You were basically fucking her with your eyes."

"Are you jealous?" he whispered and came closer to me. He reached out to place his thumb on my lip.

"Not even a little bit." And that was the truth. "But you seducing her while I'm trying to intimidate her is hardly a wise choice, don't you think?"

His green eyes looked over my face before he spoke. "You and I have always been honest with each other about *everything*."

"And...."

"And I want her," he said darkly, moving in closer to me. "I want her in bed with us, and I know you want her, too."

"Wrong again. Besides, you've known her all of five minutes—"

"That's longer than it took me to want you," he snickered while leaning in, but his lips only hovered over mine, and in that moment, we shared the air between us.

"I don't want her." I wanted him...like always. Like a fucking drug I couldn't break free from. "Besides, she's an annoyance. Who just stands in the hall gawking at us like we—"

"Are two lions fucking in a zoo?" he said softly. "Maybe it's because we were like two lions fucking in a zoo. I like this maid, and she's like a little worker bee. I can see my reflection in all the silverware. Plus she's sexy and feisty."

"Then you fuck her and come back to me." The thought pissed me off more than I liked.

"No." He shook his head. "When you stop lying to yourself, when you admit you want her too, that's when we see how much she might want us. Until then, I'll just keep making you cum in my hands..." He reached into my pants.

"Has anyone ever told you that you have the mind of the devil?"

"Has anyone ever told you that you have the body of a sinner?"

I couldn't reply. His lips were on top of mine, his tongue already in my mouth and my hands moved to grip his tight ass. With everyone else I was Maxwell: the asshole, the ice block, the boss. But with him, I was as good as a bitch in heat.

"You're turning me on just by breathing like that," he whispered slowly dropping to his knees.

I could see my reflection in the windows, my mouth opening as he gently stroked down the length of my cock, his thumb brushing the tip of me. "What do you want Max?"

"To go to work."

He squeezed licking the length of the vein now throbbing at the side of my cock. "Don't lie and don't make me do it again."

"I want your mouth on me...now," I demanded. He did as he was told allowing me to slide my dick into his hot wet mouth. He grabbed the back of my knees leaning forward and taking all of me into his mouth.

"Fuck," I hissed, thrusting forward, grabbing a fist full of his hair, closing my eyes and tilting my head back. He took my length all the way down to the base as his teeth softly glided over me. After being interrupted before, I couldn't hold myself back and my whole body wanted this and him. Over and over I fucked his mouth and his head bounced back and forth on me. Letting go of one of my legs, he reached up to cup my balls in his hands.

"Fuck. Ahh…Wes…urg!" I grunted, coming into his mouth. He held me in place while drinking all of me, as I tried to catch my breath.

When he got back up, he wiped the corner of his mouth. "That was quick."

"Shut up," I said between breaths and he just kissed the side of my face. "Another reason to be nice to the maid, Max, is the non-disclosure. You need it. Remember it's just a paper, and she could blurt things out by accident. Suing her wouldn't undo the damage she might cause. You've *come* too far…now."

"Even with a sexual reference, I still don't find your jokes funny," I frowned.

"My jokes are fine; it's just you who lacks humor," he replied, kissing my lips before casually heading into the kitchen.

I sat down on the arm of my couch trying to calm down. I was thirty-one years old, but I had the hormones of a seventeen-year-old boy.

Damn you Wes.

Without a word to him, I headed back upstairs to take a shower before heading to work.

I couldn't believe it had been four years since we first met. I was covering a story in Paris, and on my first night there, I went to a restaurant recommended by my mother. She had gone with a few colleagues and couldn't stop raving about the food.

He hadn't been lying earlier when he told the maid that his food was 'orgasmic'. It was then and was still now, but in Paris that evening, I wanted to meet the person who had created such delicacies. I asked the maître d', and the chef, Wes, came out dressed in his whites. His sleeves were rolled up and his hair was tied back in a bun.

Some people believe in love at first sight. It wasn't love. It was lust. Raw, plain old lust, the moment our eyes locked. I had always kept my lustful urges in check, but that night I had no idea what happened.

He gave me his card. I called, not even an hour later, and we were in his flat fucking like wild animals. Not just that first night. Or the next or the next, but every night for the whole week I was there.

Then I left.

Six months later, he had opened a restaurant in Boston.

He didn't ask why I hadn't called him, or if I had thought about him. That was one of the differences between women and men. Men don't ask. Yet, I showed up at his restaurant, and we picked up right where we left off. I'm sure we both thought we'd get sick of each other at some point, but we didn't stop to question what we had.

Four years later, and I wasn't even slightly annoyed with him.

"Room for one more." He opened the glass shower door and stepped in beside me, wrapping his arms around my shoulders.

We just stood there for a moment, pressed up against each other, the hot water beating against our skin.

"I don't want her," I whispered.

"Okay, just you and me."

That was more than enough.

Truly, even though parts of me mean it. I couldn't get her big hazel brown eyes out of my mind.

No more complications. Considering my family, I already had enough just being with him.

2

Maxwell Emerson.

I wasn't sure what I was doing googling his name. But once I clicked 'search' I couldn't stop reading. It wasn't like I had anything else to do on Friday nights anymore.

"Wow." You knew someone was famous when Google had a sidebar section for them. I thought it was because he was a news anchor. I was wrong.

Maxwell Alexander Emerson III, born April 10th, son of the hotel mogul and former governor, Alistair Crane Emerson, and now sitting senator Elspeth Yates, the head of YGM, the media company which not only controlled Maxwell III's conservative news outlet, The Emerson Report, but also The Boston Rover, and several other networks which weren't listed. The family's net worth was in the billions. That number was so out of the stratosphere for me that I couldn't even comprehend it, so I ignored it.

He was an only child, but his family was so cookie-cutter that the more I searched, the more depressed I felt.

So logically, I Googled the other man, Wesley. Thinking he might be just a chef…wrong again.

Wesley Uhler, was the son of famed British novelist and poet, Brenda Uhler, who had traveled the world by the time she was thirty-four. She was now married to a woman, a former professor of astronomy at Cambridge. She'd also written a few books on that subject.

I kept reading until I saw that Wesley had lost his little brother. After that, it felt too personal to read on, and I didn't want to pry any more than I already had.

Since I was nobody and they couldn't Google me back, it felt very *stalkerish*. Closing my laptop, I laid back on my mattress and stared at the tear on my apartment's ceiling. One by one, water droplets dripped from it into a bucket below. My phone rang.

"Hello?" I answered while lying down. My whole body ached.

"Hey Jane, it's Mary."

"They fired me. Didn't they?" Damn it. What was the point of talking to me if they were just going to change their mind?

"What? Who?"

Shit. I sat up. I wasn't supposed to say anything. "Sorry Mary. What's going on?"

"Do you have time to fill in for a maid that's called in sick? The client is throwing a party in three hours' time, and while I have two other maids there, I can use the third set of hands to finish cleaning in time. Can you help? I really don't want to lose these clients."

"More work is more money, Mary. You don't need to ask. What's the address?" I asked grabbing a pen and random notebook to write it down.

"317 Beacon Street. It's a Brownstone. If you take a taxi, I'll reimburse you for it."

"Music to my ears. I'm leaving now. I'll call you when I'm there." I said already pulling on my jeans and stepping into my Vans.

Grabbing my bag, I rushed out. Three hours to clean a townhouse was barely cutting it. Close. It was mid-August, and yet every time I stepped outside, I felt like the North Pole. I could already tell it was going to be a cold winter.

I had to walk for a good ten minutes before I saw a taxi. They didn't come down to my neighborhood for the same reason I had a taser on me at all times.

"Taxi!" I ran onto the street corner and waved one down like a madwoman because I was freezing.

"317 Beacon Street, please," I said buckling my seatbelt and rubbing my hands.

"You want the heater?" he asked me.

"Please," I said sitting on my hands.

It was one of those nights where it felt like everyone was out, or going into the city. My favorite thing to do was people watch. To me, everyone had a story or somewhere to go. I couldn't afford to live in this city—hell only half of us really could—but I loved it all the same.

Thanks to the driver's shortcuts, it only took us about twenty-five minutes before he pulled up at the elegant, cream-colored townhouse. Paying with everything I had in my wallet, I grabbed my bag and took the stairs two by two. A butler—yes, a fully-fledged butler with penguin tails and everything—opened the door.

"Hi, I'm one of the maids?"

He looked me up and down. "Next time use the service entrance below."

"Yes sir," I nodded as he moved aside to let me in. The very first thing I noticed was that everything was colored in beige, green and off-yellow, but that was before I saw an expensive of marble flooring.

"Oh good, there is another one!" A woman with short blonde hair in a red robe came out holding a glass of wine. "Please tell me this one speaks English. That *Earlena,* or *Erelenea* or *Earlina,* I have no idea how she pronounces it, swears she doesn't understand a thing I'm saying. She just keeps nodding like a bobble head repeating *okay, okay, okay.*"

"*Yo no habla ingles,*" I shrugged at her.

At that, she sighed and her shoulders dropped while she rubbed her temples. "You're in America now. Learn to speak English."

"Okay." I nodded to her, fighting the urge to give her a few other words. She was probably in her early to mid-thirties; there was no reason for her to be this ignorant.

She stared at me then started to shoo me away with her hand like I was dirt going into the dustbin. "Well! Go clean!"

"Yes." I ran around her seeing the second maid in the kitchen but not before hearing her sigh once again.

"Jesus. I swear, Foster, finding a good person like you is impossible nowadays," the drama queen cried out before downing her wine.

"*Eres español?*" an older woman with dark brown-gray hair asked me skeptically. The white skin—though I wouldn't call it ivory white , more like sun-kissed white—was probably the give-away.

"No," I whispered in Spanish, "but she won't know."

She laughed shaking her head, "Earlene."

"Jane," I said shaking her hand in return. "What do you want me to do?"

"Carlotta upstairs. Kitchen, dining. You living room, bathroom and outside."

"Got it," I said reaching for the gloves and the cleaning products. I wanted to put on my earphones and listen to music, but I wanted to make sure I heard her if she called out for me.

The place was a mess.

She had rim stains. The old water stains on her coffee table made me feel like I was going insane. *Use coasters people!* They were only an inch away. Her floors had cracker crumbs all over them, and to make it worse, her couch cushions reeked of wine. I sprayed them down before taking them outside to air out, hopefully before her party. I wasn't sure who the hell her maid was, but she needed to be hog-tied given the amount of crap she missed. All of these things didn't happen in a week: stains, dust behind the mirrors and on picture frames. She was slacking off. The owner might be a bitch, but we still had to do our job.

Moving over to the bathroom, I rolled up my sleeves up to use the toilet bowl cleaner when the rude owner came up behind me.

"Don't forget to use bleach," she said nearly scaring the shit out of me.

"Okay," I nodded to her.

She just eyed me before moving back to the butler. "I still can't believe she doesn't understand English," she said rather loudly.

"Watch them, Foster. If anything goes missing, I will hold you responsible. I'm going to get dressed."

Rolling my eyes, I just scrubbed since there was no point getting upset with people like her. They never changed.

"So you don't understand English?" the butler asked me as I wiped a strand of my hair back with my wrist.

Smiling at him, I shook my head. "No."

He grinned, "Keep up the good work."

"Thanks," I replied.

It took us exactly two hours and twenty-three minutes to finally finish. Amazing really, if all things were considered. My back ached as I leaned on the counter. The caterer had come an hour ago and was carefully preparing every dish along with his staff.

"Okay, I'm not sure of your sizes, but these should work." The owner was now out of her bathroom and in a tight pink floor length gown with a built-in push-up bra that screamed 'stare at my tits'. Around her neck was a long diamond necklace. Her blonde hair was swept to the side, and I wouldn't lie, she looked stunning. I had found out from one of the guys who was setting up the caviar tray, which looked disgusting, that the lady's name was Irene Monrova, the daughter of some big investor or something. She'd just come back from France and was holding a welcome home bash...for herself, which seemed really sad in all honesty.

"What?" Earlene moved to the stack of real black and white maids' uniforms. "No. We clean."

"I just called your boss, so don't worry. I'll pay extra. Come on, go change. Can anyone translate for me?" she glanced over at the food staff.

Earlene looked at her watch. "*Mi Hijo.*"

"Go," I nodded to her taking the dress from her hands. She needed to be with her son.

"Wait what? No! I need you all."

"It's okay. I'll stay and cover whatever she needs to do," I said. Carlotta came over grabbing the black dress and an apron.

"You understand English?" she glared at me.

I shrugged, "A little."

"You're not funny, and if I didn't need you right now, I'd throw you out for making a fool of me."

I wanted to tell her she was doing a fine job by herself, but I just nodded, I was tempted to add an 'okay'.

She spun around and marched over to sample the food.

"How much you think we will get paid for this?" Carlotta asked. She was probably only a few years older than me though she was a full head shorter. Foster pointed to the back room where we could change. It was filled with boxes upon boxes of unopened paintings, chairs and cabinets. There was barely space for us to change, but we managed.

And the moment I tried to button up my dress, one around my breast popped off.

38

"Are you serious right now?" I said, staring at my chest. My tits weren't even that big, but the dresses were just so tight. I looked at Carlotta whose dress fit her perfectly, and I realized this costume was not tall girl friendly.

"Can you ask Ms. Monrova if she has another one?" I asked Carlotta and she nodded, heading out.

I didn't bother covering up. If my boobs offended them, they were going to have to get over it. I was too damn tired to even care at this point.

"What is the problem? Now I'm—" Ms. Monrova came forward, stopping when she saw my black bra.

"You ruined it?"

"It was too tight. Do you have a bigger one?"

"No, I don't have a bigger one. What are we going to do? People are going to be here any minute, and there is no way you can go back out in jeans."

"If Mr. Foster could spare T-shirts and bow ties, I can make formal uniforms for Carlotta and me."

"Who's Carlotta?" She stared at utterly confused.

I pointed to the woman who had just cleaned her house beside her.

"Oh okay. I'll have Foster bring you the shirts, but hurry. Don't ruin this," she huffed before exiting. You'd think this was her wedding day.

Stripping out of the dress, I reached into my backpack and grabbed a pair of scissors and my sewing kit. It wasn't going to have a perfect seam, but at this point, I didn't care. Carlotta handed me hers as well.

"You're so good at that," she said as I cut off the tops and sewed down the extra material.

"Years of practice." If the Bunny Rabbit had taught me anything, it was how to be good under pressure. "Step in, and hold. When I get the shirts I'm going to make it a little tight but you can rip it later to get out of it."

"Miss," There was a knock at the door.

Opening it, I reached out and took the clothing from him. "Thanks Foster."

"No, thank you. Sorry for the short notice." He wasn't the one who should be apologizing to us.

Carlotta took the bigger shirt and buttoned up the clothes front quickly, as I tucked it into the skirt. Some clever cutting into the front made it look like we hadn't stolen shirts from guys. I then pulled the extra material to the back and pinned it in place. Carlotta reached for the bow tie and I took it from her and cut the neck part of the shirt before placing the bow right above her breasts.

"Good." I gave her thumbs up before skipping over to my own. I was sewing and cutting so fast that I cut my finger.

"Ah." I hissed and immediately put my thumb in my mouth, so I wouldn't get any blood anywhere. I then reached into my bag for a Band-Aid.

"Are you okay? You are good at everything." Carlotta laughed at me.

"Years of practice means years of mistakes too," I smiled while wrapping my finger. I then stepped into the skirt after I buttoned up my cutout top with a bow. It was a little tighter when I was done, but it was better than nothing.

"Good?" I asked her while spinning around.

"*Maravilloso.*"

"Yeah, let's just hope the boss thinks so," I muttered stepping out the side.

When I did, she was waiting and tapping her foot nervously. She glanced over us and took a deep breath.

"Okay, let's do this Boston. Irene is back in action."

It was a little after ten by the time I swung around to Irene's townhouse. Max had said he was only five minutes away, and I hoped he was right. Irene was going to need her cousin tonight of all nights.

There were a total of four people who came to welcome her back, not including the staff. They all looked like bloody captives, eyeing the door, but were too afraid to take any steps towards it.

"Welcome sir, may I have your coat?"

"I'm fine mate. I won't be staying long," I told him clasping my hands on his shoulder looking for anything to get me drunk fast enough to forget this cluster fuck already.

Irene and I weren't close at all. However, she frequently brought her 'friends' to my restaurant in order to show off that she knew me personally. As long as she enjoyed the food, I didn't give a bloody hell, either way. My plan was to watch Max struggle to make small talk and then sexually frustrate him across the crowd until he'd make up some bollocks scheme to leave, but that was no longer a possibility. Shame.

Drunk sex would just have to do.

"Pardon me, are you the keeper of the alcohol?" I spoke to the server at the bar cleaning glasses.

"I'll bring some now—" She whipped around nearly tripping over her own feet, the glass in her hands dropping to the floor. Catching her, I held her still. "You alright?"

"I'm so sorry!" she gasped out, brushed back her auburn hair before bending down to pick up the shattered glass.

"Thanks, but I got it," she said when I bent down to help her.

"I'm a professional at broken dishware."

"Oh really this happens a lot?" she snickered, glancing up at me. At the same moment, I looked at her, our faces barely an inch apart.

Her hazel brown eyes were stunning as she stared at me in shock. They were warm brown in the center and seemed to have this honey-colored hue towards the end.

"Sorry," she said again, backing away and standing up. "I'll get a broom."

Just like that, she escaped. I couldn't look away from her. I didn't want too. However, because the master of the universe loved misunderstandings, that just so happened to be the same moment I saw Max standing at the door. He had no expression on his face, which meant he was doing his best not to let anyone know what he was feeling or thinking.

He stared at me once more before walking towards the kitchen.

Angry sex it is then. I thought to myself reaching over the bar and helping myself.

"You cut your hands again?" I heard a maid speak when I stepped into the kitchen. The caterer and his staff were just sitting around either eating the food they were supposed to be serving or mesmerized by their phones.

"It's fine. I dropped a glass. I really need to get back and clean it up before someone gets hurt," the woman I knew to be Ms. Chapman said. She taped a bandage on her finger before taking the broom from the other woman. When Irene had asked me for the number of my cleaning service, I never thought she'd be here.

"Yes, because it's so crowded they won't see broken glass," the other woman mocked. "All that work today for this?"

"I feel bad. She really wants this to go well—"

"No. Don't feel bad for people like them. They'd never feel bad for you. They think the world is centered on them. It's good when God reminds them that they are human too."

"Get back to work!" I hollered when stepping further into the kitchen. "Or are you all just being paid to sit around? There are guests outside who need food and drinks. Go."

Jumping up, they ran one by one, with the exception of Jane who face was more annoyed than I'd like to admit.

"That means you too, Ms. Chapman."

"Of course. Sorry, Irene—Ms. Monrova is in her bedroom. I brought her food, but the door is locked—"

"Okay."

Nodding, she started to walk out, but for some reason, I reached out and grabbed her arm. She glanced up at me, and I'd admit she was pretty, beautiful even, in a strange way. But I didn't understand why Wes was so obsessed with her. Beautiful women were a dime a dozen in this city.

"I'm sorry. Do you need anything, Mr. Emerson?" she asked, not afraid at all. In fact, it felt like she was challenging me.

"You say 'sorry' a lot."

She nodded again. "It's weakness for most people. If they're angry or upset and you say sorry quickly, they automatically relax. So does smiling apparently, but I'm not very good at that."

That was a lie. Only two minutes ago she was smiling at Wes.

"Do I look relaxed?"

"Not even a little bit, Mr. Emerson. But since I haven't done anything, and I'm currently not working for you, I'm sure you can't be angry at me. So can I get my arm back or would you like to intimidate me some more?" She held her head up high at me.

"My apologies, Ms. Chapman. I did not mean to intimidate you," I said overly politely, releasing her arm.

"Yes, you did. It's alright though; it didn't work," she smirked before shaking her head and walking off. I couldn't look away. I felt like I had lost in that altercation; she got the last word, and it bothered me.

Wes stepped out into the hall drinking his glass of brandy. He didn't look at me. He didn't even seem to realize I was there, but I knew him better that. He was a nosy son of a bitch, and he most likely heard all of that.

"Mr. Uhler, it's good to see you again," I said reaching out to shake his hand.

"Likewise, sadly I can't stay long. Please give your cousin my regards. Next time she comes to Wes Hill, it's on me," he replied by shaking my hand before turning to Mr. Foster and leaving.

"Tell the guests to go, Foster. This has gone on long enough," I told him. Heading up the stairs I could see the tray Jane had left out. She had thoughtfully covered all the food with plastic wrap, even the water.

"Irene, open up. It's me," I said while knocking on the door.

No answer.

"Irene, if you don't speak, I'm going to think you're either dead or dying and have to break down the door."

"Go away!" she screamed, throwing something against the wall.

"Irene, you are not a kid. I get it. You're upset, but I can't help if you don't let me in," I said and when she still didn't

46

answer I sighed taking a seat against her door, reaching for her tray of food.

"Fine I'll wait. You know how I just *love* eating cold pasta," I joked, peeling back the wrapper and stuffing the penne in my mouth. I hadn't eaten all day. I hadn't really tried to taste it. After a second, the aftertaste was left in my mouth. Either I was far too used to eating Wes' food, or this was just plain horrible. I wasn't sure.

"One positive thing about no one showing up is that you didn't subjugate them to this!" I reached for the water when she opened to door.

Her mascara was smeared all over her eyelids, her eyes themselves bright red from all the crying.

Still in her dress, she sat down beside me. She took the plate for herself and tried a bit.

"It's good. What are you talking about?" she frowned.

That was what she considered good? What was she eating in Paris? Garbage?

"Slow down or you'll choke, and Siri no longer tells me where to dispose of bodies." This is why I didn't try to make jokes. I was worse than Wes.

"It's been three years, Max. When will everyone forgive me? Not even your parents came," she whispered while blowing her nose.

"My parents aren't known for their forgiveness or patience. Or kindness…or anything positive really."

She snickered. "Are they still pressuring you to get married?"

I didn't answer.

"I'll take that as a yes. You're going to have to tell them you're gay. The rumors—"

"Why label things? Gay? Straight? I've never thought of myself along those lines." I'd been with both men and women and I didn't really care which. For me, it was everyone else with a fucking problem.

"Well, whatever you are, I suggest you figure it out fast before your mother runs for president. Opponents have the knack of digging into personal life."

"They already do that."

"You know what I mean."

Yeah, I did. My mother was going to run for president next term, and she needed the Hallmark-ready family.

"Do you want me to stay?" I changed the subject.

She shook her head. "I really just want to forget. You should head home."

"If you need anything, call," I said heading back towards the stairs.

"And Max," she called out standing up herself, "thank you for coming."

"Always"

"Oh and Max?"

Sighing I turned back to her. "Yes, Irene."

"There is a maid downstairs, Jane. Can you tip her for me? I know we aren't supposed to, but she really did a lot for me today."

Maid Jane strikes again.

I had just put the last of the leftovers in the fridge when Max came into the kitchen. His blue eyes scanned the room and then fell back on me.

"Where is everyone?"

"I thought you told them to leave?"

"And you don't count as everyone?"

I shrugged, "I couldn't just leave the mess. Irene, Ms. Monrova, would have woken up to a dirty house the day after one of the worst nights in her life. It seemed kind of shitty to do that to her."

I wondered what his connection to her was. Were they friends?

"So you are a saint and decided to take one for the team and clean up?"

I didn't like the tone he was using, like he was mocking me.

"No, I'm not a saint. I'm still on the clock, so I get paid for every last hour thank you."

"You're putting in all this effort for an extra ten dollars." He said ignorantly.

My hands ached with the need to smack the shit out of him.

"Yes. I'm working for the extra ten dollars. That extra ten dollars is bread, milk and eggs. Food. Have you ever been starving Mr. Emerson? No? Have you ever been so hungry you feel sick and in pain? Or so poor you eat other people's leftovers in bars? No, I wouldn't think so. I don't live in a penthouse suite. I didn't grow up with a silver spoon in my mouth. I work as hard as I can to get by. An extra ten dollars is…is worth more to me than you can possibly understand. In the process of making that money, I can also help someone. Two birds, one stone, and we maids are all about those discounts."

I was so upset. Did he think I killed myself day in and day out just for the fun it? He could have his rules and his secrets, after all, none of that was my business. But he couldn't insult me for working hard. I wasn't his dog to kick around whenever he was moody.

"I'm sorry. I didn't mean to insult you," he said sincerely. "I'm sorry."

I glared at him. "You're just saying that because I told you it helps people to calm down."

He grinned, and in that second I saw how cute he was. "Being calm is good seeing as you are closest to the knives."

I sighed rubbing my shoulders. "Goodnight, Mr. Emerson."

"I'll give you a ride home."

"What?"

"For being an ass, I'll give you a ride home. You'll save on the bus fare, and I'll feel like less of an ass. We silver spoons like discounts too."

He was right and I had used all of my cash getting here.

"I live in Chelsea. Is that okay?"

"It's fine."

"Give me a second to grab my stuff," I said, walking back to the room where I had changed and stuffed my clothes into my bag before coming back out.

He just stood there waiting and we walked out into the cold air. But I welcomed the fresh air after that tense party.

"You need a second?" he asked me waiting with the door open to his midnight blue 1962 Ferrari.

I grinned. "This is *your* car?"

"No, I stole it off an old lady in Worcester." He rolled his eyes.

"I need to get myself to Worcester." I grinned, sliding in. I ran my hand on the dashboard, looking over at him when he sat down. "I saw this in a movie once, and I told myself if I ever won the lottery this would be my first—well, second purchase."

"After the lecture you just gave me you'd blow seven million on a car?"

I nearly had a heart attack. "Did you say seven million?"

"Six point nine, but I'd leave wiggle room for any tune-ups or replacements," he said, casually pulling onto the road.

I frowned. I didn't know what else to do.

"You look like a kid who found out Santa Claus isn't real," he said relaxing into the cream seats.

I gasped, putting my hand to my heart. "Say what? Who have I been sending letters to at the North Pole all this time?!"

He stared at me like I was insane and then just laughed. So did I.

"I may never win the lottery, and I'll never own this car, but at least I got this chance," I told him.

Closing my eyes, I lifted my hand up into the air as if I were on a roller coaster. "Most of us live our whole lives without having an adventure to call our own. What is life without the pursuit of a dream?"

Inhaling deeply, I opened my eyes when the car stopped at a light. When I looked over him, he was staring at me, not glaring, not angry, just in awe. He looked at me with so much intensity that I shifted in my seat and looked away.

"It's a quote from the movie—"

"*Vanilla Sky,*" he said before I could.

"Let me guess, you hated it?"

"No." He drove when the light changed. "It's actually one of my favorites."

"Really, so many critics tore Tom Cruise apart for that movie, but I personally think it's better than *Jerry Maguire*. The girls at my old job thought I was crazy. I'm rambling. I don't usually ramble." What is up with me? Whenever I was around Wesley or Maxwell, I suddenly started acting like fool.

He didn't say anything for the rest of the ride, so we mostly sat in silence. When we got to my neighborhood, I noticed his car attracted a lot of unwanted attention.

Reaching for my seat belt, I sat up. "You can drop me off at the corner. It's not that far to walk."

"What was the first thing?" he asked me.

"Huh?"

"You said if you won the lottery, this car would be your second purchase. What would be your first?"

"Why do you care?"

He didn't answer.

"Fine, I'd pay off my debt and rejoice at never getting one of those statements in the mail ever again." It was another dream out of reach though.

"I'll pay it." He said out of the blue like it was nothing.

"Come again?"

He spun the car around not answering.

"Hey Mr. Warbucks, my apartment is that way." I pointed to the other direction.

"I'm taking you to my place."

Has he lost his mind? "Yeah. Without my permission, this would be considered kidnapping."

He pulled to a stop on the side of the road. Turning to me, his eyes were shadowy in the dark interior of his car. I wasn't sure whether to run or call an ambulance for him. He sighed.

"My mother is running for president next year." Another random statement that I had no clue where it came from. "She wants her Hallmark-perfect family beside her, and it would be great if her son wasn't bisexual."

"Did you tell her she'd actually win the presidency if she embraced the rainbow?"

He snickered and leaned back. "It's more than that. My family is old, white and conservative, so are my viewers, actually. There's nothing wrong with that, my political views also line up that way. *Time* magazine called me 'the young blood and soul of the New Republican Party'. I want to run for office one day, but my party isn't ready follow a man who enjoys fucking another man."

"You want me to be your beard and pretend to be in a relationship with you," I whispered, finally catching on. But how long would that last? It seemed better to just tell the truth.

"Not just a relationship. I want you to marry me."

3

"You asked her to marry you?" Wes said he as laid back on the bed trying to figure out how the hell I fell down this hole.

"I honestly don't know what happened," I said, resting my arm on my face. "I was just going to take her home. Thank her for her effort at Irene's. Then we started to talk about how much she loved my car. She threw her hands up in the air, and the wind blew her hair back. She had this beautiful genuine smile across her lips, and she was so damn happy just to have the chance to ride in it. Then she quoted *Vanilla Sky* and in that second I thought…"

I felt him hovering him above me. Letting my arm drop to the side, I stared up at him. "You thought what?" He didn't look away from me.

"I thought if you wanted her and she wanted you I wouldn't mind. That we could all win in this. I'd get my mother off my back. You'd get rid of these fasciations you have with her, and she'd get enough money to stop working herself so hard," I said softly, reaching up to brush back a strand of his sandy brown hair.

"You want her, too," he said again with his arms on either side of my head. "That's why you asked her. Even if was just once, you ..."

I kissed him just to make him shut the fuck up. And even as he moaned into my mouth, I couldn't stop thinking of her: how she arched her back against the seat of my car and how soft her pink lips looked. I remembered the first time we both heard her moan. Everything was clouding my mind and having him this close to me wasn't helping.

So I just needed to stop thinking.

Reaching up I pushed him back, flipping him over, pinning him below me. Gripping his neck, I glared down at him. "Stop thinking about her and start thinking more about me."

Pushing me back, fighting in my arms, we rolled over and over on top of the bed, me on top, him on top until Wes grabbed a fist full of my hair, and tugged my head back, and we were both on our knees...

"I'm always thinking about you!" Wes sneered while I kissed his jaw and tugged harder. "Every fucking day you are on my mind. I can never get a damn break from you. I revolve around you! You are an addiction I can never shake so don't make me keep repeating it!"

Fuck.

"Wes—"

"Strip. Apparently you need a physical reminder," he commanded releasing his grip on my hair his eyes hard completely serious...turning me on with every breath. "Now."

My heart pounded against my chest as I did what he asked. Getting off the bed I stood up pulling off my tie—

"Slower." He leaned back against the pillows.

He knew I hated being put on the spot like this, but he also knew I wouldn't disobey him when he got like this. I unbuttoned my shirt slowly for him.

He called me an addiction.

Then, who was he to me? An obsession? A sweltering passion?

When I stood in front of him naked, I took a deep breath, trying to calm myself down. With each second my cock got harder and harder, twitching anxiously. He got up and walked past me, grabbing something from the drawer.

"You know what I was just thinking about?" he asked, when he came back standing in front of me, "How good you'd look with balls in your mouth."

Before I could speak he lifted a ball gag to my lips. Glaring at him, I opened my mouth both turned on as fuck and deeply frustrated.

I took a shower hoping to relax enough to go to bed, but it only made me more aware of everything: the fact that I was naked in a million-dollar penthouse, and also the fact that I was spending the night at said penthouse and that the owner of the penthouse had asked me to marry him. I'm not sure where I took the wrong turn, but this no longer felt like my usual mundane life.

I debated the options.

"No debt," I muttered to myself as I dried my hair. "On the other hand marriage. A fake marriage."

There was no way this could work.

"Ugh, I can't." Dropping the brush and hair dryer, I wrapped the towel around myself and stepped into the same room I'd cleaned over and over again in the last month. The king size bed with eight damn pillows just for decoration. Another window for hand cleaning. The plush white carpet I vacuumed...it was now supposed to be my room...even for just a night it was—

"Ahh...urgh... Fuck."

Moving closer to my door, I listened but wasn't sure what I was hearing. My mind told me to keep the door closed, but my hand didn't seem to get the message. I opened the door a crack just to peek out, but I only saw a dim yellow light.

Stay in.

But instead I walked out, tiptoeing across the floorboards while clenching the towel to my chest. I wasn't sure what I was expecting but Maxwell with a red ball gag in his mouth, gripping the sheets as Wesley thrust into his ass was not it. I felt myself stop breathing and was awestruck at how beautiful they were. They were like wild animals as they grunted, ecstasy coating Max's face. Just like before, his blue eyes fixed on me and yet the rage he had before was gone. When his mouth parted so did mine. I felt myself getting wet, and while I knew I should look away, I couldn't. Not with the way he was looking at me.

"Juahm ..." Max tried to speak against the ball. Wes opened his eyes and stared straight at me as he stopped a drop of sweat on his chin from dripping onto Max's back. He pulled out of him, and Max collapsed on the bed, but Wes got off the bed and moved to the door. I stared at his cock. It was fucking huge, erect and pointed right at me. I tried not to look, but I was human. Damn it! I then noticed his six-inch tattoo on his inner thigh, which read: *'I solemnly swear that I am up to no good.'* He smirked at me, never breaking eye contact as he slowly shut the door.

I was far too embarrassed to think straight. Turning around, I just ran.

Slamming the door closed, I fell back on it and panted.

"Jesus fuck," I muttered dropping the towel and rushing back into the bathroom, turning the shower on cold. My skin was on fire.

When I stepped in, I shivered, trembling under the water as it beat against me. I wanted to think of something else. For the second time now, I had intruded on their private life and I felt like a damn pervert. It was like I was mesmerized by it...two grown men in love... two men fucking. It wasn't any of my business. It was wrong and rude to gawk at them, and I knew that. Yet, I couldn't erase the scenes from my mind.

"Stop thinking," I muttered putting my head directly under the stream of ice water. But it was easier said than done.

The look of pleasure on Max's face, the way the whole bed jerked forward as Wes rammed his cock into him. The way Wes walked up to the door completely naked and proud of it. The grin on his lips when he stared me down, never breaking eye contact until the door was shut completely. How do you need forget about something like that?

"You don't," I whispered to myself, turning off the water and stepping out on to the rugs. There was no steam on the mirrors.

It was just a little wet, so I could still see my body perfectly: my hair sticking to my body, water sliding down my neck and chest only to drip off my very hard nipples, thanks to the cold. "What are you doing Jane?"

Reaching up, I smacked myself across the face because I need to wake up from whatever daydream or fantasy I was falling into.

I'm not marrying Maxwell Emerson. The very fact that I even considered his proposition proved just how desperate I was. However, I have worked every day of my life and the number one lesson I have learned is that the only person who I can count on is me. There was no saving grace or easy path. Cinderella was a fairytale.

"But I'm a maid." I nodded to myself. I pulled back my wet hair into a ponytail deciding I'd dry it when I got back home.

Moving back into the bedroom, I didn't bother to dry off. Instead, I grabbed my clothes and rolled up my sleeves. Peeking at my phone, I stared at the time. 12: 47 a.m. It was officially Saturday morning. I had to clean, and after that, I'd go back home. If I didn't vacuum and did my best to be quiet, I wouldn't disturb them. Plus they were otherwise occupied.

Grabbing the towel I had dropped, I moved to the laundry room. The blue basket was filled with socks, underwear, T-shirts and a few towels. Separating the colors and whites, I sorted them out to wash before taking the red basket for dry cleaning, and closed the washing machine door. I was grateful they had one of those silent machines.

Cracking my neck to the left and then to the right, I took a deep breath before I got to work by first sliding on my cleaning gloves. If I was lucky, I'd be done before they woke up in the morning.

"Mr. Window...we meet again." I smiled to myself staring up at the large window overlooking Boston.

"Wes!" Max grumbled at me and rolled away when my phone alarm went off. But I was far too tired to get up. "Turn it off before I throw it out the goddamn window!"

He could be such a twat sometimes. Rolling my eyes, I sat up rubbing my eyes as I reached for it.

6:10 a.m.

The thought of going to the market this morning exhausted me, but I got up anyway and stretched.

"What do you want for breakfast?" I asked him knowing he never stayed in bed long after I got up. He wasn't a morning person, but once he was up, there was no hope he'd get back to sleep. Four years of this and you'd think he'd be used to it already.

"Anything." He was lying on his stomach, the sheets barely covering his ass.

"Risotto with leeks, shiitake mushrooms, and truffles then?" I asked reaching for my jeans.

He rolled over opening the only eye to see if I was serious. Last time he said 'anything' I made him just that and he had to force him to eat it on my behalf.

"On second thought, bacon and eggs are fine," he yawned.

Nodding, I opened the door, remembering why it was closed in the first place, and saw a pile of shirts, towels, socks and underwear folded neatly at my feet. There was a note on top.

"Your fiancée is up," I said and he groaned, most likely remembering his impromptu proposal he gave last night.

"You mean our own penthouse Peeping Tom," he grumbled. Getting up out of bed, he winced and gripped his back. I grinned proudly. "Shut up."

"I didn't say anything," I shrugged. He put on his boxers finally noticing the folded laundry. I let him pick up the message. *Sorry, I wasn't able to clean your room. It will be given a twice over next time.*

I paused before glancing back down at the time. Stepping over the laundry, I looked around the penthouse. It was spotless.

"She made breakfast?" Max came up beside me nodding to the kitchen, where two trays were left out. There was plastic wrap over the plates and another Post-it note.

"It's six in the morning. When the bloody hell did she does this?" I asked walking down the stairs. I could see that the room she was supposed to be sleeping in was now empty. From the temperature of the plate of scrambled eggs, strawberry pancakes, bacon, and toast, she had left only minutes ago. This time I took the note.

"I know this is probably not up to par with the great Wesley Uhler's cooking, but I made breakfast, first to say sorry for last night *again* and second because I didn't want a lot of dishes left in the sink." She had tried to write small but still needed to use the back of the Post-it. Maxwell just stared at his plate.

"If the maid thing doesn't work, she should try a career in burglary," he stated and I understood what he meant. How could we have slept through all of this? Sitting down on the stool, he pulled back the plastic wrap to eat.

"Well?" I waited.

"Too much salt," he replied but kept eating.

Reaching for my fork, I cut into the pancakes and scooped the eggs with it before taking a bite. The moment I did, I smirked. He lied. It was good. Not better than me, but good. He just couldn't admit it.

"You're right, too much salt," I lied along with him.

"I'm guessing this means she's rejecting my proposal?" he asked still eating.

"Are you disappointed?"

His glanced up at me and was luckily saved when my phone rang.

"What?" I answered.

"Chef, we only got two truffles—"

"Two? I asked for two dozen!"

"Well—"

"I'll be there in twenty." Hanging up, I took another bite before getting up, "I have to go."

He just nodded and I licked the syrup from the corner of his lips before rushing up the stairs. When I got to the top, I paused to glance at the spare bedroom. I wondered what was going on in her mind...

"Jane you begged me for this job." Mary reminded me as I sat in her office on Monday morning. I had slept all of the Sunday, missing six of her calls. I didn't realize how exhausted I was until I laid down. I didn't even eat. I just slept.

"I know and I still want to clean, but just not that penthouse. It would be better if I could switch jobs with another maid."

"Did something happen?" She leaned toward me and I could tell she was scanning for any marks or bruises. "If something happened, I swear—"

"Nothing happened." That wasn't a lie. Nothing happened in the way she was thinking. "I just.." I needed to think of something she'd believe. "I have crush on the owner and I act awkward, okay! I don't want to be there. I need to focus."

"You, Jane 'the Warden' Chapman, have a crush?"

"No please!" I groaned at that name. The girls at the Bunny Rabbit gave it to me as a joke, but it stuck, and I hated it with a passion.

"Something smells fishy here," she pressed. I just pointed to the angelfish she had in the corner of her office, which made her glare at me. "You aren't funny."

"It was a little funny," I beamed. "Mary, you know me, and I always do my best to stay focused, so it's weird for me, too. That's why I want to get out before anything happens."

"So there is a possibility of things *happening*?" Her red eyebrow rose. At this point she was just being nosy.

"Mary. Please."

"I can't just switch you out. Mr. Emerson made it very clear that he wanted one maid only. I have to let him know."

"Fine, but in the meantime do you have anything else for me?"

She made a face her lips stretching out into a thin line. "You are so lucky sometimes."

Me lucky! Hah! Luck and I didn't even live in the same hemisphere.

"Irene Monrova, you worked for her on Friday, asked if you could fill in on Mondays, which is why I tried so hard to call yesterday."

See? This was the type of 'luck' I got.

"What's wrong?" she asked.

"Nothing. I'll go there now. It's only noon." I grabbed my scarf and bag and stood up to go.

"Are you still able to work on Wednesdays at Mrs. Crofton's and Thursdays at Mr. Wells, or do you have a secret crush on one of them too?" she mocked with a fat grin on her face.

I pretended to think. "Now that you mention it, Mr. Wells sure knows how to rock a cane, and that receding hairline, missing teeth, wrinkled old hands…it's kind of hot."

"Eww…Jane!" Her face bunched up and she even wiggled in her chair as if she was trying to shake the thought from her whole body.

"Bye, Mary, and thank you." I flashed her a smile, since she always told me to, before leaving.

Just like that, I had washed my hands of Maxwell and Wesley. I wasn't going to embarrass myself anymore. The second rule of survival I'd learned growing up was that if it got messy or dangerous, it was okay to run.

Running was good; anyone who said otherwise would be the first one to die in a horror movie.

4

Why did I answer the phone?

"Hello, Mr. Emerson? Are you there?" said the voice on the line.

"Yes, I'm here."

"This is Mary Turner from Mary's Magnificent Maids. I wanted to ask you if you would be alright with a change of maids."

Why did I answer the phone? I saw the number on the screen. I knew who it was and to add to the discomfort, I was at work. I didn't have time to worry about a damn maid. Yet I answered the fucking thing anyway.

"What is wrong with the maid I already have?" I questioned, signing off on the segment board in front of me.

"She was personally requested by another client," she replied and I could feel my jaw clenching, but I had no idea why.

"Ms. Turner, is this how you do business?"

"Excuse me?"

"Maybe you aren't aware, but I'm a private person. I do not do well with change. It has taken me over a month to get used to this new maid, and now you are telling me she has another client who wants their home cleaned at exactly same time as mine? Or maybe you do know and this is just a ploy to get more money."

"Mr. Emerson, no never—"

"Then I want the same goddamn maid on Tuesdays and Saturdays like always. Have a nice day, Ms. Turner." Hanging up, I threw phone back on my desk and leaned back.

If I wasn't sure before, I was now. She'd rejected my offer and now she was trying to quit. Here was the same woman who had the goddamn nerve to lecture me on the value of working extra, no matter how hard it is, was now quitting a perfectly good paying job.

Hypocrite.

Great! Wes was going to blame me or at the very least think I got rid of her because I was jealous. I didn't give a fuck. We never said we were exclusive. We hadn't been with anyone else in years, or at least I hadn't, but that still didn't change the fact that there were no rules between us.

"She is just a maid," I muttered to myself. *So why I am so damn pissed off!?*

"Mr. Emerson?"

"What?" I snapped when my assistant poked her head into my office. She jumped back pushing her glasses further up her nose.

"Ahmm...I...you're...the meeting is starting."

Rubbing my eyes, I nodded. "I'm on my way."

Rising, I took my phones before walking around my desk and stepping out of my office and into the pit. Over two dozen employees on this floor alone were glued to their computers, and on some nights they looked like zombies. Everyone in the media business started there until they found that one story which would help them climb up.

Walking around them, a few of them looked up and nodded to me. They were the ones who were going to sink and soon. The ones who paid no attention to me who were typing, on calls, sliding back and forth on their chairs as they shared information, were the workaholics who would make it far.

"What do we have?" I said instantly as I walked into the meeting, taking my seat at the front table. An intern ran up to place a coffee cup in my hand.

As always, Scarlet de Burgh, my producer, got up first. As she moved to the front of the white conference table, her wavy brunette hair brushed the top of her shoulders. "The Governor MacDowell scandal is a treasure trove; the more we poke, the more we find. There is correspondence with Tyson Pharmaceuticals and an RMH which all have questionable financial ties to him. All are denying. The police aren't releasing anything—"

"Who do we have outside of the police station? It's all about timing," I questioned, taking a sip of the coffee before sliding back and spitting it out. My eyes snapped to the intern I was going to fire. "What the fuck is this?"

"Your coffee?" he replied.

Lifting the lid up, I showed it to him. "I drink my coffee black. Does this look like black to you? I would ask if you're color blind, but seeing as even then you should be able to tell the difference between coffee shades, that isn't an excuse! Which leaves me with the belief that you are an idiot. Are you an idiot 'Intern's name' who I do not know or care to know? Never mind. You're fired."

"What?"

"GET OUT!" I yelled and he ran, tripping over his own feet as he went. Spinning back to the table, all of their eyes were glued on me—terrified—with the exception of Scarlet.

"Tonight, we make public that the police and the district attorney are not being transparent. We are going to put pressure on them, and I want a story to be published immediately after I go live doubling down on that. The people of this state have a right to know what the fuck their governor was doing with their tax money. If you meet resistance, call them out for being in someone's pocket. If they aren't, they will be vindicated. If they are, well…that's just another story."

No one moved. They just stared.

"You can go." I snapped. They grabbed their tablets and quickly filed out one by one, as I leaned back in the chair.

"You know this is why they call you the Maxannosaurus Rex, right?" Scarlet asked, coming up beside me, taking a seat on the table. "However, today you are a little more blood thirsty than usual. What's wrong?"

I don't know!

"Nothing," I lied.

Her bright blue eyes narrowed and she lifted her head up. "Your parents again?"

"Are you my producer or my therapist?"

"For you, I have to be both."

"I'm fine Scarlet."

"Mr. Emerson?" My assistant once again popped her head inside. "Your mother is on line two—"

"What did I tell you to do when my family calls?"

"Send them to voicemail, but she said it's important and keeps calling." No sooner had she said it my phone rang, proving that my mother had this office wiretapped. I was sure of it.

"Let's go, Lily, before our favorite dinosaur tries eating us whole," Scarlet patted my shoulder before walking out.

"For the record, if I hear anyone else referring to me as a giant lizard, I'm firing them too!" I called out as she left. She only waved back obviously not caring.

Reaching for the phone, I prepared myself for the tongue-lashing I was about to get.

"Hello Mother," I said politely.

"Mother." Her high voice stabbed into my ears. "Siri, Google 'Mother'." She must have spoken to her other phone and lifted it for me to hear. "Females who inhabit or perform the role of bearing some relation to their children, who may or may not be their biological offspring."

"Is this your way of saying I'm adopted?" *If so, it looked like life was finally looking up.*

"You drive me insane, Maxwell, and you know it! Who screens their mother's calls?"

"Anyone above the age of sixteen."

She took a deep breath. "Tonight I'm having a very *important* party. You will be there, with a beautiful young woman, preferably someone who will not embarrass you or me and is of marriage material. You will smile, you will laugh, you will pretend you are the only son of the Emerson family, and heir to everything when your father and I die. Which might be

74

soon since you are keen in breaking my heart. It will be a splendid night and then you can go back to your fortress of solitude on the top of Boston. Do you understand?"

"Where am I supposed to find this *beautiful* young unattached woman?" I asked.

"I don't know son, but the brunette producer in your office seems like a viable option for one."

"Goodbye, Mother," I hung up fighting the urge to drop my head on the table. Apparently my phone was cursed today.

"I looked pitiful the other night, right?" Irene asked me at the door while dressed an outfit I could not afford, diamond earrings only seen in catalogs, and perfect makeup while I scrubbed her toilet.

If she was what 'pitiful' looked like, I'd love to take a stab at it.

"No, you didn't," I finally answered while spraying the toilet bowl with bleach.

"I used to be really popular; people lined up to come to my parties."

I realized she really didn't give a damn what I thought, she just wanted to vent, but listening to rich people and their sob stories were not in my job description.

"People in this city...they are just so fake. You know? They all love you when you have money and power, but the moment you slip up, they leave you out in the cold."

Again this was not my business...but again she didn't give a fuck and I could do nothing about that.

"I killed someone." My head whipped back to face her and she broke out laughing. "Oh my God! Your face! Ha! Ha! HA! You looked ready to piss your pants."

"That wasn't funny."

"Now you know how I felt when you said you didn't know English." She crossed her arms.

"Touché," I nodded before standing up and flushing the toilet. "I'll keep that in mind."

"Keep what in mind?"

"That you have a twisted sense of humor," I blurted out, but she didn't care and instead smiled brightly at me.

"You know you're way too pretty to be a maid."

"I tried being a prostitute, but it didn't work out."

Her eyes widened, and this time I laughed.

"Who has the twisted humor now?" She shook her head at me.

"I never said there was anything wrong with dark humor. In fact, I applaud it." I grabbed the bucket, and moved out of her bathroom to go back downstairs.

"Jane, are you done?"

"Yes, why?" Turning to face her, I prayed to god she didn't have anything else for me to do. I'd already cleaned for five hours.

"I need help." She pointed to the two dresses on her bed. The first was a beautifully simple emerald sweetheart dress with sleeves that would fall over the shoulder. The other was an elegant champagne chiffon dress with lacy cap sleeves.

"Definitely the champagne one."

"Great, you can wear the green."

"I'm sorry. Come again?" I stared at her, hoping that she'd laugh to prove that it was another dark joke...like, ha ha ha, of course you can wear the thousand-dollar dress. Just kidding, 'you're a maid' type of joke.

But she took the cleaning bucket from my hand and put it down by the door.

"Ms. Monrova—"

"Everyone who didn't come to my party is going to be there," she said on the brink of tears, picking at her nails. "They are going to huddle together and laugh at me."

"Then don't go."

She shook her head. "If I did that, they would know I was hiding. I have no friends here anymore. If I go alone, I'll just sit there with one—"

"You're beautiful! Don't you have a guy you can call? Someone... anyone..."

She shook her head. "I've burned a lot of bridges. Besides, if I brought a guy, they'd either try to steal him away or talk about me until he distanced himself from me."

What was this? The adult version of *Mean Girls*?

"Whoever these people are, they aren't worth it."

"Yes, they are!" she snapped. "I'm sorry. I don't want to come off as offensive because I really do need your help. Nor do I want to insult you because you just don't get it. Yes, these women are catty bitches. No, I don't want to be their friends. But they are the daughters of senators, bankers, moguls and a lot of important people who can make life harder than it needs to be. I would rather be in the room being ignored than out in the cold. It's just the way it is. I'll pay you personally for the overtime."

I wanted to cry, stomp my feet, or do anything to get out of this. But I was weak-willed when it came to people who needed help. Even though this was the dumbest, most annoying and elitist type of 'help', I could remember her sobbing at her party.

"Why me?"

"You're hot, but not hotter than me. And if I go there with a new bestie no one knows and laugh my ass off at our twisted jokes, then they'd see I don't care and I can make friends. You wouldn't happen to know French would you?"

"I do."

"Oh my God!" She grabbed on to my shoulders jumping around. "This is fate!"

If fate was a stripper named Dominique, yeah maybe. I loved learning. It was my way of overcompensating for never getting to go to college. Dominique spoke it all the time and the men poured open their wallets for her. I said a few words and got better tips. 'A' plus 'B' equaled me learning French; anything to make an extra dollar. Allen then marketed the Bunny Rabbit as the only exotic strip club in the city with full-on French burlesque night and everything.

That was about my only talent, though.

"Jane?"

"What?"

"You're going to be my exotic French friend. We need to come up with a name—"

"Jane," I said.

She frowned, "What?"

"I don't change my name for anyone. Jane. Besides, are you sure you want to get caught in a lie later?"

"You really are no fun."

"Great you can take someone else." I moved toward the door but she grabbed my arm.

"Fine but at least, speak in French, please?"

How? How in the hell did I get myself into this shit all the time?!

"Okay, you might want to take a shower since you smell like bleach." She wrinkled her nose and backed away. I could only stare in shock.

So apparently I had two talents: languages and getting myself in the most unpredictable and ridiculous situations known to man.

****

"How is it possible you look better than me?" she pouted when I stepped into her room. I wasn't sure how to answer that because I wasn't sure if she was trying to insult or compliment me...maybe both.

Turning back to my reflection in her mirror, I still could not believe it was me. I wore light make up like always, but Irene had added some light, smoky eye shadow and it had made a big difference. My brown auburn hair was curled at the ends and was parted to one side to expose my neck. It stopped at the side of my breasts, the mounds of which you could perfectly see because of the sweetheart of the shape of the dress. Irene also offered me a diamond bracelet to wear, but I couldn't bring myself to take it. First because I was scared I'd lose it and have to sell her my soul, and second because it was too much. She instead suggested I wear some diamond earrings, and I gave in only because at least those would be attached firmly to my body and not just dangling off my wrist.

But the tip of the iceberg, the damn cherry on top of the ice cream were the heels... her beautiful, stunning, silver shimmering Christian Louboutin pumps that fit my feet like a glove.

Wait. I had been so swept up again that I didn't catch it immediately.

"What size shoe do you wear?"

She stood next to me fluffing her hair. "Size eight and a half. Why?"

"I wear a seven," I told her and she still didn't get it. "How do these shoes fit me?"

She froze.

I glanced down at the dress again. My breasts were bigger than hers and yet the dress cupped me perfectly.

"You had this planned all along, didn't you?" I backed away from her. She was much smarter than I initially thought. She called Mary, got me here just so she wouldn't have to go the party alone and I fell right for it.

"If you haven't noticed, I'm a little desperate," she replied, a small smile on her lips.

"You spent thousands of dollars just to have a friend? You could have gotten an escort."

She shrugged taking her clutch. "Nothing I can do now. Let's go. We're already late."

What the hell?

Part of me was impressed…another larger part of me was a little creeped out. But I followed her anyway.

Foster stood at the bottom of the stairs. Upon seeing me, his eyebrow rose. A teasing smile spread on his old face. "*Lady* Chapman."

"Don't even start," I glared. "You didn't warn me when I got here."

"You'll learn. Ms. Monrova is hard to say 'no' to."

Leaning over to him as she put on her coat, I whispered, "She isn't crazy is she?"

"Have a good evening *Lady* Chapman." He snickered before leaving me to fend for myself.

"Jane come on!" She threw me a fur jacket and I glanced at the clock. It was after nine. *Only three more hours until midnight and I could turn back into a pumpkin.*

Placing the coat on, I rushed out to the waiting Mercedes.

"I look alright…right?"

Isn't too late to be asking? "You look beautiful. Completely stunning."

"French, remember?"

Sighing I repeated, "*Vous êtes belle. Très étonnante.*"

"*Merci et toi.*" She giggled leaning back into the chair.

Rolling my eyes, I glanced out the window not sure why I had butterflies in my stomach. I was nervous but had no idea why.

"If you planned this, why did you make me clean your house first?" I asked her.

"Because it was dirty, of course"

I turned back to her. "I cleaned on Friday. You messed it up on purpose didn't you? So I wouldn't just leave?"

"You make me sound a lot more devious than I really am," she said pretending to check her phone.

She was insane. I kind of liked her for it, though.

One night playing dress up couldn't hurt right?

5

From Boston to Weston, aka the third wealthiest town in the United States, was only thirty minutes, but it felt like I had gone across the world. The houses here were bigger than half my neighborhood. It was insanity. When we drove up the long driveway and around the water fountain to the European-styled mansion, my stomach dropped and I didn't want to get out of the car.

"Welcome," the doorman said. Stepping up, I held on to the coat around my shoulders while Irene came through the other door to stand beside me.

"Be mysterious," she said in French and I hoped that meant not speaking.

"Names?" said another man at the door who was dressed in a tailored suit. Given the cold night, I was worried the poor man would freeze.

"Seriously" Irene snapped annoyed. "Irene Monrova, Elspeth Yates' niece."

The moment she said that, he straightened up. "Sorry ma'am, but we were instructed to check everyone. Please enjoy."

Elspeth Yates? Where had I heard that name before?

"May I have your coats?" A maid took it from me before I could answer. Irene didn't even blink; she just tossed it to her.

Leaning into me, Irene whispered, "Smile. The vultures are all here."

I didn't know what she meant until I stepped around the corner into the large living room. Most of the furniture had been moved for the party, but that didn't at all take away from the décor. The paintings that hung on the walls had to have been lifted straight from a museum; hell, the place was like a museum. I was actually interested in seeing more of it, but all the guests' eyes were focused on her...us...the both of us. They glared at her as if she was actually a murderer, and I felt her take a step back. She was scared and she couldn't move.

"Irene," I whispered.

"This was a bad idea. I'm sorry." I grabbed her arm before she could run. Speaking in French I said to her, "I have no idea what you did, but I spent hours today cleaning your house. I let you convince me to come to come to a party that I want no part of, in a dress I am terrified of ruining. You are going to walk in there like the motherfucking queen of England, or so help me, I'm going lose my shit."

She stared at me wide-eyed before laughing and took a step forward. "Your French is a little rough around the edges but good."

Of course, that's all she got from my speech. Shaking my head, I walked after her. When I did, two guys across the room smiled at me. I smirked, making direct eye contact with them before looking away and taking one of the glasses of champagne. I was supposed to make her look good, right?

"You're a natural," she said to me.

I learned from strippers, so of course I was a natural. For the men at least I could fake it because whether they were in a suit or jeans, they functioned the same.

"Irene! Long time, no see," A blond man was the first to come over to us and his brown eyes dropped over to me. "Who's your friend?"

"How do you know I'm her friend? We could be lovers," I said in French knowing he couldn't understand. Irene snorted and tried not to laugh.

He looked at us confused. "I'm sorry. What was that?"

"Jane," I answered him offering him a hand.

"Archibald Saint James," he said kissing the back of it, "but my friends call me Archie."

"That's quite nice of your friends, Mr. Saint James," I said and the corner of his lips turned up.

"I think so too, maybe you—"

"That's a very long handshake, *Archibald.*" We both turned to find Maxwell Emerson dressed in a fitted black suit and bow tie with his hand in his pocket. His blue eyes glared at Archibald.

Elspeth Yates...Elspeth fucking Yates...his mother! Shit!

He said nothing more, but walked up beside me and placed his hand on my waist. My eyes widened. I wanted to push him away, but I didn't want to draw any more attention. I was trapped.

Whoever said no good deed goes unpunished was talking to me.

Contrary to popular belief, I did not hate people. Did some people annoy me? Yes. Did I often lose my temper? Who doesn't? However, I hated Archibald Saint James so vehemently that if he were drowning in front of me, I'd go inside and make a sandwich.

His snake eyes dropped to my hand on her waist, and I tried to ignore the heat coming off her skin.

"Maxwell, I didn't know you were acquainted with such a beautiful *woman.*" He pressed, obviously feeding into the circulating rumor that I had to be gay. To gossip mongers, this explained why I never brought women to any of my parents' ridiculous parties thrown with the simple purpose of showing off their wealth.

Turning to Jane, I could tell she was yelling at me with her eyes. Reaching up, I cupped her waist harder and blatantly kissed her. She stared and I gave her ass a squeeze to intimate to her to play along. Closing her eyes, she kissed me back, but before it went any further than that, we broke apart. Her lips were puffy and her face flushed.

"Now you know, Archibald," I said, taking Jane's hand and pulling her away from the living room completely.

I didn't stop walking, or let go, and I could feel myself getting heated, but I wasn't sure why. The image of Archibald kissing her hand pissed me off. Or was it the shock of seeing her to begin with? Dressed like….dress….

"Let go!" She kicked me in the shin once we were in the privacy of my childhood bedroom.

"What the fuck!" I hissed, releasing her hand to grab my now thumping leg.

"That's what I want to know, asshole!" she screamed at me, kicking one more time and forcing me to back away. "How dare you put your lips on me without asking first?"

"Stop it now!" I yelled when she tried to kick me again. She just lifted her fist. "I was trying to save you!"

"From what?"

"Him! He's a fucking rapist!"

She froze with her fist still in the air. "What?"

"Fuck." I hissed sitting back on my bed rolling up my trousers, sure enough my shin was bleeding. Her heel was one hell of the weapon. "You should be thanking me not assaulting me."

"Says the man who grabbed my ass," She crossed her arms, still keeping her distance. "What do you mean he's a rapist?"

"I wasn't aware there was a differing definition of a rapist," I snapped at her while wincing when I touched the wound.

She sighed before looking around the room and opening a few doors until she got into a bathroom. I heard the water turning on for a second, and she came back out with a wet washcloth. Moving to sit on the bed beside me, she grabbed my leg and placed it on her lap.

"Why is he here if he is a rapist? I thought your mother was running for president?" she said softly dabbing my shin.

"Because he wasn't officially prosecuted for rape. His family paid them off. The victim was some broke college student. The moment she took the money, she left Boston for good. I'm sure there are more like her, but when your father owns one of the biggest financial services companies in the country, you can sweep a lot more under the rug. I kissed you because the only family you don't mess with is mine. If he thinks you're mine, you're safe."

She frowned at me and looked up with those big hazel eyes of hers. "You're this super famous reporter, so why not expose him?"

"So famous you didn't even know me when we first met?"

She pursed her lips to the side, and I was starting to notice she was horrible at controlling her facial expressions.

"I don't count since I don't watch the news. Not that I'm dumb or anything or don't care what's going on—"

"You just don't have time because you're working." She was always working. "Except you tried to quit this morning"

"I didn't try to quit."

"Really, your boss called me to tell me I was getting a new maid—"

"It's for the best."

"Don't decide what is best for me," I replied pulling my leg away from her.

She glared. "I wasn't. I was deciding what was best for me. Contrary to your ego, Mr. Emerson, the world does not revolve around you."

"So it's a no to the marriage then?"

She threw her hands up. "Yes! Do you know how crazy you sound! You don't even know me and you are in love with... I'm not marrying a stranger for money. You and your cousin both think you can buy people with money. Maybe you can. But you can't buy me."

She annoyed the hell out of me.

"You're an idiot," I said when she got up to leave.

"What?" She spun back to me.

Standing up, I fixed my tie. "You are an idiot. You think working hard is the secret to making it? How do you think half of these people got to the point where they spend three hundred dollars on a plate of pasta? Maybe once upon a time, hard work was the reason. Maybe there is one out of a few thousand people who succeeds that way now. Some people are born lucky and into wealth. Some people are born extremely intelligent or athletic. But for the majority, it's a plain hustle. Why do you make ten dollars, and your boss, who doesn't even clean houses, makes sixteen? You do whatever you can to get up the ladder and most times that means using people. You've probably been working your ass off all your life, most likely getting screwed while you're at it, too. But are you any better off than you were last year? Any opportunity you have to get ahead, you should take. If you don't, you're either scared or an *idiot*."

I was expecting her to snap back at me, but she stood there like I had slapped her across her face. Her eyes glazed over with tears she wouldn't let fall.

"Maybe you are right. I have been screwed over by bosses. It's not fair and yet I keep working. I'm workaholic Jane." She shrugged. "But I don't have anyone to step on. All I have is me, so I treasure myself more than anyone or anything in the world. So if I let you try to buy me as if I'm nothing but an item and not a person...then I won't like myself. And if I don't like myself, I will have nothing. *Nothing is painful.*"

She quickly wiped a tear off her cheek and spun around to leave. It was only when she left that I felt like I could breathe again...even so, my heart saw someone so beautiful on the outside but so broken on the inside.

"Way to go." The door opened and Irene stepped in and my shoulder drooped. She was the other beautiful broken woman in my life driving me insane.

"Why did you bring her here?"

"I wanted to see how you'd react to her all dressed up," she replied leaning against my door. "I heard you fighting on Friday, and that was the first time I've seen you so engaged with a woman. You like her."

Walking up to her, I made sure she understood I was not playing around. "Do. Not! Drag her into your mess, Irene. You are twenty-eight years old, so fix things yourself. Last time you used people, how did that work out for you?"

"Fuck you," she hissed before exiting.

Why did this shit happen to me?

Nothing is painful. Jane's voice echoed in my mind, and I suddenly felt the urge to find her. Only to apologize of course.

When I said I had an addiction to Maxwell Emerson, I was not being facetious. In the four years we had been together, I had never been with anyone else...that fact alone was insane. I, man-whore Wes, had and was in a monogamous relationship? Even my own mothers were shocked when I told them. It wasn't that I couldn't. I just never found a person I felt who could satisfy the raging lust I felt all the goddamn time, then I met him and he was raging along with me. *Feeding an addiction...living with codependency...stalking...love.*

Call it whatever you will, but I was never that far away from him. Which is why when Senator Elspeth Yates begged me to personally cater her event this evening, I said yes even though I swore to myself I'd never cater any event. When the prime minister of France wanted to eat my food, he came to my restaurant like everyone else.

Which begged the question what the fuck was I doing here?

"This needs more vinegar! Chop the basil now and wait ten minutes once the—" I stopped mid-sentence when I saw Jane rushing down the stairs. She was dressed in emerald green and her face was puffy and pink. She had her shoes in one hand and the train of her dress in the other.

"Tell me you see her," I exclaimed.

"Do you know her?" my sous-chef asked, confirming I wasn't dreaming.

"Bloody hell," I whispered. I was awed by how beautiful, even while obviously upset, she still managed to look.

"Chef?"

"Chop the basil now and wait ten minutes to grating the truffles on top of it." I said to him, not taking my eyes off her as she ignored all the kitchen staff and moved toward the back patio. Taking off my chef's apron, I moved to the fridge and took out a single chocolate and vanilla parfait with cherry sauce.

"Spoon," I snapped at one of them.

"Here, Chef."

"Nicklaus, the kitchen is yours."

"Yes chef," he nodded not looking up from his dish. It was one of the reasons why I could trust him. Pulling the door open, I was immediately hit with a blast of cold air, which oddly didn't seem to affect her at all. She sat on the steps staring up at the night sky.

"Come here often?" I asked, taking a seat beside her. Her head turned to me so fast I thought it would snap off.

"Why are you everywhere?" she groaned, brushing back her hair.

"That is not the reaction I was hoping for," I muttered, handing her the dessert and getting back up.

"No, sorry," she called out before I took a step.

"Are you sure? Because I don't do well with crying women."

"Is that why you brought the dessert?" she smiled and took a bite. She paused glancing down at it. I grinned and sat back down.

"I'm amazing. Go on you can say it."

She made a face at me struggling. "It's alright...not orgasmic though."

"It shouldn't be. At least not with the first bite," I said watching as another spoonful entered past her full lips. "A great orgasm doesn't happen remarkably fast, Ms. Chapman. It's the build-up and the path that gets you there."

She stared at me no longer eating, so I took the spoon from her mouth and scooped up more chocolate and brought it back to her lips. They parted for me. "You feel everything first, your mouth watering. The shiver has gone up your spine...the tingling in your ears and hands? Your nipples are getting harder and harder as your pussy gets wetter and wetter. You should be moaning with pleasure, savoring every inch of it to the point where it is driving you insane, not screaming out, and not giving in. It is then and only then," I fed her the last bite, "that I let you come."

She gasped and swallowed with eyes wide. She turned away from me, and I smirked like the dirty sinner I was.

"You are alright, Ms. Chapman."

"Shut up!" She put her hand over my lips covering them. "You and that damn accent and your fucking dessert are confusing me."

I waited for her to take her hands off. When she did, I told her the truth. "You aren't being confused, you're being turned on. Your nipples right now are proof of that."

"It's cold!" she snapped, placing her hands over them.

"It was cold when I came out, and they weren't like that," I pointed out. "Believe me, I would have noticed if they were."

"How can you be flirting with me when you are in a relationship?"

Good fucking question. Max was the first person to ever capture my attention like this and now here she was like a damn hurricane I couldn't ignore.

"But I guess it's fair seeing as Max kissed me."

"He did what?" The little wanker!

"Don't get jealous. He was doing it to protect me from this—" I didn't give a shit. Reaching over, I did what I'd been dying to do from the very first night she caught us. My lips were soon on hers and I could taste the chocolate, cherry and vanilla on her tongue. Her lips were just as soft as I thought, and I wanted—no I needed—more. Moaning into my mouth, she almost gave in before breaking away.

"Now it's fair," I told her, trying to catch my breath.

"You two are insane!" she snapped and got up to leave. I wanted to go after her, but due to the rather large situation between my legs, I thought better of it.

Her lips would beautiful on my cock...on Max's cock.

"Bloody fuck," I gasped out.

Why did I flirt with her? Because she was beautiful and I wanted her, but also because I knew Max wanted her too. Whatever cock-up excuse the little shit made in order to kiss her was a bunch of bollocks. He kissed her because he wanted to. The fact that he wanted to turned me on.

"Fuck! Go down!" I yelled at my cock.

Both of them were going to kill me.

"Can you believe she had the audacity to show her face?" I heard one of the women whisper when I got back upstairs. Following their gaze, I saw two women staring at Irene as she spoke with Max.

"No why? What happened?" another one whispered.

"Well, three years ago she fell for this total fraud. She kept showing him off, some hot shot Wall Street broker. Turns out she knew he was a fraud, but he was blackmailing her. She was a total junkie, and he said he was going to expose her. She convinced so many people to trust him with their money while all the time knowing they'd have losses. She selfishly just wanted to save herself. It was a huge scandal. She only avoided jail time because she's part of the Emerson family. Instead she exiled herself to France. Who knows what kind of trouble she got in there. It must have been horrible if she's back here groveling for attention again. Hopefully, she does her aunt a favor and goes somewhere else."

I didn't want to hear any more. Grabbing two full glasses off the serving tray, I took a couple of steps back before bumping into the women and spilling the wine all over their dresses.

"Oh my God!" I gasped out.

"Have you lost your mind!" Little Miss Gossip screamed at me with her hand in the air.

"I'm so, so sorry!"

"You haven't even begun to be—"

"Ladies," Max came up beside me, "I apologize for this. Please, let the maids assist you in cleaning up. I promise I'll personally reimburse you both."

"It's alright, Mr. Emerson." They tried to be cute and I wanted to roll my eyes. However, when their glare shifted onto me again, I pretended to feel terrible.

"I'm so sorry." I repeated again as they left. *Good fucking riddance.*

Max turned to me eyebrow raised, "I saw you spill the drinks on them on purpose."

"I have no idea what you are talking about," I shrugged.

"Thank you." The corner of his lips turned up and he looked, for the first time, really cute. "And I'm sorry for earlier."

"How long did I go for you to get a whole new personality?"

"I swear you just enjoy aggravating me."

"Just a little bit."

"You do know tomorrow I'll just make sure you have a shit load of things to clean," he replied.

"I quit. Remember?" I was done with their penthouse.

He shook his head. "Didn't you hear me? You don't make the rules. You are the worker bee. I told your boss I wanted you as my maid. If not, then I was done with her service. She's going to pressure you to come, because like I said, everyone is self-servicing. I bet she'll even threaten to fire you if you don't show up."

"You asshole! Why are you tormenting me?" I groaned.

"Simple. You've seen things, and I'd rather not deal with another maid. So I expect to see you bright and early, Ms. Chapman, or I'll come and get you myself."

"I hate you—"

"Maxwell." At that moment, a woman stepped forward wearing an asymmetrical black dress. Her black hair was slicked back and her blue eyes were openly staring at me. I knew she was his mother, the infamous Elspeth Yates, and she was gorgeous.

"Mother," Max said standing straighter, if possible, and also tenser. "You look beautiful as always."

"Thank you dear, are you going to introduce me to your *friend*—"

"Fiancée" he corrected and I looked around praying there was another woman beside him. Nope just me.

The fucking asshole. Did he not hear a word I just said to him?

"Actually ma'am, I rejected him. Jane Chapman. It's a pleasure to finally meet you. Your home is stunning." I reached out to take her hand and she stared at me in confusion.

"You rejected my son? Why?" she asked, not shaking my hand.

"He's a conceited, narcissistic asshole," I dropped my hand, "and on that note, I'll excuse myself."

Proudly, I walked back over back to Irene.

"Bravo," she clapped for me. "But in his defense, he gets incredibly nervous around his mother. He probably said the first thing on his mind to get her to off his back."

"Please say I can go now."

She nodded and never was I so thankful. These people and their drama were far too exhausting.

Screw the life of the rich and famous. I'll stay a maid.

6

"Home sweet home," I muttered tiredly as I turned the key to my apartment. It was after 2:00 a.m. by the time I got back. Stepping inside, the first thing I noticed was that the window was open. I never left it open.

I screamed when a man grabbed my hair and threw me into the wall. The door slammed shut as I fell to the floor. I didn't look up. I didn't want to see his face…if I saw his face—

"I've been waiting too damn long for you to get here." He clenched my hair forcing me to see look up. I shut my eyes tight. "Look at me."

Don't look. Don't look.

"Bitch look at me!" he hollered, slapping me so hard across the face that I could taste blood in my mouth. "Where is the money?"

"Anything you want take—ugh!" I cried when his foot connected with my stomach.

"Is there anything here worth two hundred and twenty-two thousand? A little bird told me they saw you riding around in a million-dollar car. Now where did you get the car from?" I didn't answer, so he hit me over and over and over again.

Coughing up blood and sobbing, I just held my arms to my chest and tried my best to stay calm even though I was panicking.

"This is a message from Aaron. He wants his money and he wants it now. If I have to come here or go to that little cocksucker, Allen, one more time…well, I won't be so polite next time," he said running his hands over my body even as I shivered in disgust.

He said nothing more, and it was only after he left did I finally open my eyes. The pain was pouring over me like waves. Crawling to my purse, I reached inside for my phone.

It felt like it took forever before Mary answered.

"It is two in the morning Jane—"

"Help," I sobbed.

Tuesday came. She didn't come.

Saturday came and she didn't show up.

It was now Tuesday again and still, no word from her. I called the maid service, and all Mary said was that she could refer me to another maid service, but Jane could not come. I even drove over to her apartment, but I didn't know which door was hers.

"What happened at your mother's party?" Wes asked sitting on the bed shirtless, no longer pretending to read the book in his hands. I hadn't spoken about it and he hadn't asked. "I know you kissed her."

I turned to face him and his green eyes were calm, serious, and completely unlike him.

How?

"She told me. She came down to the kitchen and was trying not to cry. I didn't ask why and then I kissed her."

"You did what?"

"I kissed her for the same reason you kissed her. I'm attracted to her."

"I'm not—"

"Bullocks" He shook his head and threw the book to the side of the bed before getting up himself. "Since we met her I've been trying to keep my distance for your sake, you jealous bastard. But what have you been doing? You're driving her home. You're proposing to her. You are kissing her in front of your family and friends. You are fighting back and forth. You are getting to know her favorite movies. I'm here feeling like an ass while waiting for you to man the fuck up and just admit it!"

"I'm not stopping you!" I hollered back. "If you want to fuck her, go fuck her! GO! Don't bitch at me—"

"You're not getting it," Wes said shaking his head and grabbing his shirt. "I want both of you."

"Should we just open our relationship to anyone you want to fuck now? Where is the bar? You see a pretty girl or guy and it's, 'Hey, let's all have a three-way because the man whore, Wesley, wants it?' If I don't agree, I'm the one who needs to man up? Fuck you."

"I felt something when I looked at her," he confessed as he put on his shirt and walked over to me. "In that moment it terrified me. Perhaps I've only felt that once before and still do—when I look at you. And I thought it cheapened us in some way. Or that I was...that something was wrong. Then I looked over to you. I saw that you looked at her the same way you first looked at me four years ago. When you weren't comfortable with your sexual activity. When you were so used to fucking men in the dark and hiding it that you shrugged me off when I tried to hug you. You fought with me constantly because you could not accept that we could be in a stable, normal relationship. I realized then that something wasn't wrong with *us*. If it was, you and I both wouldn't react to the same woman. I tell you all the time I feel like we were destined to meet. So who says there can't be another person with us? Society! The same people who thought being gay meant being mentally incompetent? Fuck them. If we are all attracted to each other, why fight it? I'm not just being a man whore. But thanks for the insult. I'm going to head down to my apartment. I'll see you later."

Just like that he walked out.

I didn't want him to leave. But after what he said I wasn't sure how to respond. Instead I stepped out of the room and leaned on the rail, listening as the door shut behind him. What was happening? I didn't even understand myself. Why was I so pissed that Jane stopped coming to work? Why put so much effort into getting a maid back? Why this? Why that? The more I thought the more my head hurt, so I kept putting it off.

"Error." The door beeped as someone put in the code. Glancing down at my watch I realized it was the first of October. The code changed monthly.

Did he forget?

Rushing down the stairs I nearly tripped, making me further embarrassed. I stopped to straighten my clothes before opening the door. I had expected to look directly at Wes, but instead, my head dropped down at a navy blue Patriots baseball cap.

"The code changed?" she asked softly, looking up to me.

Fuck the code.

"Jane? What happened?" I cupped the side of her face and saw the damage. Her lip was busted and torn on both sides; her left eye was dark reddish-yellow, and bruises spread across her nose. She wore a jacket, a turtleneck and leggings, but I had a feeling there was more damage to be seen.

"Sorry for taking a week off, but I'm here to clean now if you haven't gotten a new maid." She lifted a bucket of supplies for me to see, not at all answering my question. I stood there raging and it built up inside of me to the point where I was clenching my fists. "Please stop staring and let me clean, Maxwell. It's the only thing I'm good at."

Stepping aside, I let her, though I wasn't sure if I was breathing anymore. She moved to the couch where she took off her jacket and folded it neatly. She put her cap on top before putting in earphones and grabbing her bright yellow gloves.

I'm going to kill them. No, I'm going to fucking crucify them!

Pulling my phone out of my back pocket, I dialed quickly and he answered on the first ring.

"When I say I'll see you later—"

"She's back. Come up now…she's…she's hurt."

"What do you mean she's hurt?" I could already hear him walking.

"Someone beat the shit out of her!" I fought back a scream as my hands trembled. Each breath got shorter and shorter.

The line went dead. Putting the phone back in my pocket, I opened the door and waited for the elevator to come up. It took no more than a minute. He looked like I felt. His eyes hard, his lips in a thin line as he came inside and, just like I did, he froze he when saw her wiping down the coffee table.

"She's cleaning?" he hissed through his teeth before stepping forward to go to her. I stopped him and put my hand on his shoulder after closing the door.

"She's trying to make herself feel useful. She doesn't like to be pitied."

"I know that, but she's hurt!" he snapped at me. "Who did this?"

"I know what you know. She just came her and asked to clean, so I let her clean. But know this. I'm not letting her leave until I get a fucking name," I muttered, moving to take a seat on the stairs.

His jaw cracked to the side before he took a deep breath. Taking a seat beside me on the stairs, he put his hand over his mouth.

"Whoever did this...?" he trailed off, clasping his hands shut, and I understood then what was so hard for me to understand five minutes ago.

I cared about her. I didn't know why. I couldn't explain it. All I knew was at this very moment, watching her, it fucking hurt. It was torture. The Jane I knew was strong, feisty, kind, and a pain in the ass workaholic, but someone tried to break her. No, just no.

We waited two hours.

That was a total of sixty-four winces, twenty-two quick stretches, sixteen sharp inhales of pain, nine times where she just paused and stood there lost in thought, and four times whereshe wiped the corner of her eyes. When she did it a fifth time, I couldn't take it anymore.

Getting up, I walked into the kitchen and stepped in front of her. She looked at me with her big hazel eyes, and I wiped the corner of her bruised eye, and pulled out the earphones.

"Who?" I asked, placing my hand on her bruised face. "Who?" I asked again.

"I'm okay."

"Bullocks," I whispered, running my hand over her lips. "Don't brush this off. Talk to me. Who?"

Her eyes watered and she looked away. Stepping closer, I wrapped her in my arms and she just sobbed. She trembled like a child. Kissing the top of her head, Max leaned on the kitchen island, his head down, strands of his black hair covering his eyes.

"I'll go run a bath," he muttered turning away.

Nodding, I bent down and picked her up and she wrapped her arms around me not letting go like a terrified little cat. It only made this hurt more. None of us said anything as we walked up the stairs going to the master bedroom. I placed her on the bed as Max went into the bathroom.

"Do you want me to go?"

"I need help," she whispered not looking up at me. "I can't lift my arms that high."

Swallowing the painful lump in my throat, I reached to the bottom of her turtleneck and pulled it up slowly, reaching under to help her right arm out and then the left. Gently lifting it over her head...

Christ.

The bruising on her face was not nearly as bad as it was on her stomach and chest. If this was a couple of days after, I could only imagine how bad it was after it happened.

"Jane," I whispered shaking my head. I had no other words.

"I'm okay," she lied again. I wanted to tell her I wasn't. Seeing her like this, I wasn't okay, but it wasn't about me.

"Do you want to keep your bra on?" I asked, noting her bra had a clasp in the front, so she could take it off herself.

She just reached up and undid it. Like the rest of her, her breasts were bruised too. But the marks were all from beatings, and there were no teeth marks or hickeys. It didn't rule out sexual assault but...

"When I fantasized about being naked in front of you guys it wasn't like this," she tried to joke, shifting on the edge of the bed to take off her leggings. Again I noticed no hickeys, thumb or hand impressions; in fact, her legs were pretty much the only parts that weren't beaten. So whoever did this focused on her top half.

"That's the part where you say something sexual or something. You're Wes, the free-spirited wild one," she whispered to me.

"Right now, I'm Wes, one of the men trying to...trying to make you feel safe."

She laughed lightly and it was music to my ears. "You guys don't have to do anything to make me feel safe. That's why I came. I'm scared everywhere else but here. He can't get me here."

Putting her hands over her face, she cried again.

Hearing the door opening, I watched as Max came over and kneeled beside me in front of her.

"You are safe here. You can stay for as long as you want, and you don't have to clean a damn thing."

She chuckled, sniffling a couple times before dropping her hands to look at us. "Thank you."

I hated how she thanked us. Like…like it wasn't normal for her to be treated with kindness. Lifting her up again, I walked us into the bathroom.

Max had dimmed the lights and put a few candles around the tub; the TV was even on to…*Vanilla Sky.* She walked over to the tub. Max inhaled seeing the bruise on her back as she got into it; the bubbles surrounding her.

"Ask me why I like this movie?" She sat staring at the screen.

"Why do you like this movie?" Max asked leaning against the bathroom sink as I leaned on the door.

"Because the message is that no matter how bad life gets, no matter how many wrong turns or ups and downs you go through, it will always be better than dreaming your life away," she replied pulling her legs to her chest. "I'm alive for a reason even if my junkie parents abandoned me at birth with enough heroin in my system to kill a baby elephant. Even though I have hospital bills and debt up to my ears. Even though I have no money and have spent all my life alone. Even though my boss put me down as the co-owner of a club he got with drug money resulting in me getting beaten by some…loan shark. I have to be here for a reason right? God isn't just fucking with me? Trying to see how much I can take before I off myself."

My eyes burned. Blinking away the tears, I moved to go sit beside her, but Max beat me to it and perched on the rim of the tub. He put his hand on her cheek as he kissed the top of her head. "You have two reasons right here."

She glanced up at him frowning. "You just want to use me to hide your relationship."

"No," he said while shaking his head. "At first, maybe...now...now I want to know what it would be like for the three of us. I care about you. Wes is obsessed with you. However, none of that means anything without you saying what you want. You don't have to say it now. Just stay here, okay?"

"Okay."

Trust didn't just happen overnight. If it did, she would have come the moment the beating happened. She needed time and space. We'd give that to her. In the meantime, we were going to figure out how the hell to make these bastards pay.

7

Max had left an hour ago in order to prepare for his eight o'clock segment, and I had officially closed my restaurant for the day, so at least one of us stayed with her. The only problem was I had no idea what to do or say. So I did what any reasonable man should do. I called my mums. Yes, that was plural.

The phone rang a few times as I sat in the penthouse's living room. The first thing I saw was smoke when the video call connected.

"Mum? Are you alright?"

She waved her hand through the smoke, and I saw part of her dirty blonde hair before she stepped outside coughing. "If it isn't my favorite little wanker!"

"Mum, you've got to stop calling me that," I replied even though I couldn't help but smile when I saw her face more clearly. My mum, Brenda, always kept her dirty blonde hair short, and also had an earful of piercings. "What is going on? Why is the house on fire?"

"Because someone sent a *simple* recipe for their mother," she pointed at me taking a seat on the patio.

"It can't be that bad."

She turned the camera for me to see the smoke coming out the window, the handiwork of my mother, Pippa.

"All she had to do was melt the cheese!" I laughed.

"Instead, she was trying to melt our house. Come home. Save me. I eat missing home cooked meals."

I rolled my eyes at that. "Mum, you're the one who taught me how to cook."

"Yes, and you surely surpassed me, so after eighteen years of raising you, little bugger, I deserve to be pampered now in my old age."

"Look at that skin! You do not look a day over forty," I winked at her.

She frowned. "I miss you. You look skinny. How can a chef be skinny? No one eats food from a skinny chef."

"I am not skinny, I'm fit. Everyone here loves me because they think I cook healthy."

"Do you?"

"Not even a little bit. What is the point of life if you don't add a little butter sometimes?"

She and I both laughed at that.

"Stop it! You're making me miss you more."

"Brenda." I give her the very same look she used to give me as a child.

"At least, say you miss me too, you little twat."

"I miss you both."

She inhaled deeply like she was getting a power boost before exhaling, "Okay, what does my little wanker want?"

"Can't I just call to say hi? Or to make sure my childhood home hasn't burnt to the ground?"

"Wesley." She gave me *the look*, and I cringed at how effective it still was.

"Fine…I have a friend." I wasn't sure how else to phrase it, but I wish it wasn't like that. It felt cliché but she didn't interrupt me. "She's an amazing, hard-working person and a week ago she got hurt. She didn't come to me until now. Also, I don't know her very well, but I know I want to help her. I just don't know how. She's become quiet and she's not a naturally quiet person."

"Sounds like you know her a lot," she replied, her eyes softer.

"No." I frowned wishing I did. "She's just a very genuine person. If you met her, you'd like her instantly."

"Wesley, what's happening with Maxwell?" she asked and I wished she hadn't.

"Nothing, we're still together." As far as I know.

She stared at me for a long time before speaking, "Does he realize you have feelings for someone else?"

"She's just a friend. Honestly, we haven't known each other for—"

"I've known you for thirty-one years—thirty-two, the day after tomorrow—and in all that time you've only ever called me twice about specific people in your life: Maxwell and this woman. What's going on darling?"

Running my hand through my hair, part of me regretted calling. "Mum...can we just focus on her right now? I just need advice. What do I say?"

"I don't know," she replied shrugging. "If she's as genuine as you say then that's probably what she wants from you. Truth."

"Women love it when you bare yourself to them." I heard the soft giggle of my other mum, Pippa. She sat on the armrest of the chair coming into the frame, her brown hair pulled back into a ponytail. "If she doesn't want to talk about herself then be honest with her about who you are. The more she feels like she knows you, the more comfortable she'll feel about sharing her problems."

"So be a douche and just keep talking about myself?" Sounded like an awful idea.

"No, you ass, you do things together and sometimes slip like 'oh that shirt reminds me off when...' Things like that. What are the stars telling you?"

"To leave the astrology for you, I'll call you later. I love you both."

They waved before hanging up. I pulled the earbuds out of my ears and stood up as Jane came downstairs wearing one of Maxwell's button down shirts. Her hair was down and still wet from her bath.

"Sorry, I didn't mean to interrupt your call." She lifted her hands as if to push me back. "I just wanted water."

Nodding, I headed into the kitchen.

"I can get it myself." She followed after me.

"You're a guest," I reminded her grabbing the glass and the pitcher of water from the fridge. I filled the glass and gave it to her hoping she wouldn't run back to the room. For a split second I'm sure it crossed her mind, but she stayed sipping. Maxwell and I wanted to call a doctor, but we also didn't want her to feel like we forcing her to do anything.

"I was beaten up a lot," I blurted out thinking about my mum's advice.

"What?" She looked so confused. "You look like you'd be doing the beating."

"Thanks," I smirked.

"No…I didn't mean—"

"I got what you meant," I said pouring myself a glass of water before taking the seat opposite her.

"Why were you beat up?"

"Because I was a scrawny pale child, with two mums, thick glasses, and I loved to read. A.k.a., what you Americans called a 'nerd'." *The good old days!* Bitter sarcasm intended.

"I can't see it?" She waved her hands over my body, and I realized that once again I stood in front of her half-naked. I was so used to rarely wearing clothes here. *Nothing I could do about it now.*

"Puberty, contacts, and a few tattoos do wonders." I shrugged leaning forward. "But before that, it was eighteen years of being dragged into closets or washrooms, or having teachers make offhand remarks. Each time I would tell myself I would fight back. I wouldn't just let them bully me. And each time I still ended up with a busted eye or broken nose. It didn't matter if I changed schools. My mum's got into arguments about it. Brenda, she's a poet, and although she looks tough because of her temper, she's a big softy. She wanted to homeschool me, but my mum, Pippa, she wasn't having it. She said it would only make me awkward and unable to stand up for myself. They were already stressed over my little brother, Charlie, being sick with leukemia. I couldn't deal with all of it, so I left home. I went to university in London. Only stayed there for a semester, then my brother died. Instead of going home, I ran away to France."

"I'm sorry about your brother," she replied finishing her water.

I paused and stared at her empty glass.

"Do you mind if we get something stronger than this?" I lifted my glass.

"Yes, please!" she smiled lifting her glass to me.

Grinning, I took both of them and placed them into the sink before getting proper wine glasses.

"Tell me 'when'," I said to her after uncorking the red wine. Pouring it into her glass, I waited and waited and she didn't say anything until the wine was right at the rim.

"Perfect," she grinned, leaning over to sip the top so it wouldn't spill over.

"Are you sure? This is very strong."

She just waved me off and drank like she was dying for a drink. When she finally took a deep breath and licked her wine-stained lips, her glass was as full as mine.

"Okay," I laughed. She was so cute.

"Don't judge."

"Me? Never!" I shook my head before leaning over to wipe the corner of her mouth. "But what did I say about savoring the things in your mouth?"

Shite! That came off far more sexual than I wanted it to.

Her face turned red, which made blood rush to places it shouldn't...not now at least.

"You ran off to France?" she changed the subject and I picked up from where I left off.

"Yeah, I went to France, not knowing a word of French, thank you. I had no idea what I was going to do with myself. I ended up getting a job at the fish market. Day in, day out, gutting and handling fish. This chef, Chef Dieudonné, a man well into his sixties, came every day, and personally picked out all the seafood himself. One day he didn't show, so I biked in the rain to his restaurant. It was the first time I had been inside a professional kitchen. And it blew my mind." I couldn't stop fighting the fat-ass grin spreading across my face. "I can't describe it. The chaos, the excitement and the speed at which everyone worked. For the first time in my life, I thought...this...this is what I want."

"So you joined his kitchen?" she asked innocently.

I snorted wishing it were that easy. "In my dreams. Chef Dieudonné was the best. Everyone who was anyone wanted to be in that kitchen. Who was I to just demand to be there? First, I had to get into culinary school, and if you think secondary schools have bullies, wow, people were cut-throat. If you even touched another student's knives, there were fights. People sabotage other people's dishes. People sleep with instructors, men or women, they didn't care. It was just to get by. I didn't understand at first, that I was in fucking France. The country has been renowned for its food. They didn't just let anyone be a chef. You needed to be cocky, ruthless and bold. In other words, you truly needed to believe you were a god in the kitchen in order to make it."

"You are cocky, ruthless, and bold. Okay, cocky and bold I can see but ruthless?" she giggled, drinking some more.

"You've never stepped into my kitchen. I make Maxwell look like a little puppy," I winked at her and took a sip of wine.

"So you made it," she said sounding so proud of me that I felt even prouder of myself.

"Yeah, I made it. I wanted to be a chef. I wanted to be in Chef Dieudonné's kitchen. When you find a passion for something, it's amazing how tough you can be. I think back to all those beatings I took, and I realized I never fought back as hard as I could have because I didn't care enough to. School wasn't my passion. I enjoyed reading fiction but that was about it. The people there meant nothing to me. I visited home, hugged my mums and then joined the culinary school. Two and a half years later, I graduated and had offers to join kitchens all over the country."

"So you got to go to Chef Dieudonné?"

"I wish. He died, the second year I was there. He left me his knives though. It's a huge honor. Even I didn't know why, but his sous-chef told me that the chef had seen me when I had started. He said Chef Dieudonné told him that'd I'd be a chef to look out for one day. I never looked back after that."

"You are lucky," she said brushing her hair behind her ears. "I wish I could find a passion like that."

"I'm sure you're good at something and just don't realize it," I said moving closer to her.

We were silent for a while and I watched as her hazel eyes looked over each of the tattoos on my chest. Taking her hand, I put it on the side of my ribs where there was another tattoo.

"This," I said letting her hands glide down the Chinese lettering, "means 'be who you really are', or at least I hope it does. I was drunk when I got it."

She giggled and it was a melodic sound. Moving her hand on to my chest, I took a deep breath. "This is for Charlie."

I moved her hand to my shoulder. "This is because my mum, Brenda, would always put a dream catcher over my bed, and it made me feel better.

Gliding her hand down my arm, I stopped at the constellation. "This is for the first man I ever truly loved: Maxwell. A hot-blooded Aries."

She looked up at me. Her eyes were completely amused, and I had no idea why until she said, "*I solemnly swear I'm up to no good?*"

"In my defense, I was a nerd who grew up in England. Loving Harry Potter is a given."

I loved hearing her laugh. Reaching up, I brushed her hair back, my thumb softly rubbing her cheek.

"Don't look at me, I'm ugly."

That hurt. How? How could she think that?

"I've seen ugly people. I've seen pretty people who think they aren't ugly. Jane Chapman, you are breathtakingly beautiful."

"You can't like two people equally," she whispered as I leaned into her.

"Watch me." I wanted to kiss her lips, and I was sure she wanted me to, but instead I kissed her forehead.

"Door open." The automated door said and we both turned and watched as Maxwell came inside. His blue eyes looked between the both of us.

In a flash, she was on her feet giving him a quick hi, before running up the stairs and back into her room.

He sighed and rubbed the back of neck as he walked into the kitchen. "I think she just might like you more than she likes me."

Handing him my wine, I leaned against the island and stared up at Jane's closed door. "If she likes me, she has to like you because you're part of me."

"How is it so easy for you to say stuff like that?" he asked downing the remaining wine.

"That's just how it is," I replied. "That's just who I am."

"Yes?" she asked opening the door.

I lifted the breakfast tray for her. "You didn't eat last night."

"You made me breakfast?" She stared at it skeptically.

"No, Wesley did. He had to go because of a kitchen emergency or something." Part of me had a feeling he left us on purpose.

"Thank you. You didn't have to bring it up though. You guys have already done so much," she whispered, her eyes dropping as she took the tray from me.

I stood there for a second not sure what to say.

"I'm spoiled. I will concede to that fact," I blurted it out. She stared at me as if I were an alien. I felt like one because I couldn't shut up. "I do not like sharing. I do not do well with others. Dating is a pain in the fucking ass for me. Everyone is trying to put his or her best foot forward. Pretending to be something they aren't. Some people have resting bitch face. I have what Wes calls 'resting asshole personality.' For him, people just melt in his hands. It is goddamn annoying because even I do it. He is a people person and I'm the Grinch."

"Um...."

"What I'm saying is—" *What the fuck are you saying, Maxwell?* "He likes you. I like you. I don't know how to open up to people like he does, and so…so…don't go falling just for him. Okay?"

She stared as a smile slowly spread across her face, "You know everyone loved the Grinch at the end of the movie right?"

I snickered at that, "I never finished it."

"What? It comes on every year," she gasped at me like I had insulted her.

I shrugged. "I've seen clips and pieces never the whole thing."

"I'm a movie aficionado. Hearing this pains me," she pouted.

"Last thing you need is more pain. It's on Netflix, so I'll watch it—"

"Brilliant," she nodded walking past me with the tray.

"You want to watch it now?" I followed her.

She paused on the stairs glancing up at me, "Do you have anything else to do?"

No, I didn't. I went down the stairs and she followed behind me.

"Are you one of those people who talks during movies?" I asked her when she sat on the couch.

She froze with the glass of orange juice resting on her lips. "Is that a problem?"

"No. I do it, too. It drives Wes insane," I grinned as I sat beside her.

She laughed. "I get so emotionally invested I have to say something."

"I understand," I replied and leaned back, after starting the movie. Her eyes were immediately glued to the screen. "After this will you help me with something?" I didn't look at her, just watched.

"What?"

"Wes' birthday is tomorrow. I'm crap at planning things like that. We can't go out and it's my fault, but..."

"Sure," she nodded without hesitation and giggled the moment the Grinch came on the scene.

She was beautiful.

Why did I come here?

It was the first thought that went through my mind as I stood outside the door. I tried to come up with a reasonable explanation. But I didn't have one. What I had a lot of selfish unreasonable ones, though. The first, I didn't want them to forget me. Yes, I tried to quit. Yes, I said I wanted to walk away. But that horrible night of the beating, when the only two people on my phone were Allen and Mary, I realized I didn't want to be forgotten. I wanted more people to care. It was selfish, I know. My second reason was Mary kept stressing me out. She was amazing and she wanted to help, but it felt like she was proud of the fact that she could repay the favor of when I helped her.

Now that I was here, I felt like I was crumbling. They were so sweet. They both cared and I felt...I felt happy to be here. But there was a part of me that knew that good things don't happen to me.

"Jane."

"Huh?" I looked up and Max was no longer watching the movie but watching me.

"Sorry, what?"

"Are you alright? You stopped talking."

"Yeah...sorry—"

"Jane, you say 'sorry' too much." He lifted his hand to my chin and the cut on the side of my face. "What were you thinking about?"

"You," I said honestly reaching up to grab his hand, but I didn't push it away. That was the problem. "And Wesley. Most importantly, me. I told you. I'm selfish. I came here because I wanted someone to care about me. And I'm happy here."

"But?"

"But...I'm not good with happy. It's Wednesday, and on Wednesdays I clean Mrs. Crofton's house and walk her three terriers: Bailey, Coco, and Gus. But instead, I'm curled up on the couch watching the Grinch. I've never taken a day off in my life...but I want to. I want to stay here with you guys, and I'm even tempted to suck up my pride and just marry you. It scares me. I know can't just sit around all day. I can't just be here. But I'm so confused."

"You don't have to figure it out now." He brushed my cheek gently just like Wes did. "You don't have to sit around all day Jane. You can learn how to enjoy living instead of just working. What are you passionate about? Where haveyou always wanted to go or see? I bet you've never asked yourself those questions because you didn't have time to. By staying with me, with us, you can."

He made it sound so simple...so fun. "But what happens when this fascination you and Wes have with me fades away?"

He frowned at that and his hand dropped. "Have you ever watched a movie from the ending?"

"What?"

"Have you ever started a movie at the end?"

"No."

"Then why start a relationship like that? I have no clue what will happen next week, next month, or next year. All I have is right now and right now we want you here. Isn't that enough?"

My heart felt like it was drumming against my chest. "I'll think about it."

What would I be if I wasn't Jane the maid or bartender / manager / accountant / stripper's assistant? I had no idea but I was curious now.

8

"Aren't roses a bit cliché?" He frowned as the saleswoman packed up the flower petals, and I grabbed as many damn candles as I could.

"Clichés become clichés because they work!" I said while I started looking over the birthday cards for Wes. We decided to leave the penthouse after we had finally figured out what to do. However, Wes had the worst timing and came home. Neither of us could make an excuse other than I had a doctor's appointment this morning, and Max had offered to take me. I could tell he felt like something was up, but I said nothing. He was going to be at the restaurant until the evening in any case.

"Is that everything, ma'am?" The woman behind the counter looked up to me happily. I was glad she didn't react to the bruising on my face. I hoped that meant it was finally getting better. Last week, I could barely feel my own face. It was scary.

"Do you have any balloons?" I leaned over the counter to see.

"No balloons," Max cut in giving her his card.

I frowned. "You can't have a birthday party without balloons!"

"Maybe if you're five."

"I can be five." I clasped my arms together and leaned into him giving him the best puppy dog eyes I could muster. "Please?"

He glared at me and I could tell he was grinding his teeth. "Add a couple of balloons."

"A dozen please," I turned back to her. She snickered, reaching for the two different sets.

"Regular or helium?"

"Helium," I said.

"Regular," Max answered at the same time, and before I could try again to persuade him otherwise, he reached for the regular ones. "How would it look if we get home and get busted with helium balloons?"

131

"Fine." I threw my hands up jokingly and he shook his head while signing the receipt. In the back of my mind I couldn't help but notice how he had said when *we get home*. It was only my second day and he was calling it my place. I disliked how much I enjoyed it.

"Do you have anything else on that neverending list?" he asked taking the bag.

I reached for my notepad. "Flowers and candles. Check. The birthday card. Check. Groceries double-check because I'm not going to forget how confused you looked when walking down the aisle."

"I was not confused; the store was just not properly organized," he muttered a little embarrassed. A grown man in his thirties and he'd never even done his own groceries. What a life, man.

"If you say so," I replied when we got back to his car.

He hadn't driven the Ferrari, which I was thankful for, instead it was simple black Mercedes, and I hated that I was using the word 'simple' to describe it. He opened the door for me before putting the things in the trunk along with the groceries.

"Okay, we should have enough time to set up and prepare."

"You do know I could have hired someone—"

"Not romantic!" I cut him off before he could even say it. "He knows you're rich. It doesn't count if it's easy! What did you do in previous years?"

He shrugged, "We usually just…"

"You usually just what?"

"You sure you want to know?"

This felt like a trick question, but I was too damn curious. "Fine, what?"

"He's into BDSM. I like some of it, but I don't get off on it like he does. On his birthday, I let him go crazy," he replied and I couldn't look at him anymore. Instead, I just stared straight ahead as he drove. The BDSM wasn't the problem. It was the fact that I had seen them both naked, and I'd even seen him with a ball in his mouth. Now I was getting flashbacks.

"I tried to warn you."

"No, you didn't! You knew I'd walk right into that."

"Are you blushing?" He laughed at me and I grabbed my ears.

"Shut up!"

Luckily he didn't push it, which allowed me to calm down. Leaning back into the seat, I went over the list again.

"This year I'm sure he'll love what we are doing," I muttered smiling to myself.

"You're so odd."

"Why?"

He glanced over at me. "You get really happy when you help other people. Even with Irene, after you poured the wine on those horrible women, I saw how proud you were."

"I never confessed to that. As far as anyone knows, it was an accident," I winked and he rolled his eyes.

"Why did you go along with her? It isn't in your job description."

"Have you met your cousin? Everyone thinks she has no clue what's going on, but she's an evil mastermind."

"That still doesn't explain why you went out of your way to help her."

"I'm just an awesome human being." I lifted my head up before slowly reflecting on it. "I don't like seeing others embarrassed or in pain because it makes me think…oh, that could be me. So again, a completely selfish reason."

He didn't say anything. We pulled in front of his building and one doorman came around for Maxwell's keys while the other opened the door for me.

"We got it," I said rushing to take the bags in the trunk. I even handed some to Maxwell. He stared at them in confusion. "Normal people carry their own bags."

"I don't want to be normal."

I gave him a look and he sighed and took the bag from me. He was such a big baby. The doorman followed us and had the elevator already opened for us.

Rich people apparently didn't even need to push buttons.

"Why are you smiling?"

"Because I can." I swayed back and forth on the balls of my feet staring as we passed each floor. "Question: Does Wes live with you? How do the people in the lobby not know?"

"Answer," he mocked, "Wes has the floor right under mine. He's a resident. He just spends more time at my place. Besides, the doormen and maids here all have to sign a non-disclosure."

They thought of everything.

"Penthouse suite" The automatic voice said when we got to his floor. Maxwell opened the door for me, and I peeked in making sure Wes wasn't inside.

"He texted me to say he'll be home around seven," he said.

"Okay, set the candles out, but don't light them, and then join me in the kitchen. Food always has to be done first."

"You don't want me in the kitchen—"

"If it's easy, it's not romantic."

"He loves this kitchen. It's not romantic if I burn it down," he said really panicked.

Stepping up to his face, I stared him down.

"No, Jane." He glared back at me not backing down.

"Yes, Maxwell."

"No."

"Yes."

"No."

I kissed the side of his cheek. "Yes, come on. There is a fire extinguisher under the sink if anything happens."

"Do you seduce everyone into doing what you want?" He followed behind me grumpily.

"Oh, when I'm seducing you, Mr. Emerson, you will know."

"What the bloody hell is this?" I tried not to laugh the moment I walked through the door. Jane was standing there dressed in waiter's attire. Her hair was pulled back, and she had an apron around her. However, that wasn't even odd in comparison to the atmosphere in Max's penthouse. All the lights were off with the exception of the dim light from the kitchen, and the dozens of candles were spread around the living room. The furniture had been moved, and there was a now a table in the center set for two.

"Welcome to *Le Château de Maxwell.* May I have your jacket and I'll see you to your table." She reached out for my coat and folded it carefully over her arm.

I was too stunned to speak. I finally made eye contact with Max who stood just off to the side dressed in a three-piece suit...and clutching a rose in his hand.

"Am I on *The Bachelor?*" I asked with a grin on my face. As I walked to him, I could sense he felt awkward and was only pushing himself to do this. He took a deep breath before handing me the rose.

"We've never been on a date," he said seriously. "You and I aren't the type to really stress about it. However, I've been told it's still important. We can't go out, and that's my fault, so Jane helped me make a restaurant here."

"You didn't have to do this," I muttered, now feeling awkward myself taking the rose from him.

He frowned, "Just go with it. She's a tyrant."

"What was that Mr. Emerson?" Jane popped up beside us with a grin on her face. I noticed my coat was now gone.

"Is our table ready?" he asked her and it was taking all my strength not to laugh. Was this a date or a comedy skit? I had no idea, but I'll go with it.

"Right this way." She moved for us to walk to our seat. "Is there anything I can get you to drink?"

If they wanted to play, I'll go along with it.

"Tell me, what are your featured wines?" I asked, undoing the napkins and placing it on my lap.

"This evening the chef has selected a 1989 Cabernet Sauvignon, or if you would like to work up to it, we have a *Cote Rotie 'Brune et Blonde'.*"

She was good. From those wines, they, the *chefs*, must have prepared steak tonight. "What do you suggest?"

She never broke her role. "Both are equally delightful. However, I'd suggest a Rum Martinez before the wine."

"Two Rum Martinezs then," Max nodded to her and unbuttoned his vest.

"Right away, sir," she replied stiffly.

"You both are ridiculous," I told him.

"You hate it?" he frowned.

I shook my head. "On the contrary, love. I'm stunned for words."

"Doesn't seem like it," he muttered, reaching for the water. I grabbed his wrist leaning over it.

"Thank you." Did I care that we never really went out? Not really. However, the fact that he thought about meant it a lot more than he realized. Especially since I knew how awkward he felt. I didn't let go of him, but instead I clasped his hand, noticing how his fingertips fitted against my hands perfectly.

"Happy Birthday," he whispered and I felt the urge to skip the meal and go straight to bed.

"Two Rum Martinezes," Jane returned, placing them in front us not even blinking at our hands. Instead, she pulled out two handwritten menus and placed them on the table. "Please take your time."

"She's crazy," Max snickered, lifting the menu.

"She didn't tell you about this?"

"All I said was that I wanted to have a dinner date with you. She went and recreated a restaurant."

Glancing over my shoulder, I watched as she chopped something up carefully. As if this was the most important moment of her career.

"The woman doesn't know how to do anything halfway," I replied. It was one of the things that made her so damn endearing.

"Wes," he reached over pulling my chin back to him, his lips on mine before I could blink. Leaning into him, his tongue slipped into my mouth rolling my own. I loved how he tasted. Just as my cock started to come alive, he broke away.

"Tonight...I want you...I want you to fuck me so hard she can't ignore it," he whispered kissing me again.

Fucking hell.

"I want you now," I demanded, only an inch from his lips.

"We worked hard on this. You can wait an hour—"

"Look down," I told him, and when he did, the bulge in my pants was staring right back at him. "I can't make it an hour."

The corner of his lip turned up and his eyes looked over my shoulder at her before he stood up. He quickly moved around the table and kneeled down in front of me. Reaching for my belt, he puled it off before undoing the button and the zipper.

"Max....ahh," I gasped when he touched me. Slowly he stroked up and down before licking the pre-cum already forming on the tip of my cock. My breath caught in my throat. Glancing over at her, I watched as she stared, frozen still, her pink lips parting slightly.

"Come," I told her reaching out for her. "Ahh..." I moaned when Maxwell's tongue ran down the side of me, leaving kisses, too.

"Come," I whispered to her again and she did. She walked over, quietly mesmerized by Max until she stood right by my chair. Taking her hand, I kissed her wrist moving to her palm before taking two of her fingers into my mouth tasting the alcohol on them. She inhaled deeply.

"Wes—"

"You don't have to watch from afar, Jane," I whispered when she took her fingers from my mouth. She didn't back away however. Her thumb brushed my lips. "You don't have to pretend like this...*him*...us...like we don't turn you on. So kiss me, Jane."

She stared at me blankly but lowered her head down rewarding me with her lips. It was then that Max took me into his mouth.

Fuck. Fuck. My mind screamed as the pleasure rolled off me in waves. She tasted sweet to his spicy. Every corner of her mouth was mine. My chest felt like it was going to explode from the lack of oxygen, which only made Max's hot mouth feels even more glorious. I could die at this moment and never regret it.

"Wow," she muttered when we broke away, and I gritted my teeth as I grabbed on to Max's hair. I wasn't expecting her to bend down beside him. I don't think she expected to, either. However, when she did, Max pulled back licking along the side of me.

"FUCK!" I moaned when her tiny tongue licked me as well. It was like they were sharing an ice cream cone, and they both tasted me. Both of their tongues moved to the tip of my cock, and in that second they licked each other. That lick lead to a kiss, the kiss became fully fledged right at the base of my cock. Max reached up while still stroking me. Watching them kiss like this right in front of me was better than any porn in the world, and it drove me to the brink. When they broke, a string of saliva formed between their tongues and they both stared each other down. Jane was slowly turning red. She was sexy as hell.

He snickered at her before taking me back into his mouth while he placed his own hand on the bulge he now had. She stroked him through his pants while she looked away from the two of us. Her ears had turned bright red.

"Ough...Ahh...URGH!" I shivered as I came into Maxwell's mouth, and he swallowed it all eagerly. I pet both of them on the head, and she glanced up at me still breathing hard. I thought how this 'thing' was hitting her, what we'd be like...what this would be like...small steps. She'd come so far in such a short time, but we'd finally reached a turning point.

"I'll get dinner." She got up quickly, but she didn't go the kitchen first. Instead, she went to the bathroom and I could hear the water rush on.

"What now?" Max asked, rising to his feet and pulling off his tie completely.

"We wait. We have dinner. I replay the image of you both for the rest my life," I grinned facing him again. He took his glass, the drink she had given us completely forgotten until now.

"Best fucking birthday I've ever had," I announced lifting the glass to his before downing it. It burned on the way down, but that was nothing compared to the fire within me to have them both in my bed. It wouldn't be tonight, she still wasn't ready…but soon.

What the fuck Jane?

What the fuck?

I kept asking myself that even well after I had given them dinner. Disappearing, more like hiding, in the bedroom. I could still taste them both on my tongue. My nipples were so hard right now, it was painful.

What happens now? *What do you mean what happens now Jane?! You licked the man's dick, so there is no coming back from that!*

"Urgh!" I got up off the bed and went back into the bathroom to take another cold fucking shower.

Stripping off my clothes, I stopped when I noticed myself.

"Fucking hell, man." Not only had I made out with them both and licked Wes' dick, I did it looking like shit. Yes, my bruises were almost heeled. The one on my face just had a tinge of yellow. It was the one near my ribs, where I was kicked, that stood out the most now. I hoped it would be gone in another day or so. I iced it every chance I could. I didn't want them to....

I paused when the thought came to mind. I wanted them to see me as beautiful. I never cared what people saw me as before.

"I'm fucked." I had given in without realizing.

Is that really such a bad thing though?

"Carpe diem"

Seize the day.

You only live once.

What if…just what if…I did it?

She did it again.

Walking out of my bedroom the next morning, everything was immaculate. The only proof of the makeshift restaurant was the table that remained in the center of the living room. I'd need to call to have the furniture put back.

"Good morning," Wes whispered coming up behind me. He was naked and his cock was against my ass. He kissed my shoulder. "I see our favorite cat burglar has stuck again."

"She's not here," I told him.

"You checked?"

"No." I passed him one of her sticky notes. Which simply read. *I'll be back in a day or two...I promise.*

"Do you have her number?"

"No." I was with her almost all morning yesterday, how was that possible? I hadn't thought she'd run again. "You think she'll be back?"

"She hasn't lied to us before," he reminded me, and I sighed leaning against the railing. "This is your fault."

"My fault? Please, explain." Wes moved from behind me to lean on the railing.

"You dangled her in front of me."

He snickered, "Someone enjoyed that kiss a lot more than he let on."

I couldn't reply to that. Not without remembering and turning myself on. Being the bastard he was, he leaned in to speak softly into my ear.

"If you're so turned on by a kiss...imagine what it will like when your cock is so deep in her tight pussy you can barely think straight. When I'm fucking you, as you fuck her—"

"Wes," I gripped the railing.

"I suggest you figure out when your next vacation is because once it happens, and believe me it will happen," his hands slowly slid down my chest, "none of us will be leaving this house for a while."

His hand stopped right at my waist. Kissing my shoulder once more, he walked around me and back into the bathroom.

Damn him. Damn him!

Spinning around, I followed him back into the bedroom and pushed him onto the bed before climbing on top of him.

"Yes?" He grinned at me, his eyes filled with as much as lust as mine.

"I'm not your bitch," I hissed at him my chest rising and falling. "You don't tell me what happens."

"So perhaps you could just show me," he replied.

Angrily I lifted his legs up, the tip of my cock at his asshole, his chest rising and falling in excitement. Biting the back of his fingers, I thrust forward.

"Ugh…" He and I both grunted out.

"Who's to say I'm not the one fucking you, huh?" I hissed, pulling out before slamming back deeper into him. "You fucking her! Me fucking you"

"Max…fu…c…ahh…" That damn look on his face never left as he put his hands on my shoulders taking each plunge eagerly.

Emotionally and sexually, he frustrated me, and I didn't know what to do but keep fucking him as hard as I could up the ass.

9

"I didn't think I'd see you back here," Tommy, the bouncer of the Bunny Rabbit, said coming out of the club. It was still too early in the afternoon for a crowd, but give it a couple of hours. It was Saturday after all.

"Believe me I don't want to be, Tommy. Is Allen in?" I asked and he nodded, moving for me to go on in.

It felt like I had left years ago not just weeks. I was expecting the place to be different, but it was still the same old neon lit hole in the ground. The bar still had trays of stale roasted peanuts out and the drinks over the bar were still organized exactly as I had left them.

"You're back!" Allen dropped the boxes on the counter, a Cheshire cat grin on his face as he opened his arms to hug me. "I knew it—"

"I'm not back," I said, side-stepping his hug. "I wanted to make sure you were alive."

"Why wouldn't I be alive?" he frowned, with his head level with my boobs.

"Aaron." The moment I said his name, he grabbed my arm pulled me to the counter.

"Did he come to—"

"No, one of his guys did but not before beating the shit out of me!" I snapped yanking my arm away. "I could have been killed, Allen. Raped!"

"Keep your voice down."

"NO!" I was still so pissed at him that I wanted to grab a bottle and smack him over the head. "I refuse to die because of your mistakes!"

"Look. I'm figuring something out—"

"I need a number to wire the money." I cut him off before he could say anything else.

"What?" He froze.

"The money I'll get it to them soon and then I don't want to see your face again."

"What do you mean you'll get the money? Where? How? What are you doing Jane?" He leaned closer and I just backed away.

"None of your business. Goodbye, Allen." Turning away from him I walked out without looking back. There was nothing left for me here. I wasn't sure what was going to happen next or how it would work, but I needed to find out. I knew it couldn't be worse.

"Is he still alive?" Tommy smiled when I stepped out into the sun.

"Yes. I kept my hands to myself." See, I could use words not just my fist. "I want to say 'see you around Tommy', but I really hope I don't, at least not here."

"I understand. Be safe out there, but if you need me to bash a few heads, call anytime."

That was it. I walked away from the Bunny Rabbit, feeling hopeful and terrified, but I kept walking. Turning the corner to where Mary's yellow car was waiting, I saw her lean over the seat to open the door.

"Are you sure about this?"

"Were you sure when you left?"

"Best day of my damn life," she smiled, taking out her ponytail to run her hands through her red hair. She then reached over to open her glove compartment and tossed a bottle of Tylenol to me.

"I'm okay." My bruises were gone and only hurt if I bent awkwardly.

"Believe me, you're going to want to take those now. When was the last time you waxed?"

I tried to think, but I couldn't remember. Waxing cost more than a four-dollar razor. Sighing, I took two pills without water as we drove. I couldn't help how nervous and excited I was...not for the waxing but the reason for the waxing.

I was attracted to Maxwell and Wesley. There I said it. Well I thought it. Mary didn't know about Wes, but she just knew something was going on with Max and I. I didn't want to fight it anymore. I wanted to explore it. But what happens if this all blew up in my face? At least I'd get great sex? I missed sex! Not a quick fuck or pretending some guy was amazing when I was thinking about my grocery list. I wanted...I wanted what they gave me on Wes' birthday. I wanted to feel so turned on I couldn't stop myself that I acted instead of thinking.

"This woman, she's a gift from god. A total angel," Mary said parking in front of a small yet beautiful brown and gray brick house.

"This is the spa?" I asked stepping out of the car.

"Yep, my home away from home," she sighed walking up the steps.

I didn't say a word but followed her.

"Head to toe everything, Maggie," she said to the blonde woman behind the desk. I noticed her cat-eye make-up was stunning.

"How much is a head to toe everything?" I asked her, but she didn't pay attention to me giving the woman, Maggie, her card. "Mary no. I got it."

"Save it. Besides, you might be the future, Mrs. Emerson. I'm getting in my good friend points early." She waved me away. "I want Tomoko for her, Maggie, she's a golden egg."

"Thanks," I said crossing my arms. Mary was almost as excited as I was.

"I got it, room four. Please get changed into the robe." Maggie handed her the key.

The room was down the hall to the right, and Mary popped down on the chair not far from me.

"Let me guess, you're staying for moral support?" I asked while pulling my pants down. She grabbed her phone.

"But of course. You might chicken out."

It's too late for that. Taking the robe, I sat on the bed feeling as if I were about to go to a doctor's appointment.

"Do you have a doctor I can go see last minute?"

"Why?"

"I want to be safe."

"Do you?" She tilted her head to the side. "One kid and you're set for life."

"Mary!"

"Okay, okay!" She reached into her bag. "What do you want? The IUD, TCI, TVR, the patch, or the injections? Actually scratch the injections. I got those once and was in the worst pain for the next three months…that's not sexy."

"I was just running low on pills, jeez."

"Oh that works, too." She shrugged, sending the text when a short Japanese woman, with long white hair, entered the room. She was old but even her make-up style was better than mine.

"It too early for you," she said pointing at Mary.

"No. No. My friend, hot date. Rich man," Mary nodded easily and I wanted to just bury my face in the ground.

"Oh…let me see."

Oh my god! She just opened my legs as if they were nothing.

"Honey," she sighed looking back at me with a frown on her lips.

"What? It's not that bad! I shaved!"

She rubbed my legs, arms, and face. There was no limit to where she went. Shaking her head, she moved to her sink getting gloves, scissors, oil and wax. I looked to Mary who didn't seem to pay attention as she scrolled through the phone.

"Honey, you take medication?"

"She's all good Tomoko, make her shine." Mary slipped a piece of gum into her mouth. Meanwhile, my heart was starting to race.

"Meet rich man tomorrow. Today hurt." She rubbed something on my poor inner thighs and vag.

151

"Today hurt? Mary, you said she was an angel!"

"An angel but not God!" she laughed back.

Whimpering, I laid back with my hands gripping on to the bed.

"Don't worry. You love me tomorrow." She patted my shoulder before getting the wax.

"One…"

"FUCKING SHIT! WHAT HAPPENED TO TWO AND THREE?" I screamed, tears in my eyes.

"I lie."

Maxwell and Wesley, you better rock my fucking world!

10

"Days after we broke this story, my team and I have finally gotten insight into Governor MacDowell's arrest and his illegal activities. This was not mere corruption, but racketeering, bank fraud, and worst of all, bribery. This was not a case of a few handshakes in a back room somewhere. Nor was it lobbying by big banks or corporations leading to the deprivation of basic goods and services. No, Governor MacDowell's depravity went deeper than that. In order to hide Boston's growing sexual assault problem, he instructed the city police to, and I quote, "give warnings" to prostitutes whom officers deemed targets. What's the problem with this you ask? At this very moment, the district attorney is arresting, not one or two, but twelve cops who were part of a sex slavery ring in the city. These police warnings were used as recruitment into the ring. Women were promised no charges would be pressed against them. They were also promised free homes, meals, and check-ups but were instead threatened and subjected to sexual acts. The further we continue digging, the more filth we are uncovering. Who did we vote into office? How far does this go? I won't stop until I find out. Join me Monday night as I speak with one of the Governor's victims. I'm Maxwell Emerson and this is the Emerson Report." I finished as the music began and the lights were dimmed.

"Brilliant," Scarlet said in my ear and I pulled out the microphone and slammed the papers on the table. "What's wrong?"

"One victim isn't enough Scarlet! I want to pin this motherfucker to the ceiling," I snapped walking off the stage to my office.

"Max, you got him!" she said keeping up with me.

"No. I didn't." Grabbing the water on my coffee table, I laid back on my couch pulling my tie down. "She's a prostitute. That's all they will see when they tune in tomorrow. Governor MacDowell and his legal team of assholes will try and discredit everything she says. They will drown out one voice. But three, four, five? No! People will see what that monster is really like."

"What is this vendetta you have against Governor MacDowell?" She sat down beside me, and I shifted away slightly which only made her sit more comfortably.

"He's a liar and rapist, and I don't need a vendetta to go after a monster like him."

"Fine, I'll start calling around. Do you need anything?" She reached up to touch my face but I grabbed her wrist.

"I'm fine. I am just tired. I'll head home for now," I replied.

"Of course, I'll have the car waiting. Goodnight, Maxwell," she said standing up and heading out the door. It felt like forever before my temples stopped aching. Sitting back up, I finished my water before grabbing my jacket and bag. I hated working on Saturdays, but I wanted to be the first one to break the news.

"Goodnight, Mr. Emerson."

"Good show, sir."

"It was excellent, sir, really. I can't wait for Monday."

I didn't look them in the eye. I didn't speak to anyone. I rode the elevator down by myself, closing my eyes as I leaned against the wall.

Fucking Governor…I wouldn't even go there. Instead, I reached into my suit jacket and grabbed my phone. Just as I was about to call Wes, the devil himself called.

"Father," I answered as the doors opened the bottom floor.

"Your mother says you aren't answering her calls?"

"I hadn't realized she called. Please apologize on my behalf."

"Maxwell."

"Yes, sir," I answered, taking a seat in the back of the waiting car and threw my things to the right of me.

"You are not a child anymore this—"

"If I am not a child, doesn't that mean I can skip this lecture? Because, I've had a rather long night."

I could hear him deeply inhale.

"Your mother will be announcing her run in the next coming days. I expect you to—"

"Find a beautiful woman to throw on my arm? Answer whenever you call? Do whatever you ask when you ask? Am I your child, or am I a puppet?"

"Nice talking to you, *son*." he replied by hanging up and I threw the phone to the side. Leaning back into the seat, I glared out at the city streets.

My grandmother once told me we couldn't pick the families we were born into for a reason. She had no idea what the reason was, but she was betting it was because half of us wouldn't choose to be born. I knew that feeling. Not wanting to alive. It was because of him, Wes, that I—

"Sir, your phone" The driver pulled me from my trance.

Looking over, sure enough, my phone was ringing and it was him.

"What?" I said even though I felt better.

"Saw the show. What do you want for dinner?"

Wes…

"Whatever. That pasta dish you made last time," I said remembering how he hated when I told him 'whatever'.

"Okay. See you soon?"

"Sooner than you think," I replied hanging up as the driver pulled to a stop at my building. I didn't wait for him to come open the door. Instead, I grabbed my things and let myself out.

"Evening, Mr. Emerson," the doorman said to me.

"Evening, Berry." I nodded, moving to the elevator as my phone beeped. Scrolling through the emails, I noticed out of the corner of my eye a woman also got in, but I didn't bother looking up. I just waited for her to leave.

Yet she never did.

We rode up and up, until we were at Wes' floor. But she still didn't go until the doors opened on my floor.

"Penthouse Suite," the automatic voice said announcing the next floor.

"I think you missed your floor," I told her walking out.

"Mr. Emerson, when you're on an elevator with a woman in a dress like this, it's rude not to stare."

That voice.

Turning back, she stood there, in a stunning little black dress that hugged all of her curves perfectly. Her hair was in waves falling right beside her breast and her lips were colored cherry red. The red heels she had on made her smooth legs look endlessly long.

"Jane?" She looked so different. She'd gone from beautiful to sinful.

"I told you. You'd know when I was trying to seduce you...well, not just you," she shrugged walking past me and towards the door. "Do me a favor and get my bag?"

God her ass looked incredible.

"Maxwell."

"Huh?" I refocused on her face.

Her manicured hand pointed to the suitcase sitting outside the elevator. "My bag."

"Oh yeah. I got it." I stuttered like a buffoon grabbing on to the handle and following her inside.

"Doors opening," the automatic voice said.

"That was fast—" He froze staring right at her with the same expression I must have just had. "Wow."

"You both should see what I have on under the dress," she smirked moving to the kitchen.

Wes looked to me, but I was far too lost for words to even begin. I just rolled her luggage to the side of the stairs.

"Boys," she called out. And like schoolboys, our heads snapped to her. She sat down after grabbing three glasses and a random bottle of wine. Uncorking it, she poured a glass for each of us. "Come here."

"Yes, ma'am," Wes whispered, already walking to her. I couldn't say anything because before I realized it I was standing right in front of her, too. She handed us both a glass.

"You both are attracted to me," she said boldly. "I'm attracted to the both of you. Now I thought I could run away from you both but that failed. Then I thought I'd just be a friend, but now that I've seen and touched you both, it wouldn't be enough. So I've decided to make you my lovers. This could end horribly, horribly wrong, but until then I'm going to have the best goddamn sex of my life. Don't hold back and cheers," she finished before clinking her glass against ours.

God have mercy.

Jane the maid was dead. Official time of death was noon, yesterday, Friday, October 4th. Waxed away by a Japanese woman in Roxbury. Today my skin was on fire, and I've now opened the door to this whole new side of myself.

"Jane, there is no going back from this," Max said as I drank.

He didn't get it. But Wes did. The lust rolled off him in waves. He drank his wine and it spilled out the corner of his mouth, but he didn't give a shit.

Stepping back away from them, I pulled down the zipper at the side and pushed the dress down, allowing it to fall to a pool around my feet. Both of their eyes went to my breasts, beautiful un-bruised breasts. Wes walked over to me and cupped my ass with one hand before running his other hand down my stomach until it reached my underwear. He rubbed my pussy and kissed the side of my neck while I arched my body to give him more room to play.

"Max," I called out as he was just staring at us both. His nostrils flared and his breathing was slowing. He was getting excited. "Don't just watch. I want you both."

That was all he needed. He came over to me and pulled down my bra to cup my breast before using his tongue to lick my nipple. A shiver shot up my spine.

Who in their right mind would want to go back from this?

"Ahh…" I rocked on top of Wes' hand.

"Silly girl" Wes bit my top lip before saying, "You think you can walk into the lions' den and make us your pets?"

Max sniggered as he continued kissing up my chest and under my chin until his lips were right on my own. "She doesn't know what she's gotten herself into, Wes. We should show her what it really means to be our lover."

"Don't scare her, love. The kitten just got here," Wes replied while slowly kissing my cheek.

"I'm not scared," I told them, and I truly wasn't. Whatever it was, I wanted it. I wanted them. Wes took his hand away from me, and I instantly missed it.

"Taste her," he said to Max who licked me off his fingertips; it was fucking sexy. I licked my lips, too.

"You want to play?" Max said when Wes removed his fingers. He reached out for me to take his hand. So did Wes. "Let's play then."

They walked me up the stairs back into their bedroom.

"Get on the bed," Max commanded, already pulling off his belt, pants, and tie. Wes disappeared into the closet, as I sat on the navy silk sheets.

He then crawled up on the bed and forced me to lie down as he came up, just like a lion over its prey.

"Do you know how badly we've wanted you? And you come here looking like this. How are we supposed to control ourselves?"

"Don't," I whispered reaching up and bringing his lips to mine.

Our third kiss was different from the rest, and he didn't hold back. He cupped my breast and squeezed and pinched my nipples while moaning into my mouth. Not once did I look away and neither did he. I could feel his hot cock rubbing up against my thigh.

"Max," I said licking his tongue. He lifted my leg up, and before I knew it, my thong was moved gently to the side. Something slowly entered me, vibrating as it did. "Oh!...Wh...ah.."

I didn't get a chance to even think straight as he deepened the kiss. Again, hands spread my ass cheeks while another vibrator was rammed up me.

"Fuck!" I hissed out breaking away from him, my whole core now vibrating.

Sitting up in the middle of the bed, I saw them both standing in front me naked. Their cocks were hard and standing tall. Wes' twitched once anxiously.

"Ah...ah...what? What?" I wiggled on their bed, bouncing up and down at the pressure now in my pussy and ass.

"Look how wet you're getting." Wes lifted my chin up, "You're soaking through your panties, baby."

"I see...I...I see you've...thought about this." Fuck it felt so good and so frustrating at the same time.

"Let's make her beg for it," Max replied.

"My thoughts exactly."

I didn't know what he meant until I watched Wes kiss down Max's jawline. Their cocks rubbed against each other for a moment before they each grabbed each other and pumped right in front of my face. I leaned forward, I was so wet that I was dripping down my thigh, but they moved away.

"What's the magic word?" Max asked, and I couldn't look away as his thumb stroked the tip of Wes' cock. And how Wes's whole hand snaked around Max's dick.

"Please..."

"Please, what?" Wes asked.

"I want…let me…let me… let me touch you…I want you in my mouth."

"Ms. Chapman, how dirty," Max said turning to face me with his cock in my face. I licked the pre cum from the top of it and did the same when Wes' came over. I wasn't sure if it was possible, maybe it was just my own subconscious, but Max tasted hot and Wes was sweet. The moment I tasted them, I couldn't stop. Clasping onto Max's thick hot dick, I rubbed down the side of it, as I took Wes' cock into my throat. He was so big I thought I was going to gag, but even as he hit the back of my throat, I sucked. I alternated between them both. When I looked up at them, they were making out. One of Wes' hands held a fistful of my hair, the other Max's.

"Oh…ahh…" The vibrators were driving me crazy. Bringing their dicks closer together, I kissed the tips of both of them, licking them like candy.

"Eat her," Wes said pulling away from us both. His chest rose and fell.

Max didn't hesitate. He pushed me onto my back and lifted my legs up as he slid off my G-string before spreading the lips of my pussy. He pulled out the vibrator and sucked at me happily. Grabbing my own breast, I rocked against his mouth.

"Wes." I didn't have second before Wes kneeled beside me and opened my mouth before he slid his thick, hot cock back into my mouth.

I felt Max kiss up my stomach, coming up above me until his dick was rubbing against my pussy. I spread my legs further for him, and his tip slowly entered me.

"More," I begged to lick the side of Wes' cock as my tongue glided over his throbbing vein.

"Yes!"

"Fuck....fuck!" Max hissed slamming his cock inside of me. He was filling all of me.

I kissed Wes' balls and pumped his dick before licking all over the rim of Wes' cock, tempting him, until even I couldn't take it anymore. He thrust it into my mouth hard holding my head down and I didn't stop. I sucked like a motherfucking champion.

Gritting my teeth as I slid into Wes' tight ass, I did my best to keep my eyes open. I held his leg up on my shoulder, and I thrust forward with sweat rolling down my face. Jane leaned forward to lick it. She sat on Wes's face and his arms held her thighs on top of him. Never once did she look away.

Watching her...watch me like this...

"Harder," she whispered placing her hands on Wes' chest as she continued grinding herself on top of him. "Harder."

Each time she said it, I pulled out of Wes only to slam myself back in, and she licked her lips in excitement. Leaning over, I bit her bottom lip.

"Ohh…ohh…!" she gasped, throwing her head back as she came into his mouth.

Damn, she was hot.

She rolled off him.

I pulled out.

He picked her up and sat her on his cock. I watched as she eased herself slowly taking all of him.

He flipped her onto her hands and got on his knees in front of her.

I got behind him holding his waist, and with no warning, I guided my cock back into him.

"God fuck…" he hissed holding her legs up.

I had no words.

My mind was going blank.

All I could do was keep breathing and fucking.

He ripped off his second condom of the night with his teeth, and I slid it on as fast as humanly possible as I lubed up more, before sliding myself into her ass. The vibrator I put in had softened her perfectly.

"Fuck." She was tight, so fucking tight and I was seeing stars. I was in heaven, a sinful, perfect heaven. Watching her ass take me nearly made me want to come right there.

"Wes…oh," she gasped out reaching back to hold on to me as Max positioned himself between her thighs. He was shaking with excitement. I lifted her thighs apart for him, and in one swift motion, he thrust forward deep within her.

"Fucking Christ," she cried out. Her hand was grasping Max's shoulder, and her head was resting on mine. Her body sandwiched between us both.

We both started slowly, letting her adjust to us, feeling her squeeze around our cocks.

"Kiss him," she whispered to me. I smiled and leaned forward to take Max's lips. "More. Like the first time I caught you."

She was driving me insane: her mouth, her body, everything. Reaching over, Max grabbed my hair and kissed me passionately like he was dying of thirst and could drink from nothing else but me.

I can't. I thought I could take it, but I couldn't. My cock was throbbing with the need to release. Grabbing his ass to steady myself, I pulled out of her slowly before slamming back in. She moaned out something inaudible, and I could feel Max on the other side of her thrusting deeply into her as well. Neither of us stopped, and she moaned, crying out our names, coming over and over again, as we reached out peak.

Yeah, this was heaven.

"Fuck. Fuck," I cried out as I came only seconds later, Max did as well. I pulled out first and fell back on the bed. "Best damn shag of my life," I told them when I felt Jane fall beside me.

"I've heard that before," Max laughed breathing just as hard.

It was only when I could feel my toes again did I sit up to look over at Jane. "Are you alright?"

"I haven't been with anyone in a year. I'm a little rusty," she said, brushing back the strands of her hair. I glanced over at Max who sat up as well.

"We were too rough," I said glancing over her body, and Max got up moving to the bathroom.

"No," she shook her head, "you were both perfect. Thank you."

She was thanking us. The men who just spent the last three hours bending her over and fucking her like a porn star.

Max came back with warm towels and a glass of water while I reached in the bedside table for Advil.

"Advil will help with the pain," I told her.

She pouted still dazed, "But I like the pain."

Max paused glancing towards me and I knew what he was thinking, "For the love of God Jane, don't tempt us any further."

"Okay," she said innocently, but the look in her eyes said something completely different. She took the medicine from me and Max wiped her inner thighs lightly.

"Such gentlemen," she said to Max as she reached up to brush the side of his cheek. She was drunk from the sex. "Are you going to scowl at me in the morning, Mr. Emerson?"

"Max. Just call me Max. And it is the morning," he grinned after kissing her wrist.

She didn't say anything else but just rolled onto her side, yawned and closed her eyes. On our first night together, we'd learned that Jane Chapman could fall sleep on a dime.

Lying back down beside her, I stared up at the ceiling.

"This…us…we just got a lot more complicated," Max whispered laying down on the opposite end of the side of her.

"But you loved every moment of it." He didn't reply because I was right. The moment I saw her, I knew it, just like I knew when I saw him, they were mine. I wasn't sure how it would work out but I'd just figure it out.

11

When I woke up I noticed four things.

First, I was alone. Second, I was so damn sore and in the best possible way. Third, the note on the pillow beside me which simply read *'We're downstairs, take your time. W&M.'* I smiled because I knew they were trying to give me space to adjust. I could smell the bacon. Wes was most likely cooking. However, part of me did wonder what it would have been like to wake up with both of them. The last thing I noticed was my luggage was now parked in the corner with the black dress I had worn folded on top.

Slowly sliding out of bed, I almost fell. I glanced down at my legs grinning so wide I must have looked like an idiot. But I couldn't help it. They had legitimately fucked me until my legs were weak even hours later. Guys always said it, but they were the first for me to actually live up to their promise.

"Wow," I said, remembering how their hands and their lips felt on my skin. Moving to my suitcase, I took out my toilet bag before going into the master bathroom. Facing the mirror, I stared at the hickeys on my breast...and stomach, and neck. It looked I'd lost a battle with a vampire. Taking out my toothbrush, I made a mental note to thank Mary for whatever lipstick she had given me. It hadn't smeared at all, and even now, I could see the faint red lipstick on my lips. Washing it off with soap was easy too.

I took a quick shower to clean my hair before drying it with a towel.

I had outfits I could have worn including another couple cute bra and panty set, however, I didn't bother. I grabbed Max's light blue button down shirt that he had just thrown in the corner and put it on. Max was always in a suit and tie while Wes wore jeans, t-shirts and a jacket, or he walked around naked. They were opposites in everything and yet it worked.

"You got this Jane," I whispered to myself right in front of the door before stepping out.

"That's your second cup of tea already?" Max asked biting into his French toast. Both of them wore nothing but their boxer briefs.

"Why the fuck are you counting?"

"For a man who complains about British stereotypes, you sure are quick to prove them right."

"Can my British stereotypical ass drink in peace now that you've expressed your inner asshole, or do you need get another jab in?" Wes said sipping his tea.

"I'm sure there is a gay joke in there somewhere," Max replied and I laughed out loud.

They both turned to me, and it was a bit intimidating, their eyes wandering down my body and then back up to my face.

"Mornin'," I waved walking over to them, "is there anything for me?"

"No, we were actually planning on letting you starve," Max muttered, bringing his coffee up to his lips.

"Don't mind him," Wes ignored him, smiling at me as he put a plate of French toast, bacon and eggs in front of me. "Great sex short circuits his emotions, so he can't help himself."

"Fuck you," Max said back, though the corner of his lips turned up.

"I've never seen you guys like this," I smiled taking a bite of the French toast. Like everything Wes cooked, it was amazing.

"That's because someone always sneaks out by dawn." Max reached over to pour me a glass of orange juice. "And for the record, Ms. Chapman, I approve of this outfit."

"As your new lover, is it customary that I get approval for all my outfits?"

"If you're naked at all times, there is no need for approval," Wes added leaning on the table. His green eyes glanced at Max and for a split second it felt like they were having a mental conversation before he looked to me.

"What?" I asked them both.

"You're just far bolder than we expected you to be this morning," Wes replied.

"Let me guess. You thought I was acting out of character last night?" I asked them both before drinking. "That I'm a good girl at heart."

"Aren't you?" Max questioned and it was a good question. I just didn't know the answer.

Shrugging, I took another bite of toast and kept them waiting. I took another bite and Wes snickered. Max just rolled his eyes.

"What makes a girl a *good* girl?" I inquired truly wanting to know. "Someone who is 'innocent'? Well, then I strike out. I was fifteen when I lost my virginity. Up until two months ago, I worked at a strip club."

Wes' eyebrow lifted and Max tried to keep a straight face, but his lips made a hard line as he hunched over. Their facial expressions were cute.

"Not as a stripper. I was the bartender and manager. But way to keep cool, guys," I smiled brightly and they both drank their drinks as if they didn't know what I was talking about. "Anyway, I'm not sure what you're expecting. I barely know what I'm expecting. I just made the decision to be here. I went to the doctor and got more birth control. Spent far too much on the perfect dress and then I came here. When I make choices I don't back away from them. I'm very stubborn."

"You don't say," Wes replied and I glared at him. He only winked back.

"Then we can just skip to the rules part of the conversation," Max said putting his cup down.

"The rules?" I glanced between them. Wes said nothing but came around the kitchen island to stand beside me.

"Max and I are always honest with each other about everything we want and expect. It's always been us, but now there is you," Wes said tucking my hair behind my ear. "We can't pretend or go on like nothing has changed. So yes, there are rules for you, and if you want, there are rules for us."

"Okay." I put down my juice looking between them. I wouldn't lie that I was a little nervous.

"Rule one is that you don't just leave. Call or text," Max said putting a shiny new smart phone beside me.

173

"Guys, I can't—"

"Rule two: we are both rich. Max more than me," Wes grinned. "However, I'm still rich. Which means, we will spoil you with expensive gifts from time to time. Don't fight us on it. It might be huge to you, but honestly, it's not for us. Besides, Max told me how deeply you care about not selling yourself. You being with us means more than a gift."

I swallowed the lump in my throat not sure what to say. So I took the phone. "Just don't go crazy, okay? I get overwhelmed easily." This would be one case in point.

"Rule three." Max places his hand on my thigh, "No one but us."

"Is that a two-way street? No one else but me"

They both smiled at that.

"What?"

"Jane, you're the first woman either of us has ever wanted to join us. The first we couldn't stop thinking about." Wes kissed my forehead. "But, if it makes you comfortable. Yes, no else but you. It's just us three."

"Yes, it makes me feel better," I nodded. "Can I add a rule?"

They looked at each other. Max turned completely to me, and I tried not to glance down at the bulge in his boxers. "We're listening."

"I want the both of you. I like the both of you. I like when you both are together, so don't screw me if the other one isn't there." I know it was bold.

"Define screw?" Wes asked.

I grinned pointed to their dicks. "Those do not go in my ass, pussy, or mouth unless the other is there to witness. Kisses, touches, everything else is fair game. You two are allowed fuck each other whether I'm there or not, though."

"Why?" Max asked and I shrugged.

"My selfless reason is because you both were in a relationship before me. It would be wrong for me to break a bond that's already there."

"And your selfish reason?" Wes asked.

"I enjoy watching you both fuck…especially if I feel like I'm catching you both in the act."

"Tell me I'm dreaming," Wes said to Max, his cock already getting hard.

"Concentrate. Not now," Max said through clenched jaws.

"That night when I saw you, with a ball in your mouth, Wes was gripping your waist with one hand while stroking your cock with the other. He fucked you so hard up the ass your body jerked forward. I stopped breathing, Max. My nipples were so hard, it was painful. My pussy was aching…" I whispered, moving closer and closer to his lips before turning away to face Wes, whose eyes were clouded with lust. "Why would I ever want to stop that? I want more. I want to see, feel more. Tell me I can, Wes…please."

"Temptress," was all he could whisper.

Smiling, I pulled back in my chair and grabbed my juice. "Call me the lion tamer."

"And you wanted to start gently with her," Max finally spoke, his hands reaching into my shirt grasping on to my breast.

"Jane," Wes pressed his thumb on my lips, "Don't push us like this because we will fail and you need to rest."

"I've been resting for a year." Opening my mouth, I took his thumb into my mouth and sucked. "Screw resting and fuck me."

Whatever will was holding them back snapped in that moment. Like flipping a switch, Max grabbed on to me, spinning me around as my back pressed up against his chest. His cock was up against my ass with only the cloth of his boxers between us. He lifted up my leg as Wes reached down to free his dick from me and rub the tip to my pussy. I wrapped my arm around Max's neck.

"Well don't keep her waiting," Max said.

"Ahh...fuck!" I hissed out when Wes thrust forward.

"As you wish," he replied by pulling out only to ram himself back in. Sandwiched between them, I closed my eyes and licked my lips as Max kissed my neck.

I wasn't a good girl.

I wasn't a bad girl.

I was their girl.

"Jesus Christ," I gasped lying on the kitchen floor. My chest felt as if it was going to explode.

"Blimey," Wes cried out breathing in through his nose his chest rising and falling with each breath.

"You boys alright?"

Lifting up my chin, I saw her nonchalantly drinking her glass of orange juice. Her naked body was coated in thin layer of sweat. Exhausted, I dropped my head back and stared up at my kitchen ceiling.

"She's….she's not human," I told Wes who tried to laugh but ended up coughing while still trying to catch his breath.

"I must have saved Britain in my past life to deserve this," he joked petting my chest before finally sitting up onto his elbows to look at Jane. "I thought you said you were rusty?"

"It's like riding a bike. Who knew?" she said happily.

Finally, I found the strength to sit up. Jane walked over to us and placed her hands on top of our heads while running her fingers through our hair. I kissed her thigh, and Wes kissed her leg. She was a fucking lion tamer, there was no denying it. In only a day and a half, she had us on our knees with invisible chains around our necks.

"Someone's phone is ringing," she said. I was so taken with the sound of my heart drumming in my ears, I didn't hear it. Pushing myself off the ground, I leaned over the table. Our breakfast was forgotten.

"Maxwell Emerson," I answered not even checking to see who it was. I was too preoccupied with the scene in front of me. Wes was now on his feet and both of them were naked at the refrigerator door. She pulled out strawberries and he got whipped cream. He sprayed some in his mouth, and she licked the excess off the corner of his lip causing him to slap her ass so hard she jumped before giggling.

They are trying to kill me.

"Hello, Mr. Emerson."

"Who is this?" I blinked trying to refocus.

"Kevin the security guard."

"What is it Kevin, the security guard?"

"I have a Ms. Scarlet de Burgh here for you. She says it's urgent and has been trying to contact you for an hour."

Pulling the phone away from my ear, I checked and sure enough I had fifteen missed calls and over forty texts.

"Hold on," I said, looking across at Jane feeding Wes a strawberry. He bit it in half before looking at me.

"What's wrong?" he frowned.

"My producer is here, and she knows better than to bother me. It must be important," I said and he nodded.

"Do we need to hide?" Jane asked.

"I'm going to take a shower and get ready for work," Wes said. "You should use this as a chance to make her realize there is no chance in hell."

Before I could reply, he kissed me hard and quick then backed away.

"Jane, stay with him," he replied and just like that he went upstairs.

"I'm a little lost?" Jane came to me. "What is up with your producer?"

"He thinks she's in love with me."

She was quiet for a second as she leaned on the island, "And is she?"

"She's the woman that my mother would prefer I marry. At work, there are two rumors: either I'm gay or I'm screwing Scarlet de Burgh."

"De Burgh?" she made a face. "She sounds rich and pretty? Blonde?"

"Brunette."

"Oh. You do have a thing for brunettes," she smiled brushing back a few strands of my hair. "What do you want me to do, Mr. Emerson?"

It was a million-dollar question.

Good thing I could afford to ask.

"Hi," I smiled when I opened the door dressed in only Max's shirt again. It is just like I thought. The woman in front of me was drop dead gorgeous. Perfect c-cup boobs, full round hips and I'm sure she had a killer ass too. Her blue eyes widened, as she looked me up and down.

"I'm sorry I'm looking for—"

"Max, yeah? Please come in. He's getting dressed," I said opening the door for her to come in. When she did, her heels clicked against the wood paneling. She took three steps before turning to me.

"Who are you?"

"Jane Chapman, Max's girlfriend. You are his producer, right?" I extended my hand to shake hers.

"I didn't know Max had a girlfriend," she didn't shake my hand and I instantly remembered Max's mother…no wonder he didn't see her like that. I could already pick up on the similarities.

"Now you do," I shrugged putting my hand down. "Do you want anything to drink? Coffee? Water?"

"I'm fine. How long have you two been together?" she asked, walking over to put her purse on the couch.

"Long enough, but I'm not sure why you are asking? Do producers generally ask these type of things?"

"No. However, Max and I have been—"

"Friends for a while," I finished for her. "I know. I also know you like him, too."

"So, is that why you decided to face me dressed like that? To put me in my place?" she said softly, though if looks could kill, I'd be long dead. "It's rather desperate, don't you think?"

"You think I came out like this to prove something?" I laughed, more than annoyed. "Scarlet, if I was going to prove something, I'd do this."

Opening my shirt, I let her see the hickeys all over my breasts and stomach. Her fists clenched, and she tried to keep a straight face.

"You can like him all you want, Scarlet. I'm not threatened by you because you can't win." I told her as I buttoned up the shirt. "So please don't put him in a situation where he may have to let go of a damn good producer."

"Jane?"

I turned back as Max came down the stairs dressed in dark jeans and a casual shirt. It was the first time I'd seen him out of a tie. Well, in a matter of speaking.

"Everything okay?" he asked putting his hand on my waist.

"I feel a little bit awkward standing here in your shirt. I'm going to take a shower and get dressed." I kissed his check before moving to the stairs. "It was nice to meet you, Scarlet. We should meet again under different circumstances. I would really like to know about Max's work."

"Sure," she said but it sounded like a 'fuck off'.

Nodding, I headed back into the bedroom expecting Wes to be in the shower but instead he was lying on his clothes in the center of the bed.

"Come here," he said, not bothering to open his eyes.

"I didn't realize you were the jealous type," I said crawling into the bed and resting my elbow on his abs.

"What makes you think I was jealous?" he asked.

"Max asked me to destroy that woman, all because you made one comment. I feel kind of bad."

His eyes snapped open and his jaws were clenched. "Don't feel sorry her. I'm actually jealous of you. If I had gone downstairs, she wouldn't have gotten through the door."

"What did she do?" He was far too upset for this just to be jealousy.

"Max doesn't know this, but she was the one who started the damn rumor about his sexuality. She hoped it would prompt him to prove he wasn't, and since her mother and his mother are friends, I guess she thought she'd end up with Max."

"What a bitch."

182

"You will learn, Jane, I can take a lot of shit. But don't fuck with the people I care about. If Max didn't need her, I would have…" He didn't finish that statement, and I just put my head on his chest.

"Does it bother you that your relationship is kept in the closet?" I asked.

"It's a pretty nice closet."

"Wes."

"A few days ago, he asked for your help in order to make a date for me," he whispered placing his hand on my thigh. "It doesn't bother me as much because it bothers him. He cares enough that it bothers him. When he's ready, he'll make a choice. I can wait. In the meantime, we have a beautiful woman to focus on."

"Don't focus too much that you realize there isn't much here," I whispered. "I give you either a month or two before you're bored with me. But it's going to be fun."

He shifted, siting up against the pillows, "Why do you do that?"

"Do what?"

"Keep one leg out the door at all times. You've committed to being here, but you still can't help but think of running. Why?

"I'm just being practical."

"I'm in love with a man who can't be honest with his family or anyone in his life outside of this penthouse. I desire a woman I barely know but crave more than I can understand. On top of which, the man I love wants her too, and it makes me want her more if possible. How is any of this practical?"

I didn't know what to say to that. That was a lie. I did know and there was no point lying about it. "You and Max have each other to fall back on. as Max's family might be, he still has family. You have family. It's always been just me...being practical even in the face of the unpractical is self-preservation. That isn't a habit I'm going to break just because of two strangers."

"Two strangers you have no trouble sleeping with?"

"Sex is different. You know it's all about attraction."

"Fine then, tell me about yourself."

"I've told you guys everything."

"You've told me about your circumstances. I want to know who you are."

"What are the two of you talking about?"

I rolled back to see Max come inside the bedroom, shutting the door behind him. He fell on the bed beside Wes and closed his eyes when his head hit the pillow.

"Is everything okay?" I asked him.

"Ask me tomorrow," he replied lifting my legs and placing them over his lap. "So what are we talking about?"

"Jane was about to agree to play forty-seven questions," Wes grinned.

"Forty-seven, I thought the game was called twenty questions?"

"It is, but I knew you wouldn't agree to that off the bat. I'd rather negotiate from high to low," the bastard replied. "We should know the woman we're sharing a bed with. For all we know, you could be a black widow finding your prey by pretending to be a maid then using seduction before WHAM!"

My mouth dropped open, and I looked to Max who just shook his head. He'd obviously come to expect this craziness from him.

"Shouldn't you have been worried about that before you slept with me?"

"If we're going to die, at least, we got sex out of it," Max said joining in the madness.

"You both are crazy!"

"Through forty questions, you will see how crazy," Wes replied.

"Fine, but I start," I said sitting up in between them. "Wes...shit. I can't think of anything."

"Okay—"

"No, wait" I held my hands up and they both laughed at me. "Okay, what makes you frustrated, bored, and unfulfilled?"

"Cheating, that's three questions," he frowned.

"No, there is a comma between each adjective." I crossed my arms.

He looked to Max who just nodded, and I smiled so wide my cheeks hurt.

"Fine, but remember I know how to use a comma too."

"You're stalling," Max replied.

"What makes me frustrated? There are too many buttons on clothes. When am I bored? When I'm not using my hands to cook or fuck. What makes me unfulfilled? I don't know? Unseasoned food, a bad fuck"

Shaking my head, I turned to Max, "What do you dream about?"

"Sex," he answered making Wes laugh.

"Guys, all of your answers are all about sex!"

Wes nodded. "We're men. What were you expecting?"

"I hate this game," I muttered to myself.

Max looked to Wes. "Would you like to do the honors?"

"Jane Chapman, who is more handsome?" he asked with a wicked grin on his face. Max raised his eyebrow as if he was daring me to say 'Wes' instead.

"David Beckham." I was not falling into that trap.

"What—"

"Next time, be more specific, and no Max, you cannot ask the same question."

His jaw cracked to the side. I could tell he wasn't used to being bossed around by a woman. "What is your greatest fear?"

"Being forgotten. My turn." I didn't want to dwell on that. "Wes, who was your first crush?"

"Diana Bancroft," he said without hesitation and even Max was shocked by that. "In our seventh year, she came back with these massive tits. I'd never had to hide a boner for so long in my life. She was my first shag, too."

I wanted to smack him. Instead, I focused on Max. "What are your favorite hobbies? Note the answer should not involve sex or anything sexual."

He actually had to think...like really *think* before saying, "Flying I guess or collecting cars."

We went back and forth, laughing at each ridiculous answer. Max had his eyebrows shaved off by his cousin Irene who then tried to draw them back on. Wes drove on the wrong side of the road a few dozen times when he first came to America. He was also an adrenaline junkie. Max hated olives. Wes loved seafood and especially fishing for it himself. Max was actually a skilled marksman and took up fencing in high school. Rich people.

Everything felt simple and easy, fun even. Until it got to Wes' turn and he simply asked: "Why haven't you told us how much you owe to the loan shark or drug dealer or whatever?"

The question was so random and so sudden that I froze, too shocked to answer.

"Jane?"

Running my hand through my hair, I forced myself to smile even though I didn't want to. "We just got started, so I'm in no position to ask for money."

"You'd rather take a beating?"

"Guys—"

"My turn" Max cut me off. "How much is the debt?"

"I'm going to take a shower." I moved to get up, but Wes pulled me back, hovering over me.

"I told you, nothing upsets me more than when the people I care about get hurt. It's even worse when I can't do anything about it. I love seeing you smiling and I remember just days ago your face was bruised. Do not make either of us go through that again, please?"

Why? Why did they care so much? Why couldn't we just—?

"Jane? We're not asking again," Wes demanded and because I had somehow become a much weaker person since meeting them, I gave in.

"Two hundred and ten thousand."

12

"Eat it."

He sneered through his teeth while his whole body hunched over. Rage was rolling off him in waves. I'd never seen him like this. In fact, the man I knew in my mind to be Wesley and the chef in front of me now seemed like two very different men.

The short woman next to him, shaking in terror, turned to the plate on the counter beside her before reaching over to take a forkful of rice, scallops and fish. The whole kitchen was completely silent. It felt like they were all holding their breath, hell, even I was, and I wasn't entirely sure what the hell was going on. But I couldn't look away from her as she chewed and chewed until she paused making a face. Reaching into her mouth, she pulled out a thin long fishbone. When she did, a few other people in the kitchen grimaced. But not Wes, he just stared her down.

"What is that?" he asked her, eerily calm.

"A bone Chef."

"Are bones edible?"

"No, Chef."

"Are you or are you not the *poissonier* of my kitchen?"

"I am, Chef."

"THEN WHAT THE FUCK IS THIS?!" He grabbed the plate and threw it across the kitchen. It shattered on impact with the rice and fish flying everywhere. No one else was surprised, but I couldn't help but jump.

"I made—"

"Get out of my kitchen, or I'll throw you out!" He leaned forward to hiss in her face, and she took her apron off quickly, leaving it on the counter before running out the back.

He turned back around to face the rest of the staff. Like a drill sergeant, he moved to this next victim, an older man with a bandana on his head. The man looked up but didn't say anything.

"I should have made you taste it, too because you made the sauce. The sauce, the sauce I taught you how to make, a sauce I've watched you make dozens of times, tasted like SHIT!"

"Yes, Chef"

"Yes it tasted like shit, or yes you know you made a mistake?"

He swallowed. "I didn't have time to—"

"Go home, Alexander. Come back when your head isn't up your own goddamn ass!"

"Yes, Chef." He also took off his apron and left.

"What do I hate?" he asked the rest of them.

"Apologizing to customers," his army answered as one.

"What don't I tolerate?"

"Bad chefs," they replied.

He took off his apron and threw it on the table, "Think about that while I'm out there apologizing to a sixty-year-old woman over fish, you fucking cunts."

It was only when he left that they all seemed to breathe again. One of them even rested on her knees as if she had just run ten miles.

"I thought you guys said he was in a good mood the last couple of days, Nicklaus?" a woman muttered.

A tall man with pulled back hair went back to his pan with a small grin on his face, "He was pretty tame to me. Last time, he actually grabbed the pastry chef by the collar and threw him out."

I snickered at that. Here I thought Max was the asshole of the two, but apparently Wes shared that trait with him.

"Who are you again?" the woman asked her brown eyes curious. When she asked they all focused in on me like they had completely forgotten I was here.

"I'm a friend of Wes'," I said, which only made them share a few looks between each other before she nodded.

"Are you a cook?" she pressed.

"Stop being so nosy, Abbey!" Nicklaus smiled while shaking his head.

"Are you really a chef?" another guy asked. He was much younger and relegated to stacking plates in back.

"No," I shook my head. We still hadn't come up with how to describe me yet, and I was going little stir crazy staying in the penthouse. So Wes offered to take me out tonight while Max rushed to work. "I'm just a friend."

"Better mood friend?"

"Abbey!" Nicklaus snapped at her, and she just grinned and winked at me.

Nicklaus glanced up at me and his eyes drifted up and down on my body. For a second, I thought he was checking me out until a frown appeared on his lips. It was barely noticeable, but it was there. He didn't like me.

Interesting!

"Nickolas, I need salmon," Wes commanded when he walked back into the kitchen putting his apron back around his waist.

Immediately Nickolas moved, grabbing something that was like tiny tweezers and headed to a massive refrigerated walk-in closet. Wes moved around the kitchen grabbing ingredients before stepping up to the stove. He glanced up at me and mouthed *sorry.*

I'm fine. I mouthed back shaking my head. It was actually nice seeing him at work, and I wasn't the only one who thought so either. Slowly everyone stopped what they were doing to watch him.

He thinly sliced green onions so quickly that I blinked and they already were done and moved to one side of the chopping board. Next were the garlic cloves and then some leafy greens. It looked like spinach, but I wasn't sure. He never took his eyes off the food in front of him, and he never wasted a single moment. He was quick, elegant, and meticulous.

"Salmon." Nicklaus came over and placed it to the right of him.

Wes didn't look up. He tasted the brown sauce he had made sometime between when I looked from Nicklaus and him.

"Bourbon," Wes asked hand outstretched. In a flash, it was in his hand and he rubbed it onto the fish.

It was then that I saw it, the look on Nicklaus' face when Wes smiled, satisfied with whatever he had created.

He likes him.

"Chef, I can take over—"

"No. I told her I'd personally bring the dish out." Wes cut him off and stared at the stove.

It took him less than ten minutes to prepare the dish, including the time it took him to decorate the plate. When he was done, he placed the dish on the palm of his hand to avoid fingerprints and walked out. When he was gone, Abbey and a few others rushed to taste the remaining sauce.

"Ahhh," Abbey moaned while licking her spoon. "This makes it all worth it."

"Eating?" I laughed.

"Chef Uhler has been awarded three Michelin stars for the last six consecutive years," she replied, but I had no idea what that meant.

"Is three good?"

They all froze and stared as if I were an alien.

"Three is God," Nicklaus snapped at me. "At last count, there are only fifteen Michelin star restaurants in this country. Six in New York, Five in California, Two in Chicago, One in Las Vegas and one here in Boston, Chef Uhler's Wes Hill. Eating his food is an honor. Working here is an even bigger one."

I think I was just schooled.

"Would anyone else like to fuck up this evening or am I free to go?" Wes came back, completely oblivious. The cooks around what was left of his dish scattered like rats moving back to their stations.

"We're good, Chef," Nicklaus said to him as he walked over to me placing his hand on my back. Which I'm sure, Nicklaus and everyone else noticed.

"Very good then," Wes took off the chef's coat he was wearing. He then grabbed his jacket I forgot I was holding for him, took my hand and led me out the back. "Goodnight, kitchen."

"Goodnight, Chef," they called back.

Outside I shivered at the change in the air. Smiling, I backed away from him bowing.

"I was not aware I was in the presence of a god."

"I would have told you, but I didn't want to overwhelm you with my magnificence," he replied spinning me around and pulling me closer.

"I now understand why you are so cocky. All of those people bowing down to you, day in and day out. You enjoy it, don't you? Right, *Chef?*"

He pinched my sides as we walked causing me to giggle so hard I snorted.

"Ms. Chapman, are you ticklish?"

"Don't." I backed away.

A wicked grin spread across his face.

"Wes, no." I laughed, running away, and he caught up to me with ease before picking me up and throwing me over his shoulder. I couldn't stop laughing as he spun me around. "I surrender!"

"You surrender far too easily for my liking, Ms. Chapman," he replied setting me back on my feet.

Trying to put my best fake British accent on, I lifted my head up and said, "It is merely surrender to fight another day. For thy will rue the day thou made me snort."

He laughed. He laughed so hard there were tears in his green eyes. "Rue? Thou? Are you trying to be British or Shakespearean?"

"Shakespeare was from Britain," I shrugged.

"Very well, as such, I must ask will thy most beautiful of all maidens, accompany me on a walk?" he asked giving me his elbow.

"If it pleases you," I nodded linking arms with him.

"I'm glad I got to see you in your natural habitat," I said leaning into him.

"My natural habitat," he nodded agreeing.

"Your staff really like you" I said.

"You mean Nicklaus?"

"Didn't mean any one person. Wait, you know?"

"Of course, I know. I'm not as dense as Max" he replied. "Besides he's never let it interfere with his work. And I benefit also."

"Him having a one sided crush benefits you how? Other than making you feel good about yourself?"

He pouted, "I'm not that conceited."

"I believe you—ahh," I replied as he tickled my sides again. "Okay, okay."

"Nicklaus is great chef, and in the next year or two, he might be ready to go off on his own. Chefs are cocky; it's just how it is. His crush on me forces him to strive to be on the same level as me. He's working twice as hard for me and never fights back. He just wants to hone his skills. Right now I'm winning out. I'm going to miss him when he realizes he's ready to go."

"You won't tell him when he's ready?"

"If I have to, then he won't make it. I'm glad you met him; he's a good guy. I wish I was less of an ass tonight, though."

"Liar. You enjoyed showing them who was boss in front of me."

He glanced down and I stared back up daring him to argue.

"Okay, maybe a little bit."

"I knew it. I finally get you and Max."

He asked when we got to the abandoned playground. Rushing on to the swing I kicked my leg out. "Please share your wisdom with us little people, Ms. Chapman." He pushed me softly on the swing.

"You and him are both alpha males and usually that never works because...well, because one ends up destroying the other. But in very rare situations, some alphas actually enjoy that fight. Someone to push them back, challenge them. You're turned on by his assholery and he's turned on by your cockiness. No pun intended."

He grabbed on the chains and held me still as he leaned over my shoulder with his lips beside my ear.

"What are we going to do with you, Jane? You're uncovering all of our secrets one by one."

"Make sure my lips are sealed?" I turned to face him.

"I can do that," he replied before kissing me.

"She backed out?" I pinched the bridge of my nose trying to breathe. "What do you mean she backed out?"

"She's worried that it will make her a target of Governor MacDowell's supporters."

"BULLSHIT!" I slammed my hand on the table. "Someone got to her, and it was your job to make sure that wasn't possible!"

"Maybe if you weren't focused on some random woman and were here focusing on one of the most important stories in this city—"

"Get out."

"Max."

"Go home, Scarlet. You obviously need a break from this. So go before you say something you regret," I replied.

She clenched her fists so tightly that it looked like she was about to draw blood. Grabbing her purse, tablets and phones, she stomped out. I didn't bother looking back but instead focused on the people across from me. All of them were trying to pretend they did not just hear something about my personal life.

"Go over everything we have," I said leaning back my chair. But no one moved. "Are you really going to make me call on someone?"

"Governor MacDowell—"

"Your name?" I asked the dark-skinned man dressed in a horrible plaid shirt.

"Dwayne Adams...sir"

Sir?

"Mr. Adams, I don't remember you being in here?"

"I've been in the pit. Scarlet invited me here."

"Welcome to the big time, boy toy, and since you have the balls to speak up first, don't fuck up," I nodded for him to continue. "What do we have?"

He turned to the drawing of a spider web on the wall and pointed to the picture of Governor MacDowell in the center.

"Three weeks ago, we were given an anonymous tip that Governor MacDowell bribed a judge, Judge Aster, to get his brother a lighter sentence for a hunting run after a DUI. Judge

Aster, who up to this point has always had a spotless record, agreed—"

"We still don't know," said Isla, a young blonde who still felt awkward speaking up for herself here. Until now she had been basically Scarlet's shadow.

"Right," Dwayne nodded to her. "Isla was the one who confirmed the story after speaking with the bailiff. It was there that we were able to dig further down the rabbit hole to the corruption. This is where MacDowell made numerous property deals while he was a county commissioner in the area. Later, he stepped up to blackmailing city council members. Governor MacDowell still claims to be innocent of those charges. That is when you, sir, were informed by a whistleblower at the Boston PD of the city police's new order to 'give warnings' and the sex ring. We had a woman, only named 'LL', who claimed she was part of the ring. She called to tell Scarlet she couldn't do the show and has now disappeared."

"Is she alive?" I asked and they all tensed.

"You think he'd kill her?" another one them spoke up.

I stared at him as if he was stupid; no, he had *to be* stupid. "This is Boston. If you don't think that it's possible, you're not from here."

"So what do we do if we have no guest? We've been replaying and promoting this interview for the last two days. What are you going to say tonight?"

"The truth," I replied standing up. "Keep working on this. Keep hounding the police and the Governor's office. You're a friend of friend who knows someone at the Governor's office. Don't stop until you're so annoying that they tell you *anything* just to get you to leave."

"Yes sir."

Walking out, I headed back to my office. Everyone was in the pit answering phones and typing so damn hard that it was like a symphony orchestra. Making it into my office, I sat back down in my leather chair and rubbed my eyes.

"Long time no see Max."

"Jesus!" I jumped at the man sitting on my couch with his snakeskin shoes on my coffee table. "Not long enough, Teddy. Get your feet off my table."

He sniggered, stood up and ran his hands through his slimy brown hair. His gut hung over his belt, but he didn't seem to care.

"You shouldn't be here," I said to him.

"I just thought I'd come to speak with you man to man. Well, make that man to the little fairy. Why have you dedicated your time to sticking it to my father?"

"Fuck you, and your father is a criminal."

Teddy MacDowell, the very son of the devil who I was doing my best to make sure did not get away with this shit, just sucked his teeth and took a seat in the chair in front of me.

"This is starting to feel personal, Max."

"Mr. Emerson," I said before pushing the intercom button.

"Yes, sir?"

"I'm going to need security up here. Now," I said, never looking away from him.

"You were never very friendly," he frowned. "Well, at least to no one but my brother."

"Leave." I got up moving around the table to stare him in the face.

"Remember Chris? I'm sure the public would love to know about your personal life too, huh? How about we do a sit down interview! How about I tell everyone you are nothing but a cock sucking little bi—"

Before he could get the word in, I punched him across the jaw. He stumbled back, rushed me, and grabbed onto my neck.

"Sir!" The security rushed in and pulled him off.

"You've got secrets, too, Emerson! Keep coming for my family like this, and I am coming for yours, you hear me? You hear me, you little fuck boy!" he hollered as they pulled him away.

Slamming the door closed, I grabbed the lamp near the couch and threw it against the wall. Fuck them. Fuck them all!

"Max is late," she whispered lying on my lap as I brushed her hair back.

"He's a workaholic." It was true. What she didn't know is he always came back home on time. The only times he didn't was if something had happened. Something that took him back to that dark place again. If he wasn't home by now, he wouldn't come back home until early in the morning, most likely drunk.

What happened?

"You seem worried." She rolled over to look up at me.

"I'm fine—"

"Liar! If you can't tell me, just say you can't tell me." She was far too damn perceptive for her own good. Leaning over, I kissed her lips.

"I don't know enough to tell, and even if I did, it's not me who should say something."

She frowned, "I'm too tired to decode whatever that means."

"Sleep then."

"I want to have sex with you both," she said bluntly while pouting. It was one of the things I enjoyed about her. How she didn't shy away from her sexuality. How she was confident in her own skin. It was refreshing in a woman.

"I'll wake you up when he's here."

"Promise?" She lifted her pinky to me.

Linking it with mine and kissing it, I nodded. "I promise my horny little butterfly."

Her eyes closed but she smiled, "Are you promising BDSM stuff too?"

Fucking hell. "Go to sleep Jane before I break a rule."

"Yes, Chef," she giggled to herself. She was beautiful when she slept. She looked so innocent, not at all like the temptress she really was.

No. Focus. Max. I tried to calm myself down while reaching for my phone.

The phone rang once before going to voicemail. He declined me. The little shite!

Putting my phone on the table, I sat up lifting Jane's head to get up. Part of me thought about taking her upstairs...things were about to get ugly here. However, another part of me wanted her to see it. I wanted her to be so emotionally invested, so fucking knee deep in both Max's and my life, that she felt like she really was a part of it and not just a woman we both fucked for the hell of it.

Taking my jacket off, I laid it over her body. She'd switched to shorts so short they were basically underwear and a tank top so sheer that her nipples were poking through the material, along with thick furry socks. I take it back. She wasn't innocent. Even while she slept, she was still fucking toying with me.

I wanted to touch her.

I wanted to fuck her.

I wanted her.

She's mine....she's ours.

She asked for quote 'BDSM stuff' as if it was nothing. As if she understood what I wanted. Fucking her now with Max only partially satisfied me. I was trying to get her comfortable with the idea of the both of us before I further freaked her out. If she knew what I wanted to do to her sexy little body, she'd run and never come back.

If she knew how badly I wanted to see my cum on her face. How badly I wanted to tie her up, beat her pussy and ass until they were bright red...would she still see me as sweet Wesley? There was no point rushing into it. I could wait. For now.

Until then we'd have to focus on Max.

****

It was 2:47 a.m. when I heard the automatic voice alert me that the door had opened, and just like I thought, he stumbled in drunk. He threw off his jacket to the side and angrily pulled off his tie.

"Good to know you're not dead in a ditch somewhere," I said.

"Not now," he grumbled, brushing past me. Grabbing on to his arm, I pulled him back.

"You ignored my calls six times."

"Wes NOT NOW!" He pulled his arm from me.

"Fuck that! Yes, now!"

He tried to punch me, and for that, I punched him right back. My fist went right into his stomach. He stumbled back before charging forward like a damn bull slamming my back into the railing of the stair.

"Oh my God, Wes! Max! Stop!" Jane yelled but neither of us listened. We both struggled, falling to the ground until I was able to pin him under me.

"ENOUGH!" I yelled down at him he tried to fight, but I held down harder leaning forward. I spoke softer, "Max enough."

He stopped, closed his eyes and nodded. I got up but he just lay prostrate on the ground. I took a seat beside him on the floor. Jane stood there in shock.

"Jane." I offered my hand and she didn't take it.

"I don't like things like this," she whispered.

Max tilted his head to the side and stared at her for the longest time before saying, "Who likes being like this?"

She frowned but walked over and sat beside us, "What's happening?"

I couldn't answer that question, so I waited for him to speak.

"The first guy I cared about, the first guy I ever slept with, his name was Christopher MacDowell, son of Governor MacDowell, who I just exposed to the world for the monster he really is."

I had heard this story before. He was telling her.

"So Chris is upset?"

He laughed bitterly and shook his head, "I met Chris when I was sixteen. He was fifteen. We bonded over hating the Catholic school we were in. His family threw a New Year's party, one of those parties to prove how much money you have, and we both got drunk. One thing lead to another and we fucked in his bedroom. After hiding for so long, being with him was like a sanctuary. It went on for four months. We were so careful. In that time, his mother died and I started to notice bruises on his body. He told me he had started boxing. I didn't think much of it. I thought he was working through grief. What I didn't know was that his father was getting abusive. During one of our secret meet-ups, we got caught."

He just stopped talking for a moment and took a deep breath. Jane reached over brushing the side of his face, and he closed his eyes leaning toward her.

"We got caught, and his father was so pissed off that his face turned red. He called my mother and told me he was going to press charges and have me locked up where someone would do to me what I did to his son. I was so freaked that I stopped talking to Chris. He called and I avoided him like the plague. My mother…she kept it from my father, but the look of disgust she had on her face told me how she really felt. She sent me away to one of those 'pray the gay away' camps in secret. My father thought I was in Italy with friends. When I came back, I found out that Chris had killed himself. One of the maids told me he had written me a letter, but my mother had burned it. To this day, when I see her, I can't forgive her. I can't forgive myself either. I just left him with that monster. God knows how many times his father beat him before he finally…I was scared and I left him."

Maxwell wept and Jane just hugged him.

"What happened tonight?" I asked him.

"Chris' younger brother swore he'd expose everything if I didn't back down. He really thinks I'm the reason his brother killed himself."

"He's blackmailing you?" she whispered.

He shook his head. "He won't say anything. Governor MacDowell would kill before letting him expose that secret. It's just…"

The reminder of it still hurts.

She must have known that because she kissed Max's forehead, his cheeks, his nose, his lips, and he couldn't help but kiss her back.

13

"Do you trust me?" Wes had the nerve to ask her with a satin tie and a vibrator in his hands. Jane kneeled in the center of our bed with her hands placed on her thighs and her head down. She was also blindfolded. He hadn't done anything yet, and she was already trembling. I wondered how she'd react if she saw the tray of 'tools' he had just to the left of us.

"Yes," she answered, and when she did, he took her hand and led her to stand right in front of the bed, and me, naked. Lifting her wrist, he tied it tightly to the bedpost, kissing the ties before moving over to the next one.

"Do you remember the safe word?" he asked while gently pressing his thumb on her lips as his other hand traveled the length of her side stopping only when they reached her pussy. He stuck his middle finger into her.

"Yes. It's caterpillar," she replied licking her lips.

"What do you think of our little butterfly, Max?" Wes turned back to me with a wicked grin.

He knew I couldn't answer because of the ball in my mouth. He'd stripped me down and tied me to a chair so I had a front row seat to his show. *This isn't my thing.* I'd said it a hundred times, and yet watching him turn on the pink vibrator and holding it to her nipples, then her mouth making sure to wet it before slowly sliding it up her pussy….it turned me on more than I could imagine. My cock rose at the sight of her like this; my tongue fought against the ball in my mouth. She twisted her legs, clenched them together and turned her hands to pull on the ties. He grabbed on to her thighs and spread them open.

"Looks like I'm going to have to tie those down too," he muttered to himself. I couldn't look away from her if I wanted to.

The rope he had used on me was so secure that I could only sit and stare at her. Her pussy was vibrating and was making her so wet she was dripping down her own thighs. I swallowed the saliva in my mouth. I wanted to lick it. I wanted her on my tongue. When Wes returned, he spread her legs and tied them to the bottom of the bedpost.

That wasn't all.

He held a flat head horsewhip.

He stood back to admire his handiwork wearing nothing but his dark blue briefs. His hard cock was easily seen through the material. He licked his shaking hand out to calm himself down.

SLAP!

"Ahh..." she cried out in pleasure. He had smacked her tits so hard she jerked like electricity had just run through her.

SLAP!

Right on her stomach.

SLAP

Her other nipple.

SLAP!

Her thigh.

SLAP

Her ass.

"Oh..." she moaned at that one, and her chest rose and fell. "Is that all, Chef?"

His grip on the whip tightened, as my dick twitched anxiously. I wanted him to hit her more. I wanted to see her jerk forward.

SLAP!

SLAP!

SLAP!

SLAP!

"Fuck!" she gasped, breathing in through her nose. "Chef—"

SLAP!

SLAP!

Moving back to her, he grabbed her hair pulling it back, "Don't push me sweetheart or you'll never sit down again."

Instead of getting scared, she blew him a kiss, and if I could have, I would've laughed. Wes reached between her thighs taking out the vibrator slowly before thrusting it back in. Over and over again he did this until she was rocking with his motion. Throwing her head back, she ached with pleasure, and just when it looked like she was reaching her climax, he stopped.

"No," she whimpered and he ignored her by bringing the vibrator over to me and placing it right on top of my cock.

Fuck.

I rocked and more than anything I wanted to touch him, to touch myself. He knew it too, and instead of mercy, he brought the vibrator up and down my cock, a shiver going up and down my spine with it.

It felt so fucking good and so unsatisfying at the same fucking time.

Fuck! I grunted out, trying to speak out against the ball my mouth but nothing worked. Just like that, he moved away and walked behind Jane.

"Your ass is far too tight, Ms. Chapman. I'm going to have to stretch you out," he said getting behind her.

"Please…" she begged as her voice trailed off. I couldn't see, but by the way she was wiggling, I was sure he was using the vibrator to tease her asshole.

"Please what, Ms. Chapman?" he asked and she pulled on the ties and bit her lip so hard it looked like she would draw blood.

He grabbed the lube from the bedside table.

A few minutes later, she was shaking. Her pussy was so wet that it was begging for me. Again, I struggled against the ropes.

"You should see Max, baby," he whispered in Jane's ear staring directly at me. "He's so hard. He wants to fuck you. What do you think? Should I let him?"

She didn't just answer; she just took a deep breath.

He grabbed her jaw, "You need to answer."

"Yes."

"Yes what?"

"Yes, let him fuck me."

"No. I'm just starting to enjoy myself."

Fuck him!

"You need to learn patience," he told me by flicking the tip of my cock.

Readjusting the whip in his hands he turned back to her.

SLAP!

The whip hit right on the lips of her pussy. The ends of it were even getting wetter.

"Oh…"

SLAP!

"I…"

SLAP!

"YES!" She cried out and came so hard it ached me to not touch her.

Wes dropped the whip down and walked out of sight to come back with a red candle. He held it over her breast.

"Shit," she hissed as the wax dripped on to her nipple. He didn't stop until her whole nipple was covered in red wax. He did the same the same thing to her left breast.

I didn't understand what was happening until he came over to me. I looked to the flame. It reflected in Wes' eyes.

"Urgh!" I grunted out. I tried to tell him not to, but he did, and the wax dripped on my dick. It burned for only a second before quickly cooling. Over and over the hot wax dripped. It was something I would desire again.

My eyebrow twitched. I could feel it and I wanted to cry out, but all I did was take deep breaths through my nose to calm myself down. That seemed to bother him. He wanted me to lose control. Blowing out the candle, he dropped it beside my feet. Reaching down he rubbed the wax on my cock. The wax came off, but he didn't stop stroking me.

This is driving me insane. So close…I was so fucking close.

He never looked away from staring me down.

"I'm going to make you go wild," he stated as his thumb spread my pre-cum over my tip. So close…I was so fucking close. But just like he did with her, he stopped and let me go before I could come.

Instead he moved over to his tools and came back with a collar. For a second, I thought it was for me, his dog Max. But instead, he placed it around Jane's neck. With a simple tug, he undid the ties around her wrist. She fell forward slightly placing her arms on his shoulders. He didn't undo the ones at her feet. Instead he helped her on to her knees. Using the leash of her collar, he brought her over to me.

"Cum on her," he demanded at me and my eyes went wide. "Don't you want to? Make her know who she belongs to."

I couldn't speak and just stared down at her blindfolded face. I expected her to speak...she could. "Are you waiting for permission? Jane, tell him."

She swallowed and nodded. "Cum on me Max"

Fucking Christ, have mercy on me.

"Help him, Jane." He directed her by putting her hand on my cock and again she nodded. She licked from the base of my cock all the way to the tip.

Jane! She didn't stop but just licked like I was the sweetest thing in the world, like my dick was her favorite food. Just like that, she took me into her hot mouth and sucked.

I can't.

The sounds she made as she sucked. The way she latched on.

"Don't get greedy, Jane." Wes tugged on the leash. She took her mouth off me just as my eyes rolled back and I came, hitting her right in the face. It was everywhere, even in her hair. Some even dropped on her lips and she just used her tongue to lick it up. Fucking Christ, it was beautiful.

"Good boy," he said petting my head. "I'll let you have a short break before round two."

Damn him.

Whoever said dreams don't come true was most likely dreaming about the wrong kinds of things. It only took him twelve minutes to get hard again—a personal best. I had to hand it to him. He was trying to deny how much he enjoyed this and how much more he wanted.

"Oh," Jane moaned. She, on the other hand, dove head first into everything. She was the perfect submissive and it only turned me on more.

Putting the collar on Max, he didn't grumble or fight back. Instead, he stayed still when I cut the rope from him. When I took the ball out of his mouth, it dripped with saliva, and he took a deep breath, licking his lips. I used the extra rope to tie his arms around his back.

"It's only fair you taste her too," I said to him while pulling on the leash. He followed and crawled on to the bed where Jane was now tied up again. Her legs were wide and her pussy was wet and throbbing for more.

"Eat her out good. Don't waste even a drop," I told him, and he bent over giving me a perfect view of his tight, sculpted ass.

He sucked on her clit like a man dying of thirst. She moaned so loudly that it rang in my ears and her body partially rose over of the bed. She yanked on the ties as hard as she could. Walking around the bed, I bent over and licked her hard nipple. My tongue rolled around it over and over again before I returned it back to my mouth. Biting gently, I got the taste of her.

Focus Wes!

Backing away, I had to take a rest. My cock was throbbing so hard I couldn't concentrate and sweat dripped from my forehead.

I yanked on the leash, and he stopped.

"Fuck her," I needed to watch how he fucked her. Sitting up, his arms tied behind his back, the corner of my lip turned up as he tried to position himself. He tried to stick in, but either she was far too wet or he was too anxious. Reaching over I gripped his cock and squeezed it once before helping the tip into her.

It was like he forgot to speak; he had gone wild. The moment he was in, he rammed himself forward and her body jerked up. Grunts and moans poured out of his mouth and he slammed himself into her. The room was full of the sounds of his skin slapping against hers and the thick smell of sex rolling off them both.

I can't any more.

The leash slipped from my hand, and I reached for the lube and coated my cock in it before climbing on the bed. When I undid Max's ties, his free hands knew what to do.

SMACK.

I hit his ass as hard as I could just to see the red mark it left on his skin. Taking my dick, I rubbed it against his ass crack allowing his checks to massage me for a moment.

Only a moment!

"Fuck..." I hissed so loudly and so hard that spit came from my lips. He stilled his ass to welcome me in. Closing my eyes, I savored that he was clenched around my cock. Putting my hands on his hips, I pulled out some more.

"Ahh," he grunted reaching out to grasp Jane's breast as he rammed himself into her.

YES! I couldn't stop. His ass was my mine, and I'd fuck him like this until the day I died.

"What time is it?" I asked, too tired to even lift my head off Max's chest. My legs were over Wes, and I wasn't even sure how we got in this position, however, I was too tired to move.

Max reached on the bedside table for his phone. "6:08 a.m. Shit, I have to be back at work in two hours."

"Since when does it take two hours for you to get ready?" Wes answered and I could feel his chest rising and falling.

"I have a lot of sex I need to wash off me," Max grinned glancing over at him. "And wax."

I laughed at that while running my hands through my hair. "We definitely need to do that again."

They both groaned and forced me to look at them.

"What the fuck are you made of?" Max asked me.

"Give me twenty minutes," Wes replied closing his eyes.

"I didn't mean now, you big babies." I propped myself up on Max's chest. "And here I thought I had two of the most capable lovers."

"I bet you couldn't find any better lovers in the world," Wes stated and Max nodded.

Eyebrow raised, I looked between them asked, "Should I try?"

Both of their eyes snapped to me angrily.

"Kidding," I lifted my hands up in defense and they both relaxed. "I've decided something."

Wes looked at me confused, "When did you have time to think?"

"Somewhere between my third and fourth orgasm," I shot back and they both looked proud.

"Well, Ms. Chapman, what were you thinking of when you should have been screaming our names?" Max played with a strand of my hair.

"I'll marry you."

They both froze. Max even found the strength to sit up against the headboard forcing me to sit back up.

"Come again?"

"I'll marry you," I said stretching out my neck. "I don't want any more rumors about you or any more jerks blackmailing you. So I'll marry you, Maxwell…if you still want me to."

He looked to Wes who for some reason was looking pleased. I wasn't sure why. Max was his, and yet he was just going to let him get married to me.

"Jane, I won't lie. This will be helping me, but my family is messy."

"I don't have a family, so I'll make do with a messy one." He didn't know that even with everything he had told me about his family already, I was still jealous of that. Having people to call mother and father, even if you didn't get along, was better than nothing. "And then you two can actually go out."

"You think so?" Wes asked sitting up as well.

"I know so. We've all been together. Max, you aren't gay, you are bisexual. But they don't know you. With me around, they won't think otherwise. You two can be best friends, bros or whatever guys call it without worrying about anything else…but again if you don't want to…"

"I want to," Max said, waiting for Wes' response. It was to kiss the back of my hand.

"Thank you, Jane."

"Why are you thanking me? I get to marry a millionaire husband and get a sexy lover on the side who cooks," I smiled shifting to rest between them. "I'm living the dream, gentlemen."

"Then you're welcome," Max said, still trying to be an ass.

"So." I lifted the sheets. "What round are we on?"

They sniggered and rolled over to me. Wes in front, Max at my back. They were already hard again…and they were wondering what I was made of?

"Fuck me," I demanded and they didn't have to think.

Wes slid down kissing my chest and lifting my leg slightly before thrusting so deep into my pussy that I had to hold on to his shoulder. He spread open my ass cheeks for Max.

They were insane.

I was insane.

Fuck it. All three of us had lost our minds. We wouldn't stop. We didn't want to stop.

"Yes!" I cried out as Max entered me from behind.

Once again I was sandwiched between two men and it was even better than the first time.

God help us.

14

I can't believe it had already been two weeks since I moved in here. It felt much longer. I spent my days being more of a maid than I was before. However, this time, we all just coexisted. I'd also started to take some online classes in business management. It was Wes' idea, but trying to find who I was outside of a maid was not as easy as I thought. This week, I was officially coming out as Maxwell Emerson's fiancée. We hadn't done it instantly because, well, they both said they wanted me to know them before everything became chaotic. I'd learned a few things in that time. The first was what was behind the door to the 'secret room'. This was the room I thought could have been a sexual dungeon or Dexter's kill room. Turned out to be a damn gym.

They didn't want anyone in there because Max also has some unpacked boxes he needed to go through. One of them even had photos of Wes and him. Every morning they worked out together. It seemed harmless enough until I realized exercise was just another form of foreplay for them. They'd push themselves, sweat dripping down their abs and necks. Every once in awhile, I caught one of them staring at the other. Eventually, they both stared at each other, panting from their workout covered in sweat and horny. All of this equaled to shower sex...a lot of fucking shower sex.

Second thing I'd learned from them was that neither of them was ever too tired or sick of having sex. When Max got horny, Wes would stop everything to see that he got him off. When Wes was hard, Max was already on his knees. My poor heart could barely take it anymore. They both just seemed to know when I wanted them. We'd fucked everywhere in this penthouse. In the kitchen, in the living room, and in the spare bedroom, which was supposed to be my room but I was always in their bed. We fucked in the shower and while taking a bath. I was covered in hickeys all the time.

The third and final thing I had learned was that they liked me wearing as few clothes as possible. I honestly couldn't remember the last time I wore a bra here…or panties for that matter. They wanted access at anytime and who was I to deny them that?

"Your nipples are getting harder." Max glanced down at me. We both stood in the bathroom and I was supposed to be brushing my hair.

"They do that," I said brushing and he cupped my ass. He did that now, they both did, they touched me all over randomly and I loved it. It felt like they were aching to have me back on their dicks.

"Don't tempt me, Ms. Chapman, I'm—"

"Shit!" Wes cursed. "Of all the fucking times!"

I glanced over at Max who was brushing his teeth beside me. His eyebrows rose as we both walked to the bedroom door. Wes stood there in his boxers holding a light horizontal striped blue shirt.

"What's wrong?" Max asked.

"Nothing," Wes just sighed, throwing the shirt on the bed before walking into the closet.

"You are aware you're going to need to lie a little bit better than that, aren't you?" Max said going back in the bathroom.

Wes didn't reply. He just brought out more clothes; however, he was far too tense for someone who had spent a whole day having sex. Walking over to the bed, I took the first shirt he had cursed at. There was a tear under the fold of the collar. Moving to my suitcase, which I still hadn't bothered to unpack, partly because I hadn't had a moment to do so, I dug into my purse. Readjusting the towel around my body, I took a step back on the bed with the sewing kit in my lap.

"What are you doing?" Wes asked me as I searched for the right thread color.

"Sewing your shirt."

He paused, giving me enough time to string the needle.

"Why?"

"Why what?" I asked back not looking away from the shirt in front of me.

"Why are you patching up my shirt?"

"Dumb question."

He didn't answer

"Do you want to wear it?"

Again he didn't say anything, but instead he ran his hands through his sandy brown hair. "I have an interview today."

Max came out of the bathroom again with his arms crossed over his chest. He leaned on the doorframe. "An interview with whom?"

"*Time* magazine. I've made the top ten chefs in the country list," he said as if this were nothing. Even Max was shocked.

"Why didn't you say anything?" he asked stepping forward.

"It's nothing—"

"Bollocks," I whispered, smiling to myself as I continued to sew.

He turned to me with the corner of his lips turned up, "It is not *bollocks*. I don't really care about the ranking or fame or anything like that."

Max moved to look over the clothes on the bed, "So the reason you're cursing at shirts this morning is..."

"*Who* is doing the interview? I just found out that Chef Névenoé is the one who will be interviewing me," he said and I looked to Max. Max looked to me. Neither of us had any idea who the chef was, something Wes picked up on. Shaking his head, he explained, "Chef Névenoé was the sous-chef of Chef Dieudonné, the man who left me his knives. I haven't seen him since then. Now he's coming to my restaurant and sitting down with me—"

"And you're nervous," I grinned. I'd never seen him nervous.

"No, I just don't want to look like a twat in front of my hero's top student," he shot back.

"So you're nervous," Max nodded, putting his hand on his shoulder. "Do you want us there for moral support?"

"I rather not have a boner in front of him, thank you." Wes glared at him, but before he could say anything else, I sat up handing him the shirt. He took it from my hands and stared at it as if it were gold.

"M&J," he said looking at the small stitched letters I had put in the repair.

"Maxwell and Jane" I figured if you wanted us there, you would have told us earlier. But since we can't be there physically, we'll still be behind you..." My voice trailed off as they both stared down at me. It was so intense that I felt the need to swallow the lump in my throat. "Or maybe it was a lame idea?"

"On the contrary...thank you," Wes whispered and I could see he was getting hard.

"No problem. You should stick with shades of blue. The color suits you. A dark navy tie with that shirt and a gray-blue sweater over it. Casual but sophisticated."

"Jeans?" he paused thinking about it.

"Dark denim."

He stared at me but nodded as he walked away.

"What did I do?" I asked Max.

"Nothing. You should know by now Wes is a sucker for that kind of shit," he replied.

"Then why are you staring down at me, too?"

"A couple of reasons"

"Which are?"

"First, you thought of and stitched that faster than even I could think of."

"Thank you?"

"Second," he said as he leaned down to grab my chin. His lips were hovering over mine.

"You said a lot of personal pronouns, 'we', 'us'..."

"Sorry, I didn't know you'd be upset about it." I was getting ahead of myself.

"I'm not upset," he replied by kissing me and I couldn't help but kiss him back. His hands grabbed my towel to open it. "Why don't we help him relax?"

"You have to get ready for work, too."

He cupped my breast, "Are you only a submissive for Wes?"

My heart slammed against my chest. My ears felt like they were on fire.

"No," I finally brought myself to answer.

Max took my hand and walked me to the bathroom. Standing behind me he whispered, "Suck him off."

"Okay."

Wes was putting his toothbrush back into the cup before rinsing out his mouth. His green eyes met mine before they wandered down the length of my body.

"Jane…I…"

Stepping closer to him I kissed his chest and pecs, sliding down to his abs, until I pulled his jeans and boxers down. His cock almost slapped me in the face it was so hard already. "Jane," he repeated my name clenching on to the sink as I licked.

"You're too tense," Max said behind me. "When you are tense, you overthink. When you overthink, you cause more trouble for yourself."

"Ahh…" Wes hissed, placing his hand on my head as I kissed the side of him.

"You aren't the same kid this chef knew before. You're just as good. You might even be better. He's coming into your kitchen." Max kissed his ear. "Your temple. He's going to pay you respect and not the other way around."

When I looked up at him, Wes' eyes were narrowed, and he was breathing through his nose.

"You are Wesley Uhler. Don't bend over for anyone but me." Max grabbed on to his neck. Wes glared but it only made Max bite his lip. The bite turned into a simple kiss then the simple kiss became a full on make-out session. Wes ripped the towel from his waist and grabbed his ass.

Fuck it was hot.

Taking Wes into my mouth, I sucked to their moaning which was music to my ears. I wanted more of him, but, I stopped when I felt his hand on my hair pull me back. It wasn't Wes. It was Max. He held my head back, grabbed on to Wes' dick and stroked him hard. Wes bit his lips before finally his hot cum exploded on my chest.

"Keep that in your head today," Max told him while licking his fingers.

Wes said nothing but took a deep breath and rinsed himself off. His whole body was now relaxed. Reaching down, he picked up his boxers and jeans and readjusted himself. He petted my head before leaving.

"Oh," I jumped when I felt the cold towel on my chest. Turning back, Max was crouched beside me, wiping down my chest.

"You knew exactly what he needed to hear."

He laughed, "Good thing you were here. I can't talk him down and suck him off at the same time."

"I'm sure you would have figured out something," I replied getting back on my feet. The very first thing I saw was my own reflection in the mirror.

Max stepped behind me with his hands on my waist. His blue eyes meeting mine in the mirror.

"You're having second thoughts?" he asked kissing my shoulder.

Leaning against him I shook my head, "I'm just...I'm just shocked to see where I am."

"What do you mean?"

"I've never thought much of my future. I just got along from day to day. Now I'm here engaged to you and sharing two men shamelessly. I think my brain is catching up to the rest of me."

"Jane, you're family now. My family. Wes' family. You belong to us. We belong to you."

"Personal pronouns," I smiled and so did he.

"Don't let your brain catch up. It will only make you doubt, or worse, run." He kissed the side of my head. "Get dressed. I have to show off my fiancée today."

"Yes, Mr. Emerson."

"If you stare at it any longer, you'll go blind," I said to her, but she didn't pay attention to me. She just continued gazing at the 6.03-carat radiant cut diamond ring on her finger. From the moment we walked into the jewelry store, her eyes were glued to it. A fat-ass grin was spread across her face. "And here I thought I was going to have to fight you on a ring."

"I can tell you're trying to be an ass, but I'm too awed by this beauty to care," she smiled, lifting it to her face. It was hers.

"*Girls and their rock,s*" Rolling my eyes, I tried not to smile too, but she just kept grinning at me like a damn idiot.

"Stop it." Shit, now I felt like a child.

"I can't. It's so pretty."

"Oh my god," I laughed.

"The great Maxwell Emerson laughing at me, I'm honored. Mr. Driver? Please be my witness of such a fate." She sat up all but grabbing on to the man's chair.

Adjusting in the back seat I tried to regain my composure. I'd honestly forgotten about the driver entirely.

"Yes, ma'am," he nodded to her.

"Jane, Irene will come by the studio today to take you shopping."

"Shopping?" She sat back frowning. "You don't like my clothes? I tried really hard today."

I noticed. She looked beautiful in a dark green high-waist skirt complemented by one of my white shirts, which she had tailored to her size in minutes. She looked both elegant and sophisticated. The only problem was that it wasn't designer. She looked good but she didn't look like an Emerson.

"Max?"

"I prefer you with no clothes." *Fucking hell Maxwell!* She held her head up proudly. "What I mean is, I don't care what you have on. However, others will. The moment people find out about our engagement, your face will be out there. Think of it as your designer armor. The nicer you dress, the harder it is for them to attack you."

"Fine, but if anyone puts anything with ruffles in my face…"

"You ask them elegantly to take it away," I finished for her and she made a face.

"Am I going to be put through etiquette training, too?"

I didn't want to discourage her, but I didn't want to lie either, so it was best to say nothing at all.

"Max."

"We're here," the driver said and he met my eye in the mirror giving me a short nod before stepping out.

"This isn't over," Jane whispered to me when the door opened.

"Of course," I said, hoping she'd be too tired to ask again after Irene was through with her.

"What's your name?" I asked my driver.

"Calvin, sir, Calvin Roberts."

"You'll be her personal driver," I said to him. "Anything she needs, wherever she needs to go, you take her."

"Yes, sir."

"Nice to meet you!" Jane waved at him before I took her hand. The moment we walked into the building, I noticed the stares. People paused in utter shock, which proved how widespread the gay rumor had gotten.

I thought Jane would be uncomfortable, but she just held on to me walking on as if she didn't notice. I placed my hand on the small of her back when we got to the elevators.

"You're popular," she leaned over and whispered.

"Not for the reasons I want."

The doors opened, and before we could step in, Scarlet tried to step out. She jumped back startled.

"Are you alright Scarlet?" I asked when she didn't move. When she didn't even seem to be breathing.

"Yeah sorry, I was told your car was here, and I was coming down to meet you."

I nodded allowing Jane to get in first. "Scarlet, you remember Jane."

"It's burned into my memory," she smiled reaching out to shake Jane's hand. "It's nice to meet you again."

"Likewise," I watched as Jane purposefully used her ring finger to brush back her hair before shaking her hand. Like a hawk, Scarlet's eyes locked on and did not stop staring. Jane, being the ruthless woman she was, just grinned and stuck out her hand. "Isn't beautiful? Max has been teasing me all morning because I won't look away from it."

Scarlet held on to Jane's outstretched hand then looked at me, "You're engaged?"

"What I am is a million dollars lighter," I replied and Jane smacked my chest.

"It was not a million dollars."

"Close enough." I laughed as I saw her jaw drop. I hadn't let her see the price. "Yes, Scarlet, I'm engaged."

She opened her mouth to say something, then stopped and froze. It took her a few more seconds before she got any words out, "Congrats. Must run now. I have to stop at accounts. But really, congrats, we'll all have to celebrate later."

"Sure," I nodded when she pushed the button for the next level up.

"That wasn't the accountants' floor was it?" Jane asked when the elevator doors closed again and she was gone.

"No, it was not."

"I'm not being too bitchy, am I?"

"Since when is claiming your partner being bitchy?" I questioned her and she turned to me placing her hands on my shoulders. My hands dropped to her hips. "There are many more women like Scarlet. Jane, you have to sharpen your heels."

She laughed. "The things I do for you, Mr. Emerson."

"Just keep looking at the ring," I replied as my hands slipped down to squeeze her ass. I leaned to kiss her, but she just put her hand between us again staring at the damn rock.

"It is pretty," she winked knowing full well she was messing me.

"Don't get too cocky, Ms. Chapman."

"How can I not be cocky when you keep ramming your cock in my ass?" she whispered in my ear when we got to my floor.

I bit the inside of my check to keep calm.

"Is this where you work?" she asked while moving up to stare down at the pit as if she'd not just tried to make me hard.

"No, this is for the minions," I said softy and she giggled.

"Come on," I took her hand. "I wish I could give you a tour—"

"I'm fine, I'm fine. Go—"

"Tell the news?" I finished for her as she drifted off.

"I was trying to think of something cooler than that. Like: the beacon of truth in a sea of darkness?"

I stared at her. I was trying so hard not to laugh my eyes hurt.

"No good?"

"It's something…" Turning to the pit, I pointed to one of them calling out the least boring looking person I could find.

"Yes, sir"

"This is my fiancée, Jane. Show her around will you?" I asked even though I knew she wouldn't turn me down.

"Sure, sir"

Nodding, I moved over to kiss Jane on the check. "Irene will be here soon."

"I'm fine, Max, go."

"A beacon, I got it."

She was such a weirdo, but it was cute.

Chef Névenoé shrugged, "It's alright."

"It's fucking brilliant and it's killing you, isn't it?" I smirked.

"When did you get to be so cocky?"

"The moment they gave me an apron and called me 'Chef," I replied and a few of the cameramen around us laughed.

"You got me," he couldn't help but smile. "Il est magnifique, Chef Wesley."

I nodded thanks before sitting down across from him. "From you, that means a lot."

"When I first saw you looking like a drowned rat outside Chef Dieudonné's restaurant, I did not see you rising as far as you have. I tell my students that I've known you since you were a kitten in the culinary world, and they think, 'this old man is exaggerating.'"

"I bet you regret not taking me into your kitchen now," I replied, ignoring the camera zooming into my face.

He shook his head, "Not at all. You'd be the first to ask me if Chef Dieudonné would have done it this way or add this or what he would have done for that. I too wished to grow. I left Chef Dieudonné's kitchen and started my own as all good chefs do. I remember the fear I had. What of you? Your first restaurant in Paris, La Hauteur, is still one of the finest in the city."

"Thank you. Honestly, when I opened it, I was terrified. I had so many people tell me that I was too young. I was too cocky. I was too 'something.' Some of the greatest critics in the world lived in the same forty-five mile radius. I'll never forget Gabriel Gaétan, my first critic after opening. 'La Hauteur, *parfaitement fade et oubliable.*' (La Hauteur, perfectly bland and forgettable).

He laughed softly at me, "Did you weep?"

"Weep? Ha! I made a special menu, and it took me weeks to create it. I even called it 'The Gaétan' in his honor. He's quite proud. Even to this day, he comes in and demands 'The Gaétan', but it did tempt other critics to write poor reviews, though."

"You are a double-edged sword upon yourself," he said and I just shrugged.

"If stabbing oneself is the way to a perfect dish, stab on," I said.

"La Hauteur is still open and beloved. You have another restaurant in your home country and in Rome. How do you manage them all?"

"Technology is a beautiful thing. Once a week, I converse with all my chefs. We go over the menus and I get updates. To keep them on their feet, I even send critics to scare the hell out of them. I also visit throughout the year, but in disguise."

"You are a reality show in the making."

"God, no." Reality would be one half pornography and one half the cooking networks. "I prefer to keep my personal life just that...personal."

"So you do not have a special muse for your food?" he asked anyway. "I read a critic of yours who said only a man who's in love can cook as you do."

"I'm in love with food...and some may argue with me." That got a few snickers from my own kitchen staff.

"So if there is no one keeping you here, what next? You've been in Boston four years now? Where do you see yourself going? After all, the world of food is vast. India, Thailand, Africa, South America even?"

"I haven't thought about it yet. I'm really enjoying Boston."

"My advice, Chef Wesley is while you're still young you should explore more. See more and your food will thank you for it."

I hated how part of me was thrilled by the idea. Just packing up with my knives and going out there again, however, the more I thought about it, the less possible it became.

Max.

Now Jane.

It wasn't just me anymore. I couldn't just leave. I knew that, but it didn't make the feeling go away.

"You're excited by the thought, aren't you?"

"For now, Boston is my home. But who knows what the future holds?"

15

Oh my God! I screamed and jumped back wrapping my arms around my chest as Irene burst into the changing room. "What the fuck are you doing?"

"I'm catching you when your guard is down. Jesus Christ!" Her eyes dropped down to the hickeys that were all over my chest. "Is my cousin trying to screw you or eat you?"

"Irene! Get out!"

"Calm down! We're both women, besides I've already seen the evidence," she said, waving her hand over my body.

"Just because we're women doesn't mean I want you staring at me naked." I glared at her, waiting for her to leave. Instead, she just sat down on the small changing room bench and crossed her legs.

"Jane. Please explain to me how you were my maid one day and my cousin's fiancée the next?" she asked.

"Can I get dressed first?"

She handed me my bra. Dropping my arms, I snatched my bra from her. She tilted her head to the side still staring wide-eyed.

"You know you're a bit weird," I said to her snapping the clip in place.

"Direct. Not weird," she corrected. "Now that your boobs are covered, or rather Max's boobs, since he marked them up—"

"Irene."

"Jane."

Sighing, I grabbed my skirt from beside her and she took it back.

"Irene."

She got up and poked her head outside the curtain. "The pink one, yep and the…yes…she's also going to need jewelry so have William bring everything."

Spinning back around to me, she held a romantic soft pink lace cocktail dress with sleeves in one hand and a pair of beige heels in the other.

"This is what you're wearing."

"Wearing to where?"

"To meet Max's parents."

"What?" It was a little soon to be meeting parents especially after the first time I met Max's mother.

"She called me five minutes ago, and the one thing you'll learn quickly is to never say no to Elspeth Yates."

"Watch me." Reaching into my bag, I grabbed my phone.

"Jane, don't. Max needs to focus on his story. You need to prove to him and everyone else that you can't be messed with. The only way you can do that is to step up to Elspeth." She stretched out her hands again. "The only way you have a chance of standing toe to toe with Elspeth is if you are dressed perfectly. She can pick at your personality, but she can't speak ill of Vera Wang."

"What's wrong with my personality?"

"Jane, I'm trying to build you up right now. Come on, get dressed," she said. I couldn't believe her. She really did not give a fuck.

Taking the dress from her, I slide it on; however, it wouldn't zip up.

"Do Vera's models have boobs?"

"It's not her fault, your body is disproportional."

"I have boobs. I like carbs. Sue me! And can we stop talking about Vera Wang as if we know her."

"I do know her," Irene shot back before sticking her head out of the curtains again. Ignoring her as she commanded her troops I turned back to the mirror.

C cups were good cups! I knew a dozen strippers that had to pay for what god had given me naturally. All these designers cut their dress as if I were prepubescent. At this rate, I was going to have to buy a size up and take in everything at the waist.

"Frowning gives you lines."

"So does living," I shot back and she giggled.

"True. But really stop frowning. You're going to be fine. You're strong and confident. Most women would have flipped out on me by now."

"I've been doing that for the last five minutes. You just don't seem to notice," I replied, and for some reason, I couldn't help but smile. I liked Irene. She did not believe in personal space and had no filter, but it just added to her charm.

"Ma'am," someone spoke behind the curtain. Irene reached back to bring out a black and gold detailed jacquard dress with cap sleeves. Without arguing, I slipped the dress on. It fit like a glove, hugging every curve of my body, and stopped right above the knees. It was stunning.

"As always, Alexander McQueen to the rescue! God bless his soul." She closed her eyes as if she were actually praying for the man. "Now shoes. Please tell me you can walk in heels?"

"I can walk in heels."

She put a pair of stunning shoes in front me, and when I stepped into them, I really felt like someone important. Reaching up, I tied up my hair into a quick but messy bun.

"Brilliant. You have a knack for this."

"Thanks, I guess."

"Now, make-up."

Oh, my God! It was neverending!

****

Eight bags of clothes.

Six bags of shoes.

Three bags of handbags.

All this and a credit card in Maxwell's name damaged beyond repair and we were done. Poor Roberts, the driver Max had with me all day couldn't even fit it all in the trunk. He had to call another car. What was worse was the fact that we didn't even get everything Irene said I quote 'just needed,' so we ordered the items to be brought to the penthouse.

"Maxwell is going to lose his mind when he sees the bill," I muttered more to myself.

"We actually spent less than he thought we would." She lifted up her phone and sure enough, Max had texted her.

'The bank called me because of the spending you two have been doing. I'm glad. Make sure to order at least two of everything she likes in another color. Don't show her the price.'

"He's bossy even in text messages," she sighed, throwing her phone back into her purse.

245

"What else do I need to know about your family?"

"You mean to impress them?"

"Yeah, that would be great."

"I have no idea. I've been working on that since I was born."
She meant it as a joke, but I could tell she was really bothered
by it.

Saying nothing else, I pulled out my own phone just as I got
a text from Wesley.

'Are you okay? Max told me he let Irene kidnap you.'

'Save me. She's relentless. :('

'If you're really not having fun, I'll come now.'

I smiled at that.

'Thanks. But she's taking me to meet Max's parents.'

'Oh...Max didn't tell me about that.'

*'Yeah, his mother just summoned us. I'm sure she's heard about the
engagement.'*

'R.I.P'

'Not funny!' I typed even though I did laugh. *'I just want to be
back in our safe haven.'*

'Safe haven?'

*'The penthouse where we don't have to pretend to anyone or lie or
anything. When it's just...simply us'*

'Me too'

*'Before I forget, how was the interview? Is Chef Névenoé in awe of
your greatness?'*

'Damn straight!'

'How will we live with your ego now?'

'Ha. We'll find a way. But no, really, Chef Névenoé was great. He's a great person to seek advice from. He's made me think a lot.'

'About what?'

"Jane."

"Huh?" I glanced up at her.

"We're here."

"Shit okay."

I texted back quickly, and saw by the three dots that he was typing. 'Wesley let's talk when I get back home? Okay. Sorry. Gotta run, bye love you.'

"Oh my God!" I screamed staring at the text I sent.

"Jane, what is it?"

"Tell me there is a way to take a text back!" I screamed at her seeing that he still hadn't read it…then he read it. "Kill me. Please kill me."

"Jane, what is it?"

She reached for the phone, but I hugged it to my chest like it was bread at the last supper at fat camp.

"Jane, you're being weird. Weirder than normal."

I looked back at my phone and he hadn't replied. I couldn't bring myself to explain the colossal fuck up I had just done. Love you? Not even 'luv' but, actual love? Fuck me man! Ahh.

"Ma'am, would you like me to keep driving?" Roberts asked. I thought he was talking to Irene, but he was talking to me. I was a ma'am now.

"Jane," Irene put her hands on my shoulders. "Whatever emotional crisis you are going through at this moment is going to have to wait. Do you understand me? You are now going to go head to head with some of the most powerful women in this city, so you need to slay them down, like Khaleesi at Astapor."

"I've only watched the first season of *Game of Thrones*, so I have no idea what that means," I replied and she looked insulted.

"How can you only be in the first season?"

"I work a lot." Or at least, I did. Now sex was taking up a bigger part of my life.

"You and I are watching the rest later. Now come on." She took my hand and I let her as I tried to forget about my horribly embarrassing text.

Roberts held the door open for us, and I noticed we were at the Museum of Fine Arts.

"I'll be here until you're ready to leave, ma'am," Roberts said to me.

"Thank you," I nodded to him as I followed Irene up the stairs and into the building. It was past closing time, but, there were dozens of beautiful people all dressed up, wine in their hands, laughing among themselves. Just like at the first party I had attended with Irene, a few of them gave her the evil eye while others ignored her altogether, however, this time, she kept her head up.

"Ma'am, can I have your coat?" a server asked. I handed it to him as Irene did, but I was growing annoyed with this 'ma'am' shit.

"If it isn't 'Just Jane'," announced Archibald Saint James as came up to me with his blonde hair slicked back and a white scarf over his black suit jacket. Knowing what I knew about him from Max, I didn't want to spend any time near him.

"Not for long." I lifted the ring on my finger for him to see.

"Maxwell Emerson asked you to marry him?" he said in shock and louder than I wished. It drew more than a few people's attention.

"More like he wore me down. I'm searching for Elspeth, if you'll excuse us," I linked arms with Irene who he didn't bother even saying hello to.

"Awe them," she whispered. I smiled as we walked alongside some paintings. When we reached the end of the portraits, we spotted Elspeth surrounded by a group of women. Her hair was pin curled and brought over to one side, and the off-the-shoulder-navy gown she wore was stunning. When her blue eyes met mine, she immediately came over to me.

"Jane, dear," she kissed the sides of my cheeks. "I wasn't aware you were coming."

"When she heard about your event here, she was just dying to come." Irene had lied! She fucking tricked me again!

Eyes wide, I glared at Irene who just winked and unlinked her arms from mine. "*EVIL*" I mouthed to her.

"Elspeth, who is this beautiful young woman?" a slender older woman with pulled back gray hair asked.

"Ladies, please let me introduce you to my daughter-in-law-to-be ...Jane Chapman," she held me close to her, and I wasn't sure, but I had a feeling I was now in the twilight zone.

"Daughter-in-law?" The older woman gasped, "Young lady how did you capture the elusive Maxwell Emerson?"

"We're both passionate about the same things." That being Wesley. "That's all I can say. He really hates talking about his personal life."

"He's not the only one," Elspeth added. "Ladies give us a moment."

"Of course."

No, don't leave me! They strolled further down the exhibit leaving me with her. She didn't say a word but just kept heading out of the room. We walked and walked until we got to an empty wing of the museum. On the wall was an American colonial painting: a seventeen by fifteen foot canvas depicting George Washington, by Thomas Sully. In front of it were two black couches. She sat in one and I moved to sit in the other one opposite her.

"You must be a little confused," she finally said to me crossing her legs.

"What do you mean?"

"You came here expecting the evil mother who would disapprove of a nobody maid, who was once a bartender at a strip club, dating—no—engaged to my son."

Crossing my legs as well, I nodded, noting she had done a background check on me, "Are you saying I was wrong?"

"Yes," she said simply. "Marry my son. I don't care if you're a gold digger or a just an innocent girl trying to get by. Either way, you help him and helping him is all I want."

Twilight zone! The words flashed in my mind over and over again.

"So if I planned to marry your son and take him for half of all he's worth, you wouldn't care?"

"I'd say to wait at least a few years, maybe have a child before you do so. I'd love a granddaughter."

This was a trap. Something felt wrong.

"Why?"

The smile on her face dropped. "If he's with you then that man will eventually leave."

"What?" My heart started to race.

"Wesley. Right now he might be alright. But I'm going to make a big deal out of your wedding. I'm going to welcome you into the family with open arms. We'll have family dinners and vacations, and each time Max will have to leave him behind. There is only so much of that any human can take. It will get worse too, when you have a child. He'll watch as a whole family gets built around him, and he'll be just stuck in that damn penthouse hiding away. Max is loyal. He'll stay by you until the day he dies and then we'll be done with this nonsense."

I thought about it. No, I didn't just think about it. I saw it. Wesley being pushed to the side. The resentment, the pain, everything flashed through my eyes and my chest burned.

"Why would you do that? Why would you hurt him like this? He loves—"

"Stop." She held up her hand. "Max has always been confused. He's always sought out the attention of father figures to make up for the sorry excuse of a father he has."

"That's not what—"

"That is exactly what this is. We didn't show him the right way. Alistair and his constant infidelities and lack of regard' affected him. My ambition did not help. We overlooked Maxwell and he became twisted."

"Do you hear yourself right now? Loving people is not twisted."

"It is, Jane." She nodded to me while getting up. "He should be happy that he's found someone as understanding as you. I'm sure you can turn a blind eye to any slip-ups he might have. However, Wesley is a four-year problem that I've been trying to fix. So Jane, get married, and save me the headache."

She walked past me and I was stuck and unable to move.

"Oh," she added. "I apologize in advance that Alistair is currently fucking some whore and won't be making it tonight.

We'll be having dinner this weekend, so please come down to Washington. I'll send the jet."

With that, she left, and if Irene was sitting here now, she'd say the only slaying that happened here was of me and everything I thought I was doing.

I sat there quietly until I got a text. I thought it was Wes but someone else was dealing out some sort of punishment to me today.

'Break it off with Maxwell...before I show him what you really are. —Scarlet'

Attached was a picture of Wesley and me at the playground kissing.

How? Was my first thought?

Fuck them all was my second.

The door opened and she rushed in.

"Jane?" I watched as she didn't look at me but instead headed to the kitchen to grab a pair of scissors and go for her neck. "Jane! What bloody hell are you doing?"

"Get it off!" she screamed at me while trying to cut the material.

"Jane, calm down—"

"Off! Get it off me! Get me out of this thing! I want it off!" she kept screaming and I moved to the zipper which was stuck.

"Wes," she sobbed.

Taking the scissors from her, I cut up the back and the sides. I tore and tore until she was free. She gasped for air before hunching over the table to cry.

"Jane."

Wiping her face, she moved to the wine cooler. She didn't care what bottle it was. She just pulled it out and stabbed the cork with the opener. When she got the cork out, she drank straight from the bottle.

She drank and drank and drank to the point that I was amazed she didn't need air.

"Ahh," she gasped out hitting her chest.

"Jane, use words."

"I'm no Khaleesi," she said drinking again.

"Okay. Let's try using words that make sense."

She glared at me with puffy and red eyes, "I'm making sense! I'm no Khaleesi! I thought I was. I thought I could be this huffy, puffy, rich bitch and stand beside Max. But I can't. They're all cruel and I hate them!"

"Jane." I walked over to her putting my hands on the side of her face. "My beautiful butterfly."

"Don't try and make me feel better," she grumbled, putting her head on my chest. "They all want to hurt us. We didn't do anything to them. We just want to live our lives the way we want to, and they try and hurt us. Why?"

It was times like this where I really saw the innocence in her. Hugging my arm around her, I kissed her forehead.

"I don't know now."

"Don't let them push you away," she muttered against my chest. "You and Max have something real...something special and beautiful. Don't let them hurt you."

"Why are you crying for us? We're still here," I replied, feeling her warm tears on my chest.

"Because..."

"Because?"

"Because I'm just a good person!"

I smiled at that. "So it's not because you love me."

When I said that she jumped out of my arms like a scared cat and the bottle of wine slipped from her hand. I caught it before it hit the ground.

"That was a mistake!" she said quickly, holding her arms out. "I was typing really fast and I was just not thinking. The only people I've ever texted were Mary and Allen, and they're like family, so I guess I was on autopilot. I'm not one of those crazy girls who sleep with guys and thinks we're going to be together always or get married or something. Well, I am engaged to Max, but that's different, and I might not go through with it. His mother is evil. Not in-your-face evil, but the type that creeps up on you and gives you nightmares—"

"Jane, please breathe before you lose consciousness." Watching her ramble was hilarious, but she looked like she was verging on hysterical tears. "I understand. Don't worry, okay. Just tell me what happened tonight? What did Elspeth do?"

"She hugged me," she whispered.

"Hugs are good—"

"She hugged me because she wants to use me as a wedge between you and Max. She knows about you, too. She's known for a while and so she wants me to have a big wedding and a big family. She wants me to make a life for Max and shut you out. So I'm not doing it." She reached up to pull the ring from her finger, but it was stuck. "The moment I get this ring off, I'm going to throw it at her."

"How much have you had to drink tonight?"

"Not enough," she pouted.

Picking her up, she wrapped her arms around my neck and I held on. Her heels fell off. Holding her helped me to relax. Taking her up to the bedroom I laid her on the bed.

"Stay."

"I'm not going anywhere," I whispered, lying beside her.

I didn't want to think and neither did she. She curled up to me, and I listened to her ramble on. It was soothing and it was just what I needed right now.

Maxwell

"I just wanted her to meet Elspeth on common ground. You know your mother would never make a scene. But I don't know what happened when they were alone, Max. But whatever your mom said to her really got under her skin," Irene explained. I still had the mobile next to my ear when I walked into the penthouse.

"I got it, and Irene..."

"I know. I know. I'll stop butting in. I promise," she replied and I didn't bother replying. I just hung up.

"Wes?" Pulling off my tie, I stepped further inside. The first thing I noticed was Wes' shirt on the couch. The next thing was the wine bottle on the counter and her torn dress and discarded heels on the floor. Glancing up at the bedroom, in a split second, a dozen things they could be doing went through my mind.

I forced the thoughts out and walked up, listening but hearing nothing. I wasn't sure why my hand hesitated on the door, but it did and that bothered me. Pushing it open, there they were curled up asleep. Jane was resting on Wes' chest snoring softly. Wes was holding on to her tightly. Pinching the bridge of my nose, I took a deep breath before sitting on the edge of the bed to take off my shoes.

"You're back," I heard Wes whisper. The bed shifted as he got up to sit beside me.

"Yeah," I replied, undoing doing my cliff links. "Did I miss a party?"

"What?"

"The wine, both of your clothes are downstairs."

He didn't say anything and I just got up and walked to my closet.

"What do you think happened?" he followed me, stopping at the closet door and leaned against it.

"I don't know, Wes, that's why I'm asking."

"We didn't fuck without you, if that's what you were wondering," he said, but when I looked at his face, he didn't seem amused. He seemed annoyed, but not amused. "She came back in tears trying to cut herself out of the dress she was wearing. I got her free, and she went for the wine. If you don't believe me, you can check your damn cameras."

Why was he so pissed? What the fuck?

"How about we skip the passive aggressive bullshit, and you tell me what the hell is going on? Why was she crying? Did my mother—"

"Jane and I are going to the UK for the week," he just threw out.

"Excuse me?"

258

"I'm taking Jane to meet my mother for the week."

Either he was fucking with me or he was really trying to tick me off. "You both are just going to run away with each other?"

He sighed, "I'm not running. I'm giving her a moment to think after the night she had. She deserves it."

"Are we going to talk about this or are you just going to keep barking at—"

"No. I'm not talking about it. I'm leaving for a week. I don't need your permission to do that. I invited Jane. She said yes. Granted she was drunk at the time. However, if she wakes up and feels like explaining to you then that is her choice. Goodnight Maxwell." With that he walked out of the room.

"Where are you going?" I followed after him.

"My home." He grabbed his jeans and shirt off the couch and left.

Turning back to Jane, she just laid there, in the center of my bed, her hair over her face, snoring lightly.

What the fuck just happened?

16

"The sun...it burns..." I groaned pulling the sheets over my head rolling myself into a ball. My head was aching to the point where I'm sure it would split.

"It's already past noon."

"What?" I sat up and Max stood above me a glass of water in one hand and two tablets in the other. Taking them from him, I threw the pills into my mouth and drank. "Thanks, I can't believe I slept that long."

"You didn't. I just needed you up. It's still early," he replied putting the glass on the nightstand.

I would have said something about him being a jerk or would have fallen back on the pillows, but the look in his eyes as he sat down beside me told me something was up.

"What is it?"

"What happened last night Jane?"

The moment I tried to think, I felt the throbbing inside of my head. Sitting up more, I reached for the glass of water and finished it.

"Last night sucked," I frowned, rubbing my eyes looking around for Wes. "Where is Wes?"

"He needed to get something from his place. He'll be back soon. Did my mother say something last night?"

"She knows about Wes. She wants him gone and she wants me to help with that."

"You?" He looked surprised and amused. "What are you, a hit man?"

"It's not funny." He really didn't get it. "She promised to welcome me with open arms. She told me she didn't even care if I took you for half of your money so long as I'd at least give you children. She wants to push Wes out, have parties, family events, and a giant wedding and make sure Wes isn't there! She wants to throw me in the middle of you two."

"She'll try and then she'll realize Wes isn't that easy to throw off. I'm sorry she upset you but—"

"I also got a threat from your bitchy producer, Scarlet," I snapped. I wanted him to be so upset that he'd go and tell his mother to mind her own damn business.

"Scarlet?"

"She must have had someone watching me and caught a picture of Wes and me kissing at the park."

He closed his eyes and sighed. "I told you both to be careful."

"That's what you're upset about?" I yelled rising out of bed. "The fact that Wes and I got caught?"

"Yes! You're supposed to be my fiancée, the last thing I need is for anyone to doubt you Jane! We have a plan—"

"Then we need a new one!"

"Jane!"

"No! We aren't birds. You can't just lock us up here and bring us out whenever you need us. Wes is a human being, maybe he can stand all the shit your mother throws at him, but he shouldn't have to! And me! I like you both! I've said that from the start. Max without Wes is not the Max I want and vice versa."

"Jane, this isn't a game!" he hollered into my face, so pissed off that his eyes looked fierce. "We can't all just go out holding hands and pretending that it's okay! Me being gay or bisexual is one thing. Me being in a relationship with two people at the same time is a whole other thing! In the real world there are consequences and social norms that, I'm sorry, we have to conform to. You can either bitch about it, or you can find a way around it."

I wanted to punch him so badly.

"Jane."

Both of us turned and there was Wes, dressed in a casual sweater, dark jeans and boots.

"Wes."

"Can you get dressed? We have a plane to catch. You said you had a passport, right?" he asked, putting a few shopping bags Irene and I had brought by the door.

"Yeah, from when I went to Mexico. Wait. Where are we going?"

He moved to get my suitcase, which I still hadn't unpacked, "To meet my mums remember?"

"Oh." Our conversation from last night flooded back into my head.

"Yeah, I think it's best we all get some space," he nodded, looking to Max. Max only rolled his eyes and shook his head.

"Okay," I nodded and reached into one of the bags to pull out a random peach colored sweater and a pair of jeans from my suitcase. "I'll be right out."

"I'll wait downstairs."

"Wes, what are you doing?" I asked him when we both stepped into the living room.

"I told you I'm going to—"

"Visit your mums, I know. I heard you the first time. But really what is going on? You've never just run away!"

He clenched the handle of Jane's suitcase, "I keep speaking to you yet you don't seem to be listening to me!"

"You aren't making sense! One minute everything is fine. The next I come home and you're telling me that you and Jane are running off together."

He clenched his fist at me biting down on his jaw hard.

"I'm ready." Jane rushed down looking between us.

"Fine," I sneered. "Do whatever the fuck you want, but if you think I'm just going to wait here—"

"Jane, we're going to miss our flight," Wes said. And he had the nerve to tell me I wasn't fucking listening to him.

She frowned looking at both of us. Walking over to me she kissed me, and I couldn't bring myself to kiss her back nor push her away.

"Don't say any more shit you'll regret. We're coming back, and we're all going to have to own up to our words," she whispered kissing my cheek when she let go.

I immediately missed her.

"If you go, I'll get a new maid," I frowned.

"She'll never be as good as me," she winked, turning around to leave.

Wes didn't even bother looking back. The asshole just took her shit and walked to the door. "Don't stuff your face with junk food while I'm gone."

"I was eating long before you, and I'll eat long after." What the fuck was that? I didn't want to say that. It just came out and like that they were gone.

It felt like they had both slapped me across the face. What the fuck was wrong with them? Why now? Was everything fine? Why the fuck were they making everything more complicated than it needed to be?

"Screw them," I whispered, turning back to look at the view of the city. "Screw them both."

Who knows? Maybe this was what Wesley wanted all along and if that was the case, being pissed solved nothing. And this wasn't sudden. From the moment he met her maybe he had already thought of this.

Then were the last four years a lie, too?

Heading back upstairs, I peeled off my clothes one by one, throwing them wherever. By the time I got naked and entered the bathroom, I noticed both their toothbrushes were gone.

"Fuck them," I whispered and yet my chest burned.

What was this?

He stared out the window and his whole body was stiff. We'd only been in the air for about an hour, and since we'd left Max's penthouse, he hadn't said a word. So I did what I always do when I felt awkward. I started to ramble.

"I'm an orphan, so do you know how I got my name?" I asked him and slowly he turned back to look at me.

His green eyes softened as he leaned back into the chair, "How?"

"Well, 'Jane' isn't really that special, as in 'Jane Doe,' for an unknown female. One of the police officers who found me said I wouldn't stop shaking and crying, kind of how his kids got when they didn't have a Chapman's strawberry ice cream cone. They didn't like any other strawberry ice cream but Chapman's. Chapman's was the best; it made them feel better no matter what. So he called me Jane Chapman. I'm glad it's a better story then saying he found a crack baby in some corner somewhere. Of course, they didn't call me Jane Chapman at the hospital. I was Baby Doe or the Fremont Ave Baby until, one doctor said I was going to need a real name. And they all started to call me Jane Chapman. The cop who found me, Officer Hershaw, wanted to adopt me, but his wife was too sick. He came and visited me almost every month until I turned six. Sadly, that was when he was gunned down at work. So, I'm very passionate about my name. I even looked up the meaning of 'Chapman' and it means 'merchant'. I hated that definition so I changed it on Wikipedia once to mean strawberry ice cream."

He laughed taking my hand and kissing the back of it. "I'd say you taste more like mint chocolate chip but strawberry works, too."

"Don't tease me. We're on a plane. No mile-high club for you."

"Max and I have been members since 2012." It was instinctual the way he just brought him up. I'm sure he didn't even want to or thought he would. It just happened.

"Are you okay?"

"He's spoiled," he muttered, not letting go of my hand. "And a twat."

I giggled softly at that. "Is that why you're leaving? You hope he'll be less of a twat, that he'll come after you?"

"*Us*, Jane," he looked me in the eye and the corner of his lips turned up. "He's used to getting his way. He's used to everything and everyone revolving around him, so he doesn't understand how much people sacrifice for him. He needs to be alone. Maybe it will help him see the stick shoved up his own ass. Besides, you're irritated with him, too."

"I don't matter—"

"Don't you dare say that," he gave my hand a little squeeze. "You do matter. You matter just as much as he does."

Thank you, I thought but I couldn't bring myself to say it, so instead I put my head on his shoulder. Both men were so stubborn. I really didn't know how this would work out.

17

"Jane." I whispered to her brushing back her hair. "Jane. Baby, wake up."

Her eyelids fluttered open and I saw her beautiful hazel eyes. She smiled from ear to ear when she focused. "Hi."

"Hi, I hate to wake you, but we're landing." She was gorgeous when she slept. No, she was stunning all the time and it made it hard to concentrate.

"We're landing?" she repeated confused, sitting up and covering her mouth as she yawned. She paused looking around the plane. "We're landing? We're in London?" She was so excited it was cute.

"No. I'm from Cornwall. Falmouth specifically. London is about six hours away from here."

She didn't seem to care, she just beamed.

"I'm in England! Wes, I'm so excited."

"I can tell."

"Ladies and gentlemen, as we start our descent, please make sure your seatbacks and tray tables are in their full, upright position. Make sure your seatbelt is securely fastened and all carry-on luggage are stowed underneath the seat in front of you or in the overhead bins. Thank you." The flight attendant spoke, but, I doubt Jane heard her. Instead, she stared out the window.

"You can ignore the flight attendant, sweetheart, but don't ignore me."

"I'm not ignoring you. I'm merely admiring the country that created you and gave you that brilliant accent," she shot back holding my hand.

In a split second, a dozen ways I could make her moan my name and pay attention solely to me came to my mind.

"Ladies and gentlemen, welcome to new Cornwall Airport. Local time is 3:47 p.m. and the temperature is 9 degrees Celsius or 48 degrees Fahrenheit. For your safety and comfort, please remain seated with your seatbelt fastened until the captain turns off the 'Fasten Seat Belt' sign. This will indicate that we have arrived at the gate and that it is safe for you to move about the cabin."

"Are your moms picking us up?" she asked, already trying to fix her hair.

"Yes, and they are quite scrupulous when it comes to the appearance of other women. But just ignore them—"

"Wes, why did you let me sleep?" she panicked, reaching under the chair in front of her for a bag. I couldn't help it, I laughed. "What? Is there something on my face? Did I drool?"

"Jane, relax. First of all, you did not drool. Secondly, you look beautiful as you are. And third, my mum doesn't even know we're here."

"What?" Her shoulders drooped, but she glared as if she were about to kill me. Luckily the seat belt light turned off, and I unblocked mine to get up.

"What do you mean your moms don't know we're here?"

"Well, remember I did come up with this idea very last minute," I reminded her, taking my bag from overhead.

She didn't look pleased about it, but she took my hand anyway. "Do your moms like surprises?"

"They love them. It'll be like a Christmas miracle. Now, come on."

The moment we got off the plane I took a deep breath. It was freezing, but it was home. I hadn't realized how happy I'd be to be back, and more importantly, how excited I was to finally show someone where I grew up. Max had met my mothers when they came to Boston, but he never came over. He meant to, he said, but work kept getting in the way.

"Shit, I forgot to fill out the customs form," Jane muttered letting go of my hand dig in her bag. I didn't want to stop touching her; I couldn't. I placed my hand on her back and I waited and then I realized, no one stared at me. No one stared at us. A few people smiled and nodded walking by but not once did I get those looks. The 'how dare you be gay and happy in public' looks? I was just a guy waiting for a gorgeous girl.

"This isn't working," she replied trying to write on the paper over her hand. She paused and looked at me, her eyes roaming my chest.

"My eyes are up here," I smirked.

"Turn around."

"What?"

"Turn around."

Doing as she asked, I turned and she handed me her purse then used my back as a desk to write. I take it back…people started to stare this time. A few girls giggled and a few men just nodded to me as if we were speaking some secret code of understanding.

I didn't mind it at all.

"You're fucking with me," I gasped. My eyes were about to fall out of my head. It had taken us an hour from the airport to his home, and I still couldn't believe my eyes. "You live in a castle?"

"It is not a castle! It's more like a cottage that looks kind of like a castle if you are from America and don't know what castles look like," he rallied with a large grin on his face.

"Tell me now. Are you a prince? Is your real name Prince Wesley Fitz-Lloyd Uhler Dickens or something like that?"

"Jane." He was laughing, but I was serious. "First of all, that name is quite good. Second, no, I'm not a prince, and no, it's not a castle. It's probably the same size as Max's penthouse."

Opening the door and stepping on the gravel, he came out as well. I exhaled while quickly giving my hair one more brush. After we had gone through customs, I made him stop so I could brush my teeth, fix my hair and do my make-up in the bathroom.

"Relax, my mothers are harmless. A little crazy so you will fit right in—ouch," I cut him off by punching his arm.

"Don't freak me out. I'm already nervous."

Shaking his head, he walked up to the green door and knocked once, then twice, then paused before knocking up and down the door.

He took a step back and a second later a woman around my height with short dirty blonde hair, an ear full of piercings on one side, yet only a stud in the other, opened the door. Her glasses rested on her nose. She stared at us for a moment before slamming the door in our faces.

"I told you," Wes said not even surprised. "They are crazy."

A second later, the same woman came out this time with a fly swatter and started to smack him. "You little twat!" she screamed as she hit him.

"Ouch mum! Mum!" he yelled dodging her swings.

"How can you let me answer the door looking like a loon?" She hit him again. "And when you bring a guest too!"

"Mum! Okay alright! I'm sorry but now you've embarrassed me enough."

"Don't mind them."

I turned to another woman with shoulder-length brown-gray hair and green eyes. She smiled at me kindly.

"You must be Jane?"

"Yes, it's a pleasure to meet you, ma'am." I stretched out my hand but she linked arms with me to bring me inside.

"My name is Pippa, not 'ma'am.' Do I look old to you?" she eyed me carefully and I shook my head.

"Not at all, we could be twins in fact."

274

"You're sucking up to me?"

"Is it working?"

She grinned and then turned back to Wes and his other mother. He was now chasing her and tickling her sides while both of them laughed like mad.

"You two will freeze, and I'm not cutting off your toes no matter how much you beg, Wes," Pippa yelled at them.

"What?" I huffed trying not to laugh.

"When he was a kid, he was always the drama queen. He got a paper cut and he thought he needed stitches. He got the flu and he was writing a will. One day he jumped into a frozen lake and came home crying and begged us to cut off his toes, so he could save his leg."

What? Oh, my God. That didn't sound like him at all. "How old was he?"

"Six," she shrugged and we both laughed.

"Whatever she is saying, there is a perfectly good explanation," Wes said the moment he came back inside with his mother beside him. She was breathing a lot heavier than he was, and she didn't look happy about it.

"Is there an explanation for sniffing Mr. Edwards' dog's ass—"

"I was four! I don't even remember!" he gasped out exasperated, which made both of his mums laugh. Walking over to Pippa, he gave her a short hug and kissed the side of her face before adding, "She just got through the door, so please keep the embarrassing stories to a minimum."

"No, please. I love this. Back home he's the cool one. Wesley, the handsome and godly chef. I'm glad I get to see you more human."

"I prefer handsome and godly," he pouted putting his hand on my back.

Rolling my eyes, I bowed, "Yes, Chef."

"Better—ouch—Mum, this is abuse." He frowned when she pinched him.

"Hello darling, I'm Brenda." She put her hands on my face. "It is such a pleasure to meet you. Had my wanker son told us you were coming, we would have cooked something."

"You're welcome," Wes stage-whispered to me as he walked further into the house. Brenda glared at him. He whistled and I was expecting some kind of dog, but instead a grey bird came out of nowhere and flew onto his hand.

"Wesley's home," the bird said and I laughed. He came over to me and I took a step back. Again the bird said, "Wesley's home."

"What do we tell Wesley?" Pippa asked the bird.

"Get in the kitchen. Make a sandwich."

Wesley turned to face them both, "How long have you been training him to say that?"

"A while," Brenda shrugged taking my arm. "Now go, while we get to know more about Jane here."

"Mum, we've just arrived. We're tired and—"

"Jane, are you tired?" Pippa asked me.

"No ma'— no Pippa, I'm fine," I corrected myself quickly.

"See. Now go," Brenda nodded. "We'd have something ready, but someone didn't call."

"I'm going. I'm going," he replied before giving me a quick look.

"She'll be fine. Now go," Pippa pushed him. "Mozart, what should Wesley do?"

"Get in the kitchen. Make a sandwich."

"I'm going," he moved over to me and kissed the side of my head, and I tried to angle myself away from Mozart. I wasn't really a bird person.

"Get in the kitchen. Make a sandwich."

"One more time and I'm feeding you to Mr. Edwards' cat," Wes muttered walking around the corner.

"I'll get some tea," Pippa said following him.

I was going to tell her not to worry about it, but I didn't really didn't want to turn down tea from a British woman in her own home.

"So…Jane," Brenda led me into their living room which had a beautiful view of the ocean. "Tell me, when did you fall in love with my son?"

My mouth dropped open. "It's not like that. We're…we're close, but we're hardly in love or anything."

"My son wouldn't have brought you here if he didn't care about you. Relax, I'm not one of those menacing mothers who gets overprotective of their sons. Well, I am, but I doubt I have anything to worry about with you."

My palms didn't sweat. But I had a feeling there was a first time for everything.

"It's really complicated."

"I'm an author dear," she said, making herself comfortable on the couch. "Complicated love stories are the best kind."

God help me.

"Are you going to keep staring?" my mom, Pippa, asked me as she put the teakettle on the stove.

"What?"

"You keep looking toward the living room as if she's going to disappear….and you're letting the cold air out." She nodded to the door of the refrigerator I still had open.

"Shit—"

"Language"

Rolling my eyes, I closed the door and moved to lean against the sink. Mozart was now standing on his post pecking at his own wings.

"Did you break it off with Max?" she asked as if were that simple.

"No."

"Does she know?"

"Yes."

"And?"

"Mum..." I'd never needed to come out to my mums before. They never cared and I knew it was not a big deal, but this was.

"Yes?" She turned to face me.

"All...all three of us are together. Max. Me. Her. All of us."

"Wesley!" She stared in shock.

"I know." I cut her off before she could speak. "I know what you're thinking. It's not right. This is complicated. You can't love two people at the same time. One or all of us will get hurt. I know, Mum. I know. But..."

"But!"

Sighing, I went back to how I felt yesterday before Jane had told me about Elspeth's plan. "I had an interview with a chef yesterday morning. I admire him more than anyone in the industry, and he told me to go out there. To learn more and not get locked into one city, or not yet, at least. The moment he said it, I wanted to go anywhere...everywhere. I was excited at the thought of learning something new to cook."

"I'm not sure I understand the connection here," she replied, taking the kettle off the stove.

"I thought about this all day." I went on. "Where I would go? How they would feel if I did go. I felt so torn and then she texted me. She said 'I love you'. I couldn't help but smile. I was so choked up that I walked into a damn wall. Immediately, every thought that ran through my head since I had done the interview disappeared. I didn't want to go anywhere she wasn't...where they both weren't. I'm in love with her and I'm in love with Maxwell. I don't know if it's equal. How do you measure if you love someone? If they were both hanging off a cliff, and I could only choose one, I'd join them on the cliff and hope we could go together. I can't divide myself from them."

She sighed deeply. "If this is the case and all of this just happened, then why are you here?"

"Because I don't want to be pushed to the side by Max." That's why I left and that's one of the reasons I brought her. "I want him to know what it would be like for me to sit on the sidelines and watch them together in public. I want him to be the odd man out for a little bit."

"Wes, I don't know what to say."

I stared into her green eyes, "Don't say anything. Just support me. Support us. Support my choice to love two people at once. Please, Mum, we have enough people against us as it is."

She put her hand on my cheek, "Okay."

"Your moms are hilarious," I sighed, falling on top of his bed before staring at the night blue sky painted on his ceiling. His whole room was covered in books, not just comics, but the complete works of authors, not only Plato and Aristotle but also Edgar Allen Poe and Shakespeare.

"That's one word for it." He lay down beside me. "I knew they'd like you, though."

Really? I smiled. "I like them, too. Though, Brenda really dug deep. I swear, one second longer and she'd know my social security number and blood type."

"Don't be surprised if she makes you into a character in her next crime novel."

"It's so cool that she writes crime."

"That's one word for it," he repeated again.

I stood up and dropped some of the pillows onto the floor beside me.

"What are you doing?" he frowned shifting on to the side.

"Sleeping on the floor."

"Why?"

I had a lot of reasons. Well, just one. "Max. He's not here."

"So you want to sleep on the floor?"

"No...I..." Urgh. Running my hands through my hair, I thought about how to say this.

"Jane?"

"You whisked me away to England in less than twelve hours." He didn't understand what that was like for me. Even I hadn't really thought about it. "Three months ago, I never thought I'd even leave Boston. I went to Mexico with Allen once, yeah, but that was just right over the border. We saved for months and rented this beat up old Chevy. It was this once-in-a-lifetime thing for me. And now, in less than twelve hours, you've brought me to England, in first class, and I'm in a castle by the sea, even though you won't admit it's a damn castle. This is amazing, Wes! I'm so excited and happy. I want to kiss you, bissing you right now will lead to other things, and then I'd feel bad going back knowing we just cut out Max as if he was nothing."

There, I said it.

He stared at me for a long time. His face was emotionless.

"Wes?"

"I'll sleep on the floor." He got up and walked to his closet to pull out a knitted blanket. He dropped it on the pillows I had put on the floor. Before lying down, he kissed the side of my head.

"Wes?"

"Jane, don't say more please. You'll make it even harder for me." I thought I screwed up by bringing up Max. However, I saw the raging erection he had in his jeans.

"Night," I whispered.

"Night."

She had no clue the effect she had on me.

How I wanted her more because she also cared for Max.

Adjusting on the ground, I looked at my bed.

"You knew I was going to offer to take the floor, didn't you?"

She pretended to snore loudly. Smiling to myself, I closed my eyes.

18

Ring.

Ring.

Ring.

Reaching on the nightstand I grabbed my phone, "What?"

"Where are you?" Scarlet hollered in my ear so loudly I had to pull the phone from my ear. "You're late."

"For...?"

"Maxwell! The meeting!"

"The meeting is at 9—"

"Which is why I'm calling you at 8:57 a.m. wondering where the hell you are!"

8:57 a.m.? I pulled my phone away and stared in shock as the time went from 8:57 a.m. to 8:58 a.m. I had never overslept, not in the last four years at least. Wes always got up early which in turn got me up, too. Rolling over, I sat up looking around me room…my very empty room.

"Max?"

"I'm on my way." Hanging up on her, I got up.

I'm not sure why I walked out of my room, as if I really needed to check that they both weren't there. I stood at the door for a while until I felt my phone ring again. Lifting it up, I had a few missed messages from Jane.

'Max we just got here. Just thought you'd want to know'

'I know you're upset…both of you are upset but…just…I don't know.'

'I hope you're alright. We both miss you, goodnight Jane.'

Her most recent message being, *'I know you're already up, so good morning. Sorry, I didn't text earlier. Pippa and Brenda took me into town today. I got a wool sweater from a real life sheep! I met her. Her name is Tabitha. She has her coat back and I think we look like twins."*

Attached to her message was a picture of her and Tabitha. Smiling, I shook my head. Only she could grin like that because of a sheep.

'Which one is Tabitha?' I asked, texting back heading into the bathroom.

'Ass.' She replied. *'Glad you finally texted back. Are you alright?'*

'I'm perfectly fine. Working is keeping me busy so you don't have to keep texting me. Enjoy your trip.'

'...Okay.' She wrote back with a frown face. *'But I'm going to keep texting. After all, I'm not the one paying this phone bill.'*

'Do what you want. How is Wes—" Erasing the second sentence, I put the phone down and the back of my neck.

Ring.

Looking at the phone, her next text pissed me off more than I could even imagine: *'Wes says he's glad you didn't oversleep without him.'*

'His ego may have made him think I'm unable to live without him... he's completely and utterly wrong. I didn't even notice.' I sent it before I even realized.

Why can't I ever say the things that were really going on in my mind?

****

"We've got nothing and 48% of our viewers believe that you are personally attacking Governor MacDowell with no real facts," Scarlet said as she walked around the table. "Maybe we should drop the story."

"No," I shook my head. "No one else is talking about this. The moment we stop applying pressure is the moment he gets off."

"Max, we aren't prosecutors," she groaned, rubbing the side of her head. "The story has started to cool down. We have no cards left to play, and our only trump card to date, the interview with one of the supposed girls, vanished weeks ago. I have no idea where she is, or if she was even serious about being forced to sleep with him."

"She could be—"

"There are no dead prostitutes or missing persons in the city either. We need to move on," she cut me off, and when I looked around the table, I could tell they all thought the same.

"Fine," I muttered, rising from the desk. "We pushed too close. That's all."

"Max—"

Ignoring her, I got up with my phones and walked out. I made it halfway to my desk when Dwayne Adams, who I decided must have a fetish for plaid shirts, approached me.

"Sir, we aren't just going to drop this, are we? I really think we have something here."

"Didn't you hear them? We have nothing."

"I'll find something," he said quickly.

"Why?" I turned to him.

"Why?"

"Why are you so committed to this story?" I asked him. I knew my personal feelings were clouding me in this, but what was in it for him?

"He's guilty."

"Bullshit," I cut him off. "What's the real reason?"

He didn't speak, so I just left him to follow me into my office. Once inside, he closed the door.

"I want to nail this asshole to the wall," he stated.

"I see that but you're still not saying why—"

"Have you heard about the BWA that the Governor past four years ago?" he asked.

"The Balanced Wellness Act." I nodded. "What about it?"

"Since it's been put in place, welfare for men and women has been cut by more than half. Working people, because the governor struck down the new income rise, are really struggling. Some are even going to soup kitchens now. It is so bad that people want to protest, but they can't afford to take the time off from their low-paid work. In the past, any that tried were sent to jail on trumped up charges. Governor MacDowell called them 'throwaways'. On top of that, he slashed over a billion in spending while cutting taxes for millionaires. He claimed minorities were the problem for rising crime rates, but most of the arrests were for petty crimes like stealing food. Now that we know he's also a fraud and predator, we're going to just let this man walk? I can't! I won't."

For a split second, I remembered Jane's lecture on what ten dollars meant to her. *"Have you ever been starving, Mr. Emerson? No? Have you actually been so hungry that you feel sick and in pain or eat other people's leftovers in bars?"* Her words played over in my head.

"Fine," I nodded at him while leaning back in my chair. "Keep looking."

"I won't let you down," he said moving to the door.

"Adams?"

"Yes, sir."

"Don't go digging through the man's trash or anything." I thought for a second. "Or at least, don't get caught."

"Yes, sir."

When he left, I leaned back and took a deep breath. However, that was as much as I got to relax before Scarlet, the very last person I wanted to be alone with at the moment, came inside.

"I know you're annoyed," she said.

"You have no idea," I muttered. If I was going to do this, I was going to do it now. "We *are* going to catch him."

"I know that but until we get something concrete—"

"When we do, we'll be back on top, and then you can leave the company on a high note."

She paused before tilting her head to the side, "What do you mean leave?"

"I mean I want to fire you, but I also don't want to make this bigger than it needs to be."

"Max! What?"

"What?" I finally looked up at her and rose from my seat. "What did you think would happen when you tried to blackmail Jane? You didn't even try to hide it. You confronted her openly with what thought in mind? That she'd run away and not tell me?

She clenched her fists and approached me. "That woman is cheating on you, and you want to fire *me*? She's an obvious gold digger—"

"That isn't your business!" I snapped. She was pushing me and forgetting I had no fear of pushing back. "Over the years, I've tolerated your crush because I thought you'd eventually get it. I don't want y*ou*. I don't care that we went to school together. I don't care that our mothers are friends or if we look good together. None of that changes the fact that when I look at you, I feel nothing. Or at least, I didn't. Now I'm just annoyed. Leave Jane alone."

"You—"

"If I see that picture anywhere, Scarlet, you should know me well enough by now that when I go after someone, I never let up." Her eyes glanced over as she glared at me.

"Is that all, Mr. Emerson?"

"Yes, you can leave now. I have a headache." I moved back to my seat and closed my eyes. When I heard the door slam, I let go of the deep breath I was holding.

"Mr. Emerson, your father is on the line," my secretary announced.

For God's sake!

What would I give to be in Cornwall right now? No.

As soon as I thought it, I sat back up.

I couldn't start thinking like that especially after one fucking day!

I was fine.

"Yes, Father." I answered the phone while rubbing the side of my head.

"Your mother tells me you've actually found a woman you'd like to marry," he said with a lighter than normal voice.

"Yes."

He took a deep breath, "Congrats. I was starting to worry some of these faggot rumors were true. I just came back to the city so tonight—"

"She went to visit a friend. She'll be back home next week."

"That's fine. I'll be in town for a while. Maybe we could meet. I wanted to talk to you about this Governor MacDowell scandal coverage you've been doing."

"I'm busy working on said story. Maybe some other time"

"Maxwell." There it was. That disappointed and frustrated tone I was used to. "There are some stories you should just leave alone. You've done well. He's going to take huge flack for the corruption. The other stuff is just—"

"Is it just an illegal sex ring?"

He didn't speak.

"Tell me you're not involved in this."

"I'm telling you, son. Leave it alone."

This was my family? These people! Why? What did I ever do to deserve these fucking people?

"You're an odd one, Jane," Pippa said as we walked along the beach.

"I get that a lot," I replied.

It was a cold October day, but it was still beautiful. Ahead, Wes walked alongside Brenda, and both of them were laughing about something. I could tell that they were more like siblings than mother and son. She teased him and hit him like an older sister would.

"When is your birthday?"

"The twenty-first of December." I didn't know why she was asking, but she nodded as if I'd said something important.

"The twenty-first of December," she repeated. "So you are a Sagittarius, which means you're fiercely independent and straightforward almost to a fault. You seek adventure in all things and tend to be intelligent and enthusiastic. But most importantly, you are generous."

"That's right, you're an astrologer. I knew I was a Sagittarius, but I didn't know it was so positive."

"That's because I started with the good," she replied with a grin. "Those born under the sign of Sagittarius are also stubborn, restless, quick-tempered, careless—"

"Okay, let's go back to the positive."

"—And unable to handle criticism," she added the last part while linking arms with me. I could feel myself frowning; I wasn't trying to prove her right.

"I'm sure every sign has its ups and downs."

"Of course. Take my son." she nodded up at Wes who was walking towards the ocean, "Libras are romantic, sociable and charming."

I could totally see him. "And the negatives"

"They need approval from others, can be superficial, and hate being in situations where they aren't in control."

"I can see all of that, too."

She smiled and looked up at the sky as the sun started to set. "You know most women would feel a little shameful about sleeping with two men. And I doubt they'd even be able to show their faces to either of their mothers and yet, here you are, confidently proud, trying your best to get us to like you."

I shrugged. "I'm not the best person to speak to on matters of morality. I didn't exactly have the best role models. I try to do what makes me happy and safe. Everyone who judges does so from the outside. They don't help me pay my bills, they don't come to feed me when I'm sick. Why live for people who don't care about me unless I'm doing something they don't approve of?"

"Like I said, independent, straightforward, and intelligent," she repeated staring out at the sea. I couldn't look away from her. She was attractive in a strange way. I'd noticed that of Wes' two mothers, she was the calm, collected one. It was kind of funny how she was the one who loved all this zodiac sign stuff.

"I'm a Virgo. Do you know what that means?" she asked and I shook my head. "It means my negative traits say I'm judgmental, too logical and analytical, inflexible and interfering."

Not this again! I sighed already knowing where this was going. "Let me guess you're judging me and this situation with Wes and Max."

"It's hard not to," she unlinked her arms from mine.

"You're also going to try interfering somehow?" Because apparently I'm mom repellent. And here I thought they liked me, well, liked me in a more normal way than Max's mother.

"I might. Haven't you thought of what may happen next?"

"Next?"

She nodded breathing in through her nose, "I'm talking about when Wes and Max get over this issue they are having. Let's say you all choose to continue like this. One of you is just bound to get jealous. Boston is a big city and Maxwell is well known. So if you were to be on his arm one moment and then Wes' arm the next, people wouldn't understand. We are still fighting for equal rights in the LGBTQ community. Now you want to add polygamy to the mix?"

I didn't like that word: polygamy. But I didn't have another one.

"We aren't thinking like that—"

"No, you're keeping your head in the sand even though it is obvious you are in love with Wes, seeing as you check to see where he is every four minutes. And you're also in love with Max since you've kept him in the loop all day. That and you grin like a crazy woman when you mention either of them."

Save me please...someone...anyone...

"We're just having fun." I took a step away from her, not an obvious one, more like I was hoping we'd just keep moving closer to Wes and Brenda.

"Sagittarians are overly logical too. So I know you don't believe that."

"Not all of us fit into a perfect model of an ancient circle of animals in the sky," I snapped, running my hand through my hair.

"Jane? Mum?" Wes came over looking for us. "Everything alright?"

"Everything is fine, we were just talking about the stars. Where did your mum go?" Pippa asked, looking over her shoulder.

"She went inside to get something for us to drink." He nodded back to the house.

"I'll help. If I'm not out in ten minutes, send a rescue party." She kissed his cheek before walking up the beach towards their home.

Turning away, I stared back at the ocean; part of me wanting to run towards it.

"What were you both really talking about?" Wes asked stopping beside me.

"The stars."

He groaned, "She didn't go overboard with the zodiac stuff again? I swear if it were an official religion, she'd be the head pastor."

I didn't answer. I wasn't sure what to say. Her words were digging deep into my head.

"You leave me no choice," he whispered, and when I turned to him, he was taking off his clothes.

"Wes! What are you doing?"

"I'm distracting you from whatever just happened?" he replied taking off his sweater and undershirt and throwing it to me.

"Wes, don't—"

Off came his underwear as he ran towards the ocean.

"Woah!" he screamed and his ass was the last thing I saw before he dove in. One second later, he came up for air. "It's not that bad. Come in!"

"Really? 'Cause your teeth are chattering."

"Don't be a pussy!"

"I'm not a pussy!"

"PUSSY!"

Laughing so hard, I nearly peed myself as he ran out. I took off my sweater and jeans and ran into the sea. For a split second I felt nothing, and then it hit me. It was like hugging the iceberg that sunk the *Titanic*.

"OH MY GOD!" I screamed. "COLD! SO FUCKING COLD."

Fuck this shit! I ran out of the water as fast as I could, grabbing my wool sweater and wrapping it around myself.

"Jane!" He laughed, running with me all the way back into the house.

"What the..." I heard one of his mother question, but I couldn't even see her face. I just went for the warmth. In the house, I jumped up and down hugging myself.

"You know cold water makes your wee-wee shrivel up, right?" Pippa said feeding a cracker to Mozart, who sat on her shoulder.

"You're not helping," Wes, who just cupped his dick, ran back upstairs, leaving me there. She stared at me and then started to giggle.

"Oh, to be twenty again." She shook her head walking outside.

Running upstairs, I made it into his room and heard the shower running. Stripping off my bra and underwear, I ran in and turned my back to him. The heat of the shower was just what I needed.

"Dumbest idea ever," I muttered to him, "it felt like I had icicles hanging off my tits."

"Yeah, but it was fun." He hugged me for a second before letting go and turning around. "Right, no Max, no sex."

"Yep," I said and so we stood in the shower ass to ass, trying to defrost.

Of all the places this asshole wanted to meet me, it had to be Wesley's restaurant. In the reception area stood a young man, most likely in his twenties.

"Do you have a reservation this afternoon?" he asked, his dark brown eyes fleetingly wandering up and then back down my body.

"Emerson."

He looked at the computer and nodded, "Your company has arrived. Would you like me to take your coat?"

Nodding, I took it off and his hand grazed over mine. I didn't react or even pretend to notice. Gay men often did. Since people weren't always open with their sexuality, they put out little feelers. Is there eye contact? Did he notice this touch? If he did, did he react? All of those small things helped figure out how to openly approach someone.

"Follow me please." Still not looking at him, I took out my phone and texted Wes quickly. *'Your maître d' is putting out feelers. I've counted three crotch glances, a once over and a graze of the hand. Apparently I'm worth the risk.'*

"Maxwell." My father didn't bother standing when I arrived. I hated how much we looked alike. Same blue eyes, black hair, even though his was gray on the sides, and we even stood at the same height.

At least balding wasn't in my future.

"Let's make this quick," I muttered and took a seat. The host left, but not without trying to make eye contact. The guy apparently didn't get it. Finally, he walked away when I pretended I didn't realize he was still there.

"Tactless as always. You are your mother's son," he replied, drinking his whiskey.

"Would you prefer I was a womanizer and cheat?" I questioned without emotion. I didn't really care. At one time I pitied my mother, now, however, I wasn't going to go down that rabbit hole.

"Don't nag. It's a female trait," he corrected.

"Still worried I could be one of them faggots?"

His jaw cracked to the side, "Well, are you?"

"I should say yes just to watch you have heartache. However, that's not why I'm here. You and the governor, what are you both hiding?"

"As I said on the phone, leave this alone, Max."

"As I said on the phone, I won't, Alistair." Leaning over the table, I made sure he could look into my eyes. "If you were involved in any of this, I'll tear you down with him."

"You hate us both that much?"

"Thanks for the lunch." I got back up. "But, I realize you still make me sick, so I'm going to eat my lunch alone."

"Maxwell. I'm warning—"

"Enjoy your lunch. I hear the food here is to die for." I didn't want to waste another moment with him.

'Your maître d' is putting out feelers. I've counted three crotch glances, a once-over and a graze of the hand. Apparently I'm worth the risk.'

"What the fuck?" I hissed sitting up.

"What is it?" Jane came out of the bathroom drying her hair with a towel.

"Nothing, I'm just firing someone," I muttered more to myself than to her. The first text he sends and it's this shit. He was fucking with me on purpose.

I tried to think of what to say to that, but nothing came to mind. Dropping the phone, I laid back down.

I fucking hate this shit.

"Wes?"

"I'm fine," I snapped.

"Just call him." She sighed and laid beside me, resting her head on my chest. "You and I both know he's not going to give in."

"I can't." If I did, we wouldn't work. He would never get. Picking up the phone again, I held it above both of us and took a photo.

"What are you doing?!"

"Replying." I sent him an image and texted: *I doubt he or anyone else could make up for the two of us.*

"You two are working on my last nerves!" she kicked me while grabbing a pillow from under my head.

"Where are you going?"

"I'm sleeping on the couch downstairs. From now on, I'm not indulging you either. Keep your hands to yourself. Don't hug me. Don't kiss me. Nothing until you two stop acting like children and start acting like my men again." She slammed the door behind her.

She wanted us to just kiss and make up? I'd love to. But how could I make up with someone who didn't realize the problem to begin with?

19

"Door open," the automatic voice said.

Stepping around the kitchen island, I went to the door expecting it to be them but instead, Irene stumbled in with a bottle of wine and bag of Thai food.

"Not who you were hoping, huh?"

"How did you get in here?" No one knew the code with the exception of...

"Jane," she replied, letting herself into the penthouse. "And before you get mad at her, she said your password would be changed tomorrow anyway, so let's eat."

I didn't have the energy to argue, so I ignored her and entered the living room.

"Max, this place is a pigsty!"

Sitting down, I flipped through the time logs in front of me.

"Where do you keep your plates?"

He was there on the twenty-second. Why does this keep overlapping?

"You can ignore me all you want, but I'm not going home."

LL. Goddamn it, if I see this name one more time.

"Max!"

"WHAT?" I hollered at her not realizing she was next to me. She jumped back eyes wide. "I'm sorry Irene, but I'm working. This is important to me. I can't deal with whatever shit you've fallen into right now."

She glared for a second then downed both glasses of wine. She bunched up her fists and took a deep breath before speaking. "First off, you asshole, I came here because Jane begged me to. She said you weren't replying to her texts or calls anymore. She was worried and is coming back tonight. I'm sorry it had to be me, your screwed up cousin, but since Jane has no one else's number, mostly because you make it a habit of pushing everyone who cares about you out of your life, I thought I'd actually come and check up on you seeing as how it's been three days since I last saw you on air either. Glad to know you aren't dead, you dick."

Three days? I reached for my phone, but it was dead.

"I've been working," I whispered, staring at it. "Honestly, I didn't realize that she'd been trying to contact me."

I'd pushed everything out of my mind in order to focus. It was easier that way. The moment I got off track, I found myself moping around, and I didn't have time for that. There was so much going in my head, it felt like it was going to explode.

"Well, just call her, okay? I'll leave so you can get back to whatever this is…" She waved over the papers and photos in front of me. Moving over, she kissed my cheek. "Get some rest before she comes back too…maybe clean up. I know she was a maid, but a 'welcome-home mess' isn't the way to go."

"Thank you for your wisdom, Irene."

She winked before going back to the kitchen to get her bag. When she got to the door, she turned back to me and smiled. It was real genuine smile; I hadn't seen one on her face in years.

"I met someone. Someone great," she told me. "I really wanted to tell you."

"Why to tell me?"

She looked annoyed at that. "You're really going to make me say it."

"Say what?"

"I love you, you big idiot. Honestly, you've always been important to me. Like my big brother. I know I'm always a mess, so telling you that I've met someone, a normal, everyday, good person, from a good family, who really cares about me, is important. Maybe I can introduce you to him and all that when you aren't busy with work."

"Yeah." I didn't know what else to say until she got in the elevators. "Irene."

"What?"

"I love you, too."

She smiled waving back at me, "I know! But it's good to hear."

Waiting for the elevator doors to close, I walked back inside. Flipping the phone around in my hand again, I went up to my room where the charger was plugged in the bedside lamp. In the last three days, I couldn't remember coming up here. I had slept on the couch for the most part. Entering the bathroom, I nearly gave myself a heart attack as I pissed. The man in the reflection looked not at all like me. I hadn't shaved since they left, there were food stains all over my shirt, and my black hair was standing straight up in every direction.

"Jesus Christ, Max," I muttered to myself, flushing the toilet and stripping down. I had just turned on the water to wash my hands when I heard it.

BUZZ

BUZZ

BUZZ

BUZZ

BUZZ

BUZZ

My phone was vibrating so much that it fell off the stand. Picking it up, a stream of messages came in nonstop.

Wes: *'I doubt he or anyone else could make up for the two of us.'*

I had no idea what he was talking about, but the picture of them together bothered me.

Jane: *'You and Wes are both pissing me off. Just talk about it okay. It's night here so talk to you later.'.*

Jane: *'Morning'*

Jane: *'Feel like talking today?'*

Jane: *'I guess not.'*

Jane: *'Wes misses you, he's just can't let himself give in.'*

Wes: *'The host has a husband. You sure you weren't just imagining he was hitting on you?'*

Oh! I completely forgot that I texted him about that.

Jane: *'Max! Back to the most important thing in the world...me. I think I found something I actually like doing...Guess what?'*

Jane: *'I'll just tell you then. I went to this dress store. This old woman has been making dresses for the girls here for the last twenty years...She's hilarious. I think I might want to make clothes! Sure, I'm not going to be the next Ralph Laruen or anything. But maybe a small store somewhere. The moment I thought it, it was like everything become clear, and I got this big fat duh. I've been making, sewing and fitting almost all of my own clothes since I was thirteen. What do you think?'*

Wes: *'Jane feels like she found her meaning in life. The least you can do is text back.'*

Jane: *'I get you're pissed at Wes but don't stop talking to me!.'*

Jane: *'Are you okay?'*

Jane: *'Max. I turned in to see you on the news. You weren't on tonight?'*

Wes: *'Are you alright?'*

Jane: *'If you're fucking with me Max, I swear to God I'll beat the shit out of you.'* - Wes

'Call us.'

Wes: *'We are coming back home. Nothing better has happened to you.'*

Ten missed calls from Jane.

Thirteen missed calls from Wes.

"Your voicemail is full, please clear the messages. The first message," the automatic voice spoke before I heard Jane's voice.

"Hey, I'm calling just to check up? You're kind of freaking us out. Call us back, okay?"

"Next message," This one was Wes. He took a deep breath. "You win. I give in. Call me."

"Next message," It was a Jane again. "Wes is in love with you. You know that. He knows that. I think what happened was...your mom freaked him out. She honestly freaked us both out. When you love someone you want to share that openly, and you don't want to hide, you don't want to become a dirty little secret or worse, completely pushed out. Part of me feels like this is my fault. I'm sorry—"

"Next message," Jane. "I'm sorry because I butted in between the both of you. I'm also sorry because I'm really happy I did. I'm happy with you both, so you not answering the phone is terrifying. I have abandonment issues. You can't check out like this. It fucks me up emotionally."

"Final message," Wes. "We'll be back in Boston sometime around midnight. We'll talk then. I love you."

"End of messages."

I sat there so overwhelmed that my lungs burned, or at least, I thought it was lungs from the aching pain my chest. But it wasn't. My heart ached. It ached to hear them sounding so scared. It ached to know they cared so much. I just ached, and the harder I tried to calm myself down, the more painful it became.

I called Jane back first knowing both of them would get the messages when they landed.

"Jane," I spoke to her voicemail feeling like an absolute idiot. "I'm so sorry. I never meant to ignore your text or calls. I've been working on this story...that's bullshit and not an excuse. I feel like a complete shit. You opening a boutique is an amazing idea, but don't count yourself out. You really could be the next Ralph Lauren. We'll talk about it when you come home...yeah home, because I'm glad you're in the middle, too. I'm glad we both have you. Sorry again."

Hanging up, I dialed Wes but he didn't answer, and I ending up speaking into his voicemail. "I'm an ass. You knew that when you first met me. But I'd never fuck you like this. I'm sorry I have been out of it. When you get home we'll talk...fuck this... I'm coming to the airport. I'll even bring flowers or some shit...'cause...'cause... I love you too, Wes. Screw what my mother says."

Rushing back to the phone, I dialed quickly.

"Hello, Mary's Magnificent Maid's—"

"It's Maxwell Emerson. I need a maid, maybe two, at my penthouse this evening. They need to be done by midnight. I don't care the cost. Is that possible?"

"Of course, Mr. Emerson."

"Good, I'll send you the code," I said hanging up on her.

I then entered the bathroom and grabbed my razor and comb. I honestly felt nervous. How the fuck was going to explain how I got so wrapped up in work that I chose to forget about them for three days when they cared enough to panic about me. I really was a fucking ass. I knew they'd be pissed and that we'd all end up fighting...but after that...we'd be fine.

"The fucking what!" Wesley took a deep breath before hanging up his phone as we walked through the airport terminal. "What fuck is wrong with him?"

"He sounded sorry," I replied, not realizing I was taking a deep breath too.

He'd really scared us. The first day passed and I didn't think about. The second I was annoyed, and I could tell so was Wes. But he kept telling me he was probably just working. He even texted him most times throughout. When we went to watch the news coverage online and he wasn't on, I saw it on his face…something wasn't right. The third day when Irene said she hadn't heard from him, and when we still couldn't get through, we barely even finished packing, we just grabbed our passports, said goodbye to his mums, and drove the rental back to the airport. Wes, being the hotshot, was able to get the last flight out.

"I'm going to kill him," Wes muttered to himself, but I was sure he was still on edge.

"Try not to do it, the airport is full of the witnesses. He said he's picking us up right—"

"Breaking news, BRMJ is reporting Maxwell Emerson and son of hotel mogul and former Governor Alistair Crane Emerson and sitting senator Elspeth Yates also, the headline reporter of YGM's *The Emerson Report* was in a car accident at 10:49 this evening…"

Everything seemed to become muffled as Wes and I turned to the screens in the terminal. I thought I was dreaming or misheard or the reporter made a mistake, but it wasn't just that one reporter. It was all of them. All the reports had a picture of Max plastered there like one of the headshots you use when people die. Then there were terrifying scenes of his midnight blue 1962 Ferrari…or what was left of it.

Slowly, I ripped my eyes away from it to stare at Wesley. He stared openly, his mouth parted and his green eyes wide. His whole body was so still it was scary. The only thing that moved was his eyes, looking from screen to screen before he finally blinked. Lifting up his phone, he started to dial, walking quickly at first.

"Max," he said into the phone. "Max, answer the phone. Max, this isn't funny. The news…have you seen the news? Call me back."

He hung up and dialed again and again until he started to run. And I ran with him while all around us the screens kept repeating the same thing.

Maxwell Emerson, 31, in critical condition.

It felt too sudden, too quick, too…not right, and because of that, it felt like a walking nightmare.

20

"Sorry, ma'am, we can't let anyone in this side of the hospital," the security guard told me.

"I'm his fiancée! MOVE!" I screamed at him. He just held his arms out as if that would stop me.

"I'm sorry, ma'am, but I have no way of proving that—"

"You have ten seconds to move or I'll break you," Wes sneered at the man who only called for back-up.

"Jane!"

I turned around to find Irene with her eyes so red I knew it had to be true. It was really true. She ran to me. Running up to me, she wrapped her hands around me and squeezed tightly.

"Have they told you anything?"

"They won't let us through!" My head felt like it was on fire and I couldn't breathe.

"Us?" she frowned, finally noticing Wes. "Chef Wesley? What are you doing here?"

"Good question." I knew that voice. Walking behind the guard blocking our entrance was Elspeth dressed in a black suit. Her hair was pulled back and her eyes were bloodshot. She looked so human in that moment, and not the monster who tried to destroy everything less than a week ago.

"How is he?" Irene was the first to speak up. She let go of me and walked up to her. "I don't understand. I saw him just a few hours ago!"

Elspeth tried to speak but just flinched. Her eyes were tearing up and her hands were shaking, but she tried to hide it by clenching them closed.

"Aunt Elspeth!" Irene screamed at her.

"He's in pretty bad shape," she finally managed to say, fixing the pearls on her neck. She coughed once and rolled her shoulders back. "It's a miracle he's alive…that's what the doctors are saying. But it's still…it's still…it's bad."

"I need to see him—" Wes stepped forward, but she stuck her hand out.

And just like that the grieving mother was gone, and the monster was back. "The only people allowed in are family. His family being: his mother, Irene, his cousin, and Jane, his fiancée. Who are you again?"

"Elspeth!" I screamed at her. She could have stabbed me in both eyes, and it would have been less painful.

"Jane, what is it? Come on." Irene pulled my arm, but I pulled my arm back and stood next to Wes who was breaking. His pale face and his whole body motionless.

"Don't do this, Elspeth, it's not right—"

"Either you stay here with him, or you can see my son. God knows..." she said, closing her eyes. "You may regret it, if you don't."

I slapped her.

I wanted to do more than slap her, but when I lifted my hand again, Wes caught it.

"Go. I'll wait out here," he replied.

"Wes—"

"Go. I need a second anyway."

"Wes—"

"Jane, please."

Nodding, I let go. Elspeth, the heartless human that she was, just turned back around. Irene looked between us with a confused expression as I walked down the hall. Pausing halfway, I turned back at Wes, but, he was already walking quickly away.

With every step I took forward, I felt my stomach knot up until finally we were in front of Max's room. I could hear the machines when they opened the door, but I couldn't see in. I couldn't bring myself to take that step.

Elspeth walked to the window beside the bed. There was a man, I remembered him from the Google search I had done earlier, Max's father. He sat in the chair opposite the hospital bed with his hand on his face.

"Oh my God," Irene cried, throwing her hand over her mouth.

That's what it took for me to go in, and when I saw him…when I could barely see him under the bloody bandages, I shook. I cried out so loudly, yet I couldn't even hear myself. Walking up to him, I put my hand on his scraped hands.

"Max," I whispered. "Max."

I barely made it the toilet on time. Hunched over, I couldn't stop vomiting. My whole body shook as I kneeled over the rim. The sobs that came from own lips didn't seem human at all to me, but I couldn't stop.

So this was hell?

"I don't want any members of the press around here. Any slip-ups and I swear I'll have your heads," Elspeth directed at what I could only guess her security detail. When they finally left, she turned back to come into the room. I stood there staring back into her broken eyes.

"Let him in," I demanded.

"I'm not doing this with her—"

"Let him in!"

"NO!" she screamed at me. "If that is too hard for you to understand, I'll have you thrown out."

"You're going to throw me out into a sea of reporters, Madam Senator? Good, because I've been told I'm very photogenic. Crying on cue? I've got that down pat. How could I phrase this? 'My future mother-in-law hates me, because I'm a poor nobody. She's always been against me, and now she won't even let me by his side.' I'm no media mogul, but I'm sure the press will eat that up. It's better than the real story, isn't it?"

She rubbed her forehead, "Are you're going to do this now? My son is laying broken…dying, maybe, in bed…and you're going to—"

"I'm doing it for him. It's not about you! It's never been about you!" Why didn't she get it? Why didn't anyone get it?

"Excuse me, young lady," Max's father stood up, "but who do you think you are speaking to? Get out."

Taking a deep breath, Elspeth came into the room and I closed the door behind them.

"I'm…I'm one of Maxwell's lovers," I told him, knowing I was pushing it. But I couldn't think straight. The only people who mattered to me right now were Max and Wes…and both of them were suffering.

"One of?" Irene looked up from Max's bedside.

"Jane, enough." Elspeth grabbed my arm tightly, but I yanked it back from her.

"Mr. Emerson, your son, Maxwell Emerson, he's not in love with me. We are in a relationship, but…but he's in love with a man by the name of Wesley Uhler. They've been seeing each other for the last four years."

"Excuse me?" his eyebrows bunched together.

"Nothing, she was just leaving—"

"Touch me again lady, and I will show you that I have a very ugly side." I moved away from her looking back to Maxwell's father. "Your son, your adult son, is bisexual. He's in love with a man, and if Max was able to speak, he would tell you that he wants him here."

"Young lady, you're very confused."

"Days ago your son took me to his station and introduced me as his fiancée. People know who I am. You can be disgusted. You can pretend like it's not true or that this is all just some sick game or whatever. But either way, you will let Wesley in here, or I will walk outside and air the Emerson's dirty laundry for the whole world to see. I don't have a family. I don't have anyone who'll ask me what the hell am I doing or hate me for my choices. I don't have some bullshit façade to stand behind. But you do. So either you let him here in secret, or I'm going to start talking the ears off some reporters. Your choice."

He looked to Elspeth, but I was far too pissed to look at her right now.

"This one time—"

"He comes in whenever you're not here."

"Don't push it."

"Do you know why people don't negotiate with a suicide bomber?" I asked him. "Because it doesn't work. Any person willing to destroy themselves cannot be negotiated with. So you either kill me now, or you do what I ask. If two men in love freak you out so much, you can wait outside. But Wesley has the right to be in here for as long as he motherfucking wants."

He tilted his head to the side, and I knew I'd won. That's how much these people really cared about protecting their image over their own son's happiness.

Fuck them.

I could hear my phone ringing, but I couldn't bother to get it or get up from the bathroom floor. I just sat there trying to think. Why the fuck had I left? Everything I was so worried about seemed ridiculous. Maybe for a split second I got jealous of Jane. How freely she could be part of his world while I had to just keep waiting. Maybe I foolishly thought that he would just confront his family, and we'd be able to work through all of this. Now all of it seemed so insignificant.

"Wes?" The door to the stall opened and Jane stood above me, her phone at her ear. She stared for a long time before coming in and closing the door behind her.

"I don't deal with death well," I confessed to her while rubbing the tattoo of my brother. It was burning as if to prove my point.

"That's good," she whispered, pulling her legs to her chest, "but he isn't dead. A little banged up here and there, but he isn't dead. Once we are both beside him talking, he'll need to stay alive just to get the last word."

I smirked at that, "You should go be with him."

"I'm not going without you."

"Elspeth—"

"I made a deal with them. You can go in."

"How?"

She shrugged, "Once you've dealt with a dozen strippers and gotten beaten up by a drug dealer, negotiating with some rich snobs isn't anything. Now come on. Max is probably waiting to hear your voice. But first—"

She dug into her purse, pulling out the bag they give us at first class. "Clean up a little bit. He's going to wake up and you're going to be the first person he sees."

Getting up, she took my hand and took me to the sink. Taking the bag from her, I brushed my teeth. She rested her head on my back.

"He's going to be okay. He doesn't have a choice."

I knew it then. In a world filled with monsters, fakes, and liars, Jane was an angel. Our angel.

Irene had gone with Max's parents to get something to eat or whatever, and I was grateful for that. This was too private. Sitting beside him, Wes held on to his hands sobbing. He kissed the back of Max's hand over and over again. Giving them space, I stepped outside, closing the door behind me. Wrapping a scarf around myself, I walked down the hall with no destination in mind. My heart felt so heavy that it actually felt like it could sink through my feet and then maybe even through the floor, never stopping until it fell into the center of the earth.

Finally finding a place to sit, I tucked my knees up to my chest, trying to relax.

"We have heard multiple stories on the current status of Maxwell Emerson, headline reporter here at YGM, however, none have been confirmed. We currently know all of Emerson's family are with him at the moment. Maxwell Emerson was, just days ago celebrating his engagement to long-term girlfriend, Jane Chapman. Our hearts and prayers are with our leader tonight." A young man spoke on the television not too far from me. On the screen, there was a photo of Max right when we got off the elevator at his building. He was looking at me and grinning and, of course, I was making some sort of face.

Reaching up, I tried to wipe my eyes, but the tears just kept coming. The worst thing about me is that when I started to cry, there was no ending it. I'd cry until I couldn't cry any longer.

I don't know how long I stayed like that. It was only when my phone started to ring that I got up.

Ring.

Ring.

Ring.

I knew the number. I just didn't want to answer now. Ignoring the call, I laid back when it started again.

Ring.

Ring.

Ring.

"Allen. Right now isn't the—"

"Jane. It's important. I can come to you."

"Allen, it's always important. Right now I can't deal with—"

"It's about Maxwell."

21

I lifted my head from his hand when I heard the door open. It was Elspeth. She looked to me and then merely walked to the window. I had the feeling she was telling me to leave, but I couldn't bring myself to do that.

"Thank you," I said instead, not looking away from Max even though it hurt to see him this way. "Thank you for letting me in."

"The only reason you are here is because that woman has no sense of decorum or respect. I'll never be okay with…with you, or this."

"Why?"

"Why?" she repeated

Putting his hand to my forehead, I nodded, "Why can't you be okay with this?"

"Why aren't people okay with abusing children? Or hunting animals? They just aren't. I don't agree with your way of life. It doesn't make me a bad person. It does not make me the villain."

"So in other words, you don't know." I finally glanced back her. "You see us, and you're just disgusted to the point where it doesn't matter what either of us feels. Your feelings matter more so, therefore, we must live with your disdain."

"I'm sure you are a good man, but you are not for my son."

"It's a good thing it's your son's choice, isn't it?" I reminded her. "Have you ever thought that if he could conform to what you wanted him to be, he would've done it already? Has it ever occurred to you how painful it is to break the mold? Not being the child you want him to be. He knows that. There is part of him that wishes he could be. But he just can't. So he struggles to walk the middle, to be the Maxwell Emerson you all expect him to be and the simple Max he is."

"Don't speak for my son."

"Someone has to!" People like her drove me insane. "He's been trying to talk to you himself, but you refuse to listen! All of you refuse to listen."

"Mr. Uhler!" She held her hands as if she were to choke me. "Let's just leave this matter, why don't we? There is only so much a wicked witch can handle in one night."

We both fell into silence.

He was her son.

He was my love.

We were both hurting, and so silence was really the only choice.

Sitting in the hospital cafeteria with a cup of cold coffee, I waited for Allen to get here. He didn't say anything more than it was about Max on the phone. The side of the hospital where Maxwell was recovering was basically under lockdown thanks to Elspeth. I didn't want to leave either, so the cafeteria was the only option.

"Hey, boss."

I looked up from my cup to not only see Allen but Lady, Crystal, and Bambi from the strip club. They all were dressed like they had just finished their shift, and the only things covering them was their coats.

"Guys, what are you doing here?"

One by one they all pulled up a chair. Allen began, "I never got to thank you or say sorry."

"The money."

"Yeah, the money." He looked like he aged in the time while I was gone. His face was wrinkled and his shoulders were hunched over, making him look even shorter. "And sorry for not only getting you into this mess but also, there was a moment, a split second when the wire came in and I saw all them zeroes. My heart skipped. I thought about running. Just taking off, leaving Boston, the Bunny Rabbit...you...behind."

"Allen!"

"I didn't!" He raised his hands up to protect his face. Which would have been funny if I didn't feel like such shit. "I didn't run. I didn't spend a dime. I paid off the debt we owed, and now The Bunny Rabbit is a clean business."

"That's great..." My voice drifted off, still looking at the girls who couldn't bring themselves to look me in the eyes. "So why are you all here? What does this have to do with Max?"

"That has nothing to do with me. Okay. Nothing, I don't even want to be dragged through this shit. I said sorry and all that, so I'll leave the ladies to you." He jumped up and left us all there.

"Pussy," Bambi's heart-shaped face bunched as she made a face at him.

"Jane. Mama Jane, you know that's what the girls really call you," Crystal smiled as she pinched her own hand. "You always stand up for us. You always have our backs. When you quit, we all really missed you. We kept begging Allen to give you a raise, so you'd come back."

"Hell, we were all even willing to split our earnings with you," Lady smiled shaking her head at me. "You should be honored."

"I am. But guys I'm still a little confused."

"Maxwell Emerson has been trying to get in contact with us," Crystal spat out. "That's why we're here."

"Why would Max be trying to get in touch with strippers?"

"What do you mean strippers? You think you're better than us or something now?" Lady snapped, crossing her arms. Bambi shoved her elbow in her side.

"You know the last person who will ever look down on you guys is me. I'm just trying to figure this out."

"I can't do this," Lady muttered. Her eyes had glazed over with tears she wouldn't let fall. She got up and quickly left.

"You know the story YGM has been trying to do on the governor?" Crystal whispered. "The one about the girls getting pulled off the streets for warnings."

One by one, the dots started to connect. "You...all of you...you're...but I thought it was prostitution."

Crystal dropped her head and so Bambi spoke next, "It was before we started at the Bunny Rabbit. We worked this corner of Fairmount. We got busted by some undercover cops. They took us in, booked us…it all seemed normal. Until they promised they wouldn't charge us. We'd get all this stuff if we did what they asked."

"I don't know how many men's cocks I sucked that night," Crystal said rubbing her throat. "At first, I thought it was no big deal. Hell, I was out on parole. I didn't want to go back, but then it spiraled out of control, and we were stuck in this thing. It was hell and obviously we couldn't go to cops, you know. We just dealt with it, but one girl tried to talk and it just got worse."

"Crystal," I grabbed on to her hand. "I'm as powerless as you are. I want to hear this story as your friend. But I need you to talk about it with—"

"The news," Bambi nodded, brushing her short hair behind her ear. "Yeah, that's why we're here. We got out, kind of easy when you get pregnant. They don't want you anymore. We got money to keep quiet, and we were going to. Lady was pissed. She tried to contact the news, but I figure she'd got scared."

"We saw you on the news, the picture of you and Max, and we wanted to help, and this is the only way we know how," Crystal shrugged. "We just don't know where to go next or who will believe us."

"I do," I replied. I took out my phone and called Irene.

"Jane, did you leave—"

"Irene. I need Scarlet de Burgh's number." As she told it to me, I remembered how much this story meant to Max. He'd been so opposed to us leaving that he didn't speak to us for three days. This made us come home early, which made him rush to get us. It was a circle now coming back around.

"Thank you." I could feel myself crying again. I was just a ball of tears apparently.

"What are you doing?" Irene followed Jane as she rushed into the room. Her eyes were blood shot as she looked around frantically. Elspeth sighed and muttered something to her and Alistair, Maxwell's father, stepped in but didn't look at me.

"Where is the fucking remote?" Jane snapped, running her hands through her hair.

"Young lady haven't you caused enough—"

"I can explain. I just need the remote," she said back to him.

"Jane," I called out and handed her the remote from the bedside table.

"Thank you." She took it and flipped on the television. She searched through the channels before stopping at YGM. A commercial was playing.

"Turn this off."

"It's for Max," she said softly, walking over to the other side of Max's bed and touching his head. "You got him, everyone will know now. You got him."

Confused, I leaned forward, "Jane? What are you talking about?"

"This is YGM Breaking News." We all turned to the television where a black man in a plaid shirt, navy tie and suit jacket came on screen, *"Weeks ago, here on this stage my boss, Maxwell Emerson, broke on the Emerson Report the scandalous behavior of Governor MacDowell. Everyone was gripped to their televisions. How far would this scandal go? What other wrongdoing was left to be exposed? It was an incredible tale, and we did not want to believe our governor was not only a thief and a fraud, but also a sexual predator. As hours became days and days became weeks, we were able to forget Governor MacDowell. Lay him in the graveyard along with the other corrupt politicians. After all, there was nothing but speculation of the 'give warnings' sexual assaults. Interviews were dropped. Sources were gone, and it looked as if this was just another fabricated story. Other stations began to drop the story from their headline news. But even as ratings dipped and our news team was being pressured to move on from this developing story, my boss, Maxwell Emerson, stood firm. He believed that this man, Governor MacDowell should not just fade into the background but be punished for his actions. Tonight, Maxwell Emerson has proven why he is the man deserving of this chair, your trust, and as he fights for his life in the hospital, your prayers. Not one, but three women, have come out this*

early morning with proof, not only of Governor MacDowell's involvement, but with many others. Thank you, ladies, for speaking out."

Seated beside him were seated three women of varying ethnicities. A grin spread across my face as I turned back to Max. "God, how are we going to live with your ego now?"

"I'm going to need to call my lawyer," Alistair muttered, reaching into his jacket pocket.

And they were disgusted with us?

Well, I was even more disgusted with them.

22

DAY ONE

"Mwlels..." That's what it sounded like, a muffled voice speaking into my ear. I tried to move, but my body felt as if it was strapped down. The more I tried to move, the worse it felt.

"Camms...ha...ah..." I couldn't understand the words, which only made me more frustrated and panicked.

"Maxwell." Finally, something I could understand. "Maxwell, I'm Doctor Raji."

Who is this?

"Can you hear me now?"

I didn't know what he was doing, but the pressure in my ears decreased. I tried to tell him so, but my throat burned. Fighting it, I spoke with what felt like sandpaper in my throat, "I...w..."

"It's okay. Take your time." Opening my eyes, I had to shut them immediately; the lights nearly blinded me.

"Where...where...?"

"You're in Boston General Hospital. You were in a car accident five days ago."

"Car accident?"

Five days?

I tried to think back, but all I saw was the lights...the lights from the van...the van? What?

"Mr. Emerson, can you feel this?"

I wasn't sure if I was feeling something or not. So I didn't speak.

"What about here?"

Still nothing and I knew that wasn't good.

"Calm down, Mr. Emerson. It's fine. We still have a long way to go. But you've already taken the first step by waking up."

Five days? He said five days.

Closing my eyes, I thought back again. I'd...I'd have gone to...Jane and Wes.

"My...family." I wasn't sure what else to call them.

335

"Everyone is here. I'll bring them in, once we are done."

There was click and the bed rose slightly allowing me to sit upright. It wasn't just Doctor Raji, but a whole team of doctors, I counted six, around my bed. All of them just staring.

"Mr. Emerson, I know it hurts, but try to breathe in for me." He put his stethoscope to my chest. Breathing again, I focused on my legs. I had two of them, thankfully. But I barely felt either of them. They were like dead weights.

"I hit someone?" I finally brought myself to ask, again the minivan came back to mind.

"The police say that you sped through a yellow light. Another driver crashed into you. She's fine and her daughters have been discharged. Your family paid their bills. It was just a bad accident."

"My family." I asked again.

"We can stop for now and bring them in. But try to relax," he told me.

I wanted to ask, how could anyone relax in a situation like this? But all I could do was nod and even that hurt.

"Maxwell." The first people who came in weren't really the first ones I wanted to see, but I was still grateful.

"Mom," I said, as she kissed my check crying.

"I tell you I love you, and you go wrap your car around a lamppost. Such an ass," Irene said brushing the tears from her eyes.

"Sorry." I didn't have the strength to be witty.

She hugged me before taking a seat beside me.

"Dad?" I looked over to my mom.

She frowned, "He's…he's not going be able to come for a while."

More hookers!

"He's been indicted. The Emerson family curse strikes again," Irene muttered bitterly.

"What?"

"Sexual exploitation. He rolled on Governor MacDowell, to save himself though, which is—"

"Irene, enough." My mother sneered at her and took my hand. I was far too confused, and the thought of asking questions right now only gave me a headache. I didn't care about any of that.

"Jane," I whispered, looking to my mother. "And Wes."

She didn't reply, but she kept holding my hand.

"They're waiting in the hall. They haven't stopped waiting for you. They love you a lot," Irene answered and part of me was shocked but a bigger part of me was relieved.

"I…I…I need to see them."

She walked to the door, and I didn't have to wait a second before they both came running in. Their clothes were rumpled, and their faces were pale.

"You guys look…like…shit," I gasped out, why that took so much energy to say, I don't know. My mom let go. She didn't say a word. She just left with Irene.

"Yeah, well," Wes sat beside me. He kissed the side of my head, then lips. "My boyfriend nearly gave me a heart attack, twice actually."

"Speak for yourself," Jane said, now sitting on the opposite side of me. She took my hand before saying, "I always look good. Your eyesight isn't doing well right now."

Inhaling felt like I had swallowed glass. I wanted to say something, but all the words that came to mind seemed subpar at best.

"Never again," Wes said with his eyes dropping. He looked like he'd lost weight and his whole body was shaking. He looked at the ceiling and blinked a few times.

Jane was just as bad. Once again, just like the day I went to pick them up, which only felt like yesterday to me, I was in awe of them.

"I'm sorry," I whispered.

"Idiot," Jane bit her lip. "Don't be sorry. Just be alive."

"Okay."

"Okay," Wes nodded again.

DAY TWO

Yesterday I was so shocked, amazed, and grateful to be alive. Grateful that they were both here that I didn't really or truly think of myself. I'd learned a couple things today. I learned that my story, both of the scandal and me being awake, was all anyone could talk about on the news. It left me with a sense of pride, which got me through the second piece of news I was currently hearing.

"You've broken bones in both legs and have substantial nerve damage," my doctor explained to me and my mother who was right beside me. Jane and Wes had gone home earlier, and only because I begged them to. They looked just as bad as I felt. "However, bones can heal, so that isn't the problem."

"What is this problem?" my mother asked for me.

"You have what we call an incomplete spinal cord injury," he replied, pulling up a chair beside me. "Now what that means is you do not have total paralysis or loss of sensation, nor was your spinal cord totally damaged or disrupted. This means there are better chances of additional recovery, but I want you to prepare for the long haul. It will get worse before it will get better."

"What do you mean?" *How could it get worse?*

"Physically, your brain knows how to walk and how to function. When the body doesn't respond, it can be frustrating. There may be times when you try to move on your own and fall. You will need around the clock care for the first few months. A live-in nurse, if you chose to hire someone, for your rehabilitation. We must also take into consideration that phantom pains and mood swings are common. There is…there is… also the chance you won't walk again."

After that I just stopped listening to him.

When I was nine, my grandfather lived with us. He'd lost his ability to walk when he was in his twenties, and that was the start of the 'Emerson curse', as Irene loved to call it, how Emerson's ruined everything around us because of our own greed. The story went that my grandfather had slept with another man's wife, who shot him in the back. He'd always fall, getting out of his wheelchair, and being the little shit I was, I'd just watch him. I thought that what he got was because he was also a jerk to everyone, including my mother. He'd throw things and curse at the maids; it was like he hated living and made sure everyone else around him did so, too.

"Maxwell."

I glanced up at my mother who smiled gently and brushed back my hair, "Whatever you're thinking, get it out of your head. You're going to be fine. I know you. You're far too stubborn to let this stop you."

"Yeah"

DAY THREE

"Ah!" I cried out, grabbing the sheets.

"Max? What is it?"

"Don't touch me!" I screamed breathing in through my nose trying to fight the pain in my left leg. It felt like someone was trying to cut it off. "AHFF! AHH!"

Wes called out, but I couldn't think about anything other than the pain.

"It hurts. It fucking hurts! Make it stop! Please!"

"Max, hold on. The morphine will kick in soon," one of the doctors said, and I wanted to give him the definition of 'soon'.

It felt like hours before the pain disappeared, but I couldn't bother to open my eyes. I just laid there breathing in and out, forcing myself to go to sleep.

"He's been in pain all day," Jane whispered.

"It could have been any number of things. But you need to understand he's going to be in pain for a while. All we can do is manage it."

The door opened and closed.

"Just manage it?" Wes sighed sitting beside me. "I hate seeing him like this, Jane."

He hated it? What about me?

He was supposed to be getting discharged today and being the sap that I am, I actually considered getting him a flower. Not a whole bouquet, just a single rose. However, I knew he'd complain. Instead, I made him a burger. He'd been bitching about hospital food…well, he'd been bitching about almost everything, but the food was the only thing I could fix. Jane, on the other hand, got him a teddy bear saying that he could, at least, beat the shit out it when he was pissed.

"Here we go," Jane breathed deeply.

"Max…" I started to say when we got to his room, but he wasn't there. Just his nurse remaking the bed he should have been on.

"Mr. Uhler and Ms. Chapman." She turned toward us but not before picking up two letters. "Mr. Emerson wanted me to give these to you."

I stared at the letters but not taking them. "Where is he?"

She shrugged her shoulders. "He said to give this to you, and he discharged himself."

I dropped the burger on the table near the door, and I tore open the letter, partially confused. After all, who the hell still wrote letters by hand? Why didn't he call?

Dear Wes,

You're probably wondering why I didn't call or text. However, I also know you enjoy things like this. It takes more effort than writing a simple email, right? Jane once told me that saying sorry, it makes someone calmer when they were upset. Apologizing has an impact. So, I want to tell you I'm sorry in so many ways for just leaving like this. I tried. I really did, but the thought of going through this with both you and Jane beside me didn't make me feel better. It actually made me feel sick. Sick to know that I'd snap at you for no reason. Sick to know I'd be jealous every time I saw you walk from one end of the room to another. Sick enough to be so miserable that I'd only make the both of you miserable, too.

I'm not breaking up with you, so don't even go there. You belong to me...and Jane. The fact that I'm a selfish prick doesn't change that. I just need to ~~fix myself and heal,~~ work through this. I don't know how long that will take, but know I'm thinking about the both of you.

Yours,

Maxwell Emerson.

P.S. The rule about not being with Jane unless we are all there? We hit pause on that. You and Jane should be together.

Even to the end, he was still a selfish little shite.

"Break up letter?"

I turned to see Jane leaning against the door just looking at me. Her letter was still unopened in her hands. She smiled sadly and her hazel eyes never left mine.

"Maxwell's version of a 'wait for me' letter," I told her.

"If there aren't three of us, there is none of us?" she seemed to be asking, and I wanted to tell her. I wanted to tell her, we'd just wait, but I couldn't. Maybe I was in shock. I just stared back at her.

"It was fun," she said kissing my cheek. "We were fun. Thank you."

"Jane, let's just go and—"

"Draw this out?" She shook her head. "It's better to just rip the bandage off and stop where he stopped."

"Where are you going to go?"

"Wes, I'm giving you a way out. No hard feelings. No trying to explain to me how it isn't working. Just do what I know you want to do right now."

Kissing her one last time, she didn't kiss me back. Was it me or did she feel cold? I wasn't sure, but it was different now. Running my hands through my hair, I tried to fight back the headache forming. I tried to deny the fact that I was relieved...relieved I could just run away from all of this.

"I'm sorry. If you need anything, call me. Stay in Max's place—"

"Go, Wes."

Kissing her forehead one more time I walked out the room. I thought I was fine. I thought I was prepared for anything...so why was I shaking so much?

And just as quickly as we started, we were over.

Reaching into my bag, I pulled out the very thing that even a dirty Mary Poppins would be disappointed with.

"The IUD, TCI, TVR, the patch and the injection…and I went with the pill," I whispered to myself, staring at the positive pregnancy test in my hands. "Nice one, Jane."

To Be Continued...

Dear Reader

Thank you all for reading please rate, share, and review! I truly hope you enjoyed the beginning of Jane, Max and Wesley's romance!

Please join the Anatomy of Jane fan group on Facebook for more information on book two The Anatomy of Us.

About the Author

Amelia LeFay is a character of my own imagination. She's a single woman in her mid twenties in love with sex. Dirty sex, rough sex, sex of any type. She's not a whore or a slut. She believes a woman should be allowed to sexually express herself any way she wishes.

She stands for Gay Rights, Women's Rights, the rights of Minorities, and Environmental Protection.

She can be a bitch, but doesn't think there is anything wrong with that.

She has uneven boobs, stretch marks on her ass, astigmatism, and thighs that rub together as she walks. (Which means no pair of jeans lasts as long as she wishes they would.)

But most importantly, Amelia is a Dreamer…she has dreams so big it scares even her, because if she fails…if she can't make it…she feels like nothing.

"Life is to be lived, not controlled, and humanity is won by continuing to play in face of certain defeat."—Ralph Ellison

Please stay in touch via any social media outlets:
http://amelialefay.com/
https://www.facebook.com/amelialefay/
https://twitter.com/LefayAmelia

Made in the USA
Coppell, TX
06 April 2025